TEMPEST

Book 3
THE CHRONICLES OF THE NUBIAN UNDERWORLD

Dear Reader:

Shakir Rashaan continues his Chronicles of the Nubian Underworld series with its third installment, *Tempest*. The author, a real-life practitioner of the BDSM culture in Atlanta's Fetish community, offers an edge-of-your-seat thriller as secrets are exposed, revenge is exacted and erotica is plentiful.

Ramesses, his wife, Neferterri, and their submissives find paradise in the Bahamas where Ramesses introduces participants to his private island. Its grand opening is full of kinky sexcapades and explosive scenes of the dominant and submissive lifestyle. Showcased are such techniques as fire play to hot wax to a collaring ceremony. This journey will leave readers fanning to cool down while experiencing an uninhibited world in the tropics.

Be sure to check out Shakir's first two titles in the series, *The Awakening* and *Legacy*. An excerpt from *Obsession*, the first title of his next series, Kink, P.I., appears in the back of this book.

As always, thanks for supporting myself and the Strebor Books family. We strive to bring you the most cutting-edge, out-of-the-box material on the market. You can find me on Facebook @AuthorZane or you can email me at zane@eroticanoir.com.

Blessings,

Zane

Publisher
Strebor Books
www.simonandschuster.com

ALSO BY SHAKIR RASHAAN
Legacy
The Awakening

ZANE PRESENTS

TEMPEST

Book 3
THE CHRONICLES OF THE NUBIAN UNDERWORLD

A NOVEL

SHAKIR RASHAAN

SBI

STREBOR BOOKS

NEW YORK LONDON TORONTO SYDNEY

Strebor Books
P.O. Box 6505
Largo, MD 20792
http://www.streborbooks.com

ISBN 978-1-59309-548-2
ISBN 978-1-4767-4890-0 (ebook)
LCCN 2014936767

First Strebor Books trade paperback edition February 2014

Cover design: www.mariondesigns.com
Cover photograph: © Keith Saunders/Keith Saunders Photos

10 9 8 7 6 5 4 3 2 1

Manufactured in the United States of America

For information regarding special discounts for bulk purchases, please contact Simon & Schuster Special Sales at 1-866-506-1949 or business@simonandschuster.com

The Simon & Schuster Speakers Bureau can bring authors to your live event. For more information or to book an event, contact the Simon & Schuster Speakers Bureau at 1-866-248-3049 or visit our website at www.simonspeakers.com.

"The moment you believe you can control a storm is the moment the storm lets you know who is truly in control."

—*Shakir Rashaan*

For My Beloved:

For loving the extrovert…
For understanding the Pharaoh…
For comforting the teenager…
And for taming the Beast in the darkness and making him yours…

I love you more than life itself…

"To live is to suffer.
To survive is to find meaning in the suffering."

—*Friedrich Nietzsche*

ACKNOWLEDGMENTS

You know what happens when storms subside, right?

Another one pops up in its place, only this time, it might be…well, you'll find out soon enough when the next installment, SAMOIS, comes out! ☺

You're gonna love the spin on that installment…an Amazon-esque fantasy weekend at NEBU where the women are in power and the men are submissive? What woman wouldn't enjoy that type of fantasy? Sub bois at your beck and call, taking care of every whim… oh, the beauty of it all!

But first, you have to witness the current storm that's on the horizon.

Some of you already know the routine when I say this next part, but for the ones who are just getting on board, let me get this part out of the way:

This is (somewhat) a work of fiction. That means that some of this stuff was made up, and some of it includes players whose names have been changed to protect the (not so) innocent. Any reference to anyone, living or dead, is liable to happen, but please believe that I made sure not to include them on purpose…you know, things happen, right?

Anyway, let me give you an idea of what's in store for you with *Tempest*:

Island paradise…

Debauchery outside of the country…

Temptations abound…

But, those temptations come at a price, and you'll find out in the next few hundred pages what that price will be.

I'm going into areas that not many are willing to go into, and I'm fine with that. I kinda like being a bit of a trendsetter in that aspect. To be deviant, affluent, and black is already a rarity, so, to actually give people a window to see those that are black and into WIITWD is worth every word that I write in this series and beyond.

In the last two books, I was blessed to be able to thank family, friends, and other folks who have been in my corner, and there are so many more that I would love to thank personally, including the many supporters who are a part of the Temples of NEBU FB group.

To Zane and Charmaine, I truly cannot thank you enough for the opportunity to bring a flavor within the erotic genre that very few authors have traveled. I intend to continue to give you quality projects in a way that only I can bring!

As usual, I know I'm missing a whole gang of folks, so just do me a favor and insert your name in this next statement:

I'd like to thank _____ for the support and love. I hope to continue to put books out that you will want to tell your friends and family about.

Thank you again, and enjoy *Tempest*.

SPECIAL NOTE TO READERS

The grammatical errors that you might see within the dialog between the characters are not oversights. This is the type of speech and text that is used in some facets of the BDSM world. As one of my submissive friends put it, "The lowercase letters in a slave's or submissive's name are a demonstration of the hierarchical relationship. It is a reminder to the submissive that he or she is the bottom part of the hierarchy, meant to be led, and the Dominant's name is always capitalized, as He or She is the Top part, meant to lead." In keeping with the essence of the series and the essence of the BDSM community, preserving the speech was paramount. It is my hope that you, the reader, will understand and appreciate the symbolism.

PROLOGUE ⚸ RAMESSES

The hypnotic firelight danced against the luminous moonlight, seducing it like a lover welcoming the object of her desire home from a long day's work.

The familiar thudding of the floggers laced with fire against the lower back and across the ass of the young submissive being "sacrificed" to the spirits of the evening kept the crowd mesmerized. She moaned and cooed as each strike against her quivering flesh left indelible marks that she would surely show off in the morning light.

Next, the intimacy of the fire gloves…

The soft whines soon turned into gasps and screams as the gloves caressed her exposed skin. Her eyes looked entranced as she focused on the flickers of the flames licking against her tender flesh.

"Mmmm, Master, that feels so good," keket called out into the darkness as Master Osiris continued his delicious torture of his Alpha slave. With the precision of a surgeon, he took great care to avoid the most sensitive areas of his prized possession while simultaneously shooting flames between her thighs.

"Mmmm, shit, Master, you're making me wet," she announced to the crowd, bringing a smile to his face. He already knew the moment he took her down from the Cross she hung from, she would be his for the taking.

To the left of Osiris, where he lit up the night sky, another equally skilled Master of the Arts, Master Amenhotep, was performing in a rare appearance with paka, showcasing His legendary skills as an electrical play aficionado. As the casual observer watched the current resembling lightning in the distance, the electricity seemed to flow freely from His fingertips onto her waiting flesh below.

paka screamed as the electrical surges coursed through her extremities, causing her toes to curl as the currents teased and lapped at her clitoral recesses. He changed to using gloves that resembled those of a cat's claw to elicit a stronger response from her, and she did not disappoint the moment metal touched skin.

"Ahh, *fuck*, Master!" paka yelled out as He continued to rake across her flesh, leaving marks to detail His journey through her body. He was determined to leave no piece of flesh untouched, as hearing His wife's screams only fueled His sadistic desire to torture her body.

The crowd was comprised of some of the more renowned kinksters and libertines in the U.S. and abroad. Despite the coolness of the evening, they enjoyed the festivities and the night's entertainment. Everyone was transported to this oasis, tucked away in the Caribbean, for a week of debauchery, sensual decadence, and unbridled passion and delights of the flesh.

Amenhotep likened the get-together to Hedonism in Jamaica, but the patrons in attendance knew the moment they stepped off the private chartered jets, this would be a little more intense than what Hedonism could ever hope to be.

As the scenes continued, a drum circle provided the soundtrack as the rhythmic thumping against the tightly woven canvases was complemented by the delectable sight of scantily clad women dancing in harmonious sync with the drummers.

Hips swaying…

Pleasurable posteriors of the thickest variety rolling and grinding…

Weapons of "ass" destruction finding their targets with near tactical precision…

There would be no limit to what may transpire in this tropical paradise.

"I think the natives are beginning to get restless, Beloved," Neferterri observed as she stroked the back of amani's head. He was completely enthralled by the sights in front of him, more so after noticing shamise among the dancers.

"You're right, Beloved, I think it is time to let things take their natural course for the rest of the night." I smiled as sajira knelt contently in the sand against my outside hip. I honestly didn't want to move because I enjoyed the energy and essence she gave for me to indulge in, but business needed to be attended to.

As I stood, I gave a hand gesture to the drummers to slow their pace so my voice could be heard over the drums. Upon hearing the change in cadence and volume, Osiris and Amenhotep stopped their scenes, much to the chagrin of their respective properties. They turned in my direction to provide their full attention.

I walked toward an open area so the crowd could hear me over the waves crashing in the background, with sajira crawling behind me, waiting to take her position once I settled on a space suitable for my announcement.

shamise, noticing that I was about to speak, led the dozen or so dancers toward me, kneeling at my feet before taking my hand to kiss the back of my palm. The rest of the dance troop took kneeling positions around me, waiting for my cue to alert the drummers to cease. After kissing my palm, she leaned over to share a kiss with sajira before taking her position at the opposite side of me.

"Welcome, honored guests and beloved friends, to the grand opening of the *Isle ne Bin-bener*, or the 'Island of Evil Pleasures.' My Beloved and I, along with our House and the staff and personnel on the island, hope that you enjoy your stay with us this week," I announced as Neferterri and amani made their way into the circle the dancers formed. I shared a brief, but passionate, kiss with her, eliciting whistles and shouts from the crowd. After breaking the kiss, I stared into her eyes for a few more moments before continuing my speech. "While your travel and accommodations have been provided, any luxuries you indulge into, including any of the non-service slaves, will be at your expense. Breakfast will be served bright and early tomorrow morning, and anyone who wishes to tour the island will be afforded the opportunity to do so. Enjoy your evening, and we bid you a good night."

ONE ❧ RAMESSES

"Oh, fuck, that feels sooooo good!!"

It's amazing what paradise can do to loosen inhibitions and bring out the animalistic nature of a person.

In this case, make it a lot of persons.

Taking in the island debauchery in its myriad forms and splendor, I struggled to keep from participating in the festivities. With shamise perched at my hip stealing glances up at me, I felt her heat rising to the surface. Her eyes had always been my weakness, so returning the glances only served to intensify my want to take her into the midst of the crowd and have my way with her. I gripped her hair in an attempt to balance myself, more so to keep my mind into what our role was in this, the opening night of a week-long Hedonistic atmosphere.

Listening to the screams as they collectively pierced the warm night air awakened my inner Sadist. shamise knew my mannerisms all too well, and like a kitten begging to be stroked, she rubbed her hands against the inside of my thigh to edge me further into the abyss of my libidinous nature.

"Come on, Daddy, take me, please?" she cooed from her kneeled position. "I'm Yours, at Your command, for Your pleasure. Make me beg for Your lashes, to mark me in ways no other man can. Please, Daddy?"

As much as I loved my darling slave, she knew she wasn't going to win this exchange. My command was her will, but I dictated when that command would come to fruition. I needed to reclaim my senses, and the only way to do it was to meet the challenge head-on.

"Come with me, precious, we need to survey the landscape and observe what is happening." I tapped her shoulder as I commanded. "There will be plenty of time to partake in the play time, I promise."

Before she could pout in protest, I brought her to her feet and led her to the first scenes we walked toward.

Master Osiris was still in the midst of his scene with his slave, taking advantage of the gentle breezes to continue his fire scene. He alternated using the fire wands with his adept ability to breathe fire onto his slave's beautiful cocoa brown skin. She continued to writhe and grind her hips in rhythm with the way the tongs licked at her flesh, trying her best to stifle the moans she was prohibited from allowing to escape from her lips.

Osiris continued his symbiotic link with her as he turned her body to face him. He placed a fire glove on his hand and set it ablaze, watching it dance against the darkness of the night sky. I saw the familiar flash in his eyes as I knew what would come next.

He moved the flame closer to her nipples, verbally forcing her to look into his eyes as she felt the flame caress her left nipple for a brief second. She bit her lip to keep from screaming from the heat against the most sensitive parts of her body.

shamise was entranced, watching one of her peers look completely lost in the bliss created by her Master. I grinned at her focus, at how she wanted badly for the same thing to happen to her as soon as possible. She moved closer to my body, trembling beneath my body.

"She looks like she's really flying; isn't she, precious?"

"Mmmmm, yes, Daddy, she looks absolutely radiant. Her skin is glowing from the heat of the fire on her skin."

We noticed as Osiris took the alcohol solution in the basin next to them and drew a pattern with his finger from the top of her neck to her panty line. He then took a small Q-tip and lit the cotton head and placed the flame against the top of the pattern and waited for the flame to catch.

We stood in awe with the rest of the crowd as the pattern being drawn across the front of her body flashed a pattern that resembled Osiris's house crest, which included the ever-present ankh that is the staple of those of us who are a part of the *Neb'net Maa'kheru*.

shamise flinched for a moment, as she had firsthand knowledge of the pain and pleasure that came at the end of the flame burning across her skin. I lifted her face to meet my gaze, grinning at the way her eyes sparkled against the flames glowing across from where we stood.

"It's time to move to the next station, baby," I whispered in her ear as to not disturb the scene. I took her hand and led her across the sand toward one of the tents nearer to the main buildings.

We ran into a few familiar faces, greeting guests the entire walk to the next area. shamise almost squealed when she recognized two people she hadn't seen in a long while, and she ran toward them to hug.

"Candy! Jay! What are you two doing here?!?!" She hugged Candy as tightly as she could, kissing Jay on the cheek as I walked behind her. I placed my hand on shamise's hip, giving my shotgun partner pound while kissing Candy on her cheek. "i thought you two were still in Atlanta?"

"Actually, we would have still been there, if your Daddy hadn't have gone ahead and footed the bill." Jay traded glances with me, letting the cat out of the bag, as it were. I didn't want anyone knowing I was sponsoring anyone, but I knew shamise wouldn't betray my trust. "We've been keeping a low profile for the past year, trying to heal from the craziness with Jasmine and the kidnapping, but things have never been stronger between us."

"Yeah, it took me some time to get him to where I like him, but it was worth the effort," Candy remarked, still staring in my direction. "You look good, Daddy; I was wondering if the good life was beginning to have its effect on you. *Damn*."

I swear, that woman will always be good for my ego. I tried to hide the smile on my face, but there was no way I wouldn't validate her compliment without a grin or something. Even though they were together, she's still "Daddy's girl."

"Hey, hey, you're supposed to only have eyes for me, remember?" Jay playfully slapped Candy's ass for effect.

"And I do…except when *he* is around." Candy laughed, provoking a giggle from shamise. "Whether you like it or not, there's one man on this planet I will always drop everything to make sure he is okay, and you're looking at him."

Jay put his hands in the air in mock defeat. "Hey, I'm not mad at my boy. I know he's got the swagger on this side of the fence; just remember who's your Daddy when we're at home and we're good."

I tried my best to remain as stone-faced as I could up until Jay's last comment. My mind wondered if he realized who he was trying to convince, and I kept my other thoughts to myself. Sometimes, what a person doesn't know won't hurt them. In this case, Jay was better off staying on a need-to-know basis when it came to his girlfriend.

"You might wanna put a few karats on that finger before you start worrying about who's calling who Daddy, playa." I smirked when I played my trump card, shutting him down. "Until you put her on lockdown, she's gonna act up. Trust me on that."

"Yeah, yeah, yeah." Jay rubbed the back of his head, trying to find the words that would get him out of the proverbial sticky situation. Candy folded her arms over her chest and gave him the side-eye as he struggled to find the words to make everything right. "I got that handled as soon as we get Stateside."

"You better, or this next year won't be as smooth as the past year," Candy stated.

shamise couldn't stop herself from giggling, and I gave a silent cue by tapping her on her hip, alerting her to calm down. I admit, it was funny to watch them argue like an old married couple, but I needed to have my submissive conduct herself accordingly, regardless of who was in our company.

"Anyway, if it pleases my Daddy, i would like to find some time to talk to you two. We have got to catch up sometime this week; i haven't seen you guys since i came back home." shamise turned her head and looked up at me to get permission. I nodded my head, bringing a smile to my baby girl's face.

"Cool, we're looking forward to it." Jay wrapped his arm around Candy's waist to pull her off in a separate direction. "We want to enjoy the island for a couple of days before we try to relax and sit down."

"Consider that done, now go enjoy the island; we have other matters to attend to." I walked in the direction I was in with shamise in tow as we waved goodbye to them. It was good to see Candy glowing again, and I took solace in the fact that Jay was the one taking good care of her. Call me selfish, and I had no problems being proud of that, but I took good care of the women in my life.

We walked along the torch-lit pathway, enjoying the couples who dined in the intimate tents that were placed near the paths. She kissed my neck and held my hand the entire walk, blushing every time I playfully smacked her ass or tugged on her bikini bottom while whispering nasty things in her ear. She relished in the attention, almost tuning out anyone that walked by us to engage in friendly conversation.

I'll admit I enjoyed it, too. I enjoyed doing this type of thing with both girls and with my Beloved; it strengthened the bonds and connection I have with all three of them. I made a note to continue doing that once we got back home.

Once we got to our next destination, I slowly pulled the tarp back, leading shamise inside to bear witness to the change of scenery and stimulation overload she would soon experience.

What she saw took her breath away.

Along with the small crowd inside the large tent, shamise saw nearly a dozen slaves, regardless of gender, being subjected to what could be described as a modern-day kinky rendition of the legendary "Night of a Thousand Lashes" from the *Arabian Nights* collection of tales.

Be it by dragon tails, cat-o-nine tails, whips, and everything in between, the collective sounds of submissive and slave alike being whipped into oblivion by their Master or Dominant were like a symphony being played live at Carnegie Hall.

I slipped my arms around her waist, trying my best to bring her mind and body closer together into a wondrous mix of pleasure and pain. "You know why I'm torturing you; don't you, baby girl?"

"Yes, Daddy, i know why."

"Tell Me why."

"You love torturing me, Daddy," she purred. "You know how i react to being teased and tortured, and You love it."

"That's My good girl." I kissed her cheek. "You also know I won't torture you for too much longer; don't you, baby girl?"

"No, Daddy, i know You won't." shamise couldn't stop grinning as her focus shifted to a submissive being whipped by dragon tails. "i couldn't imagine You torturing me to harm me, ever. Neither You nor my Goddess."

"There's one more thing I want you to see." I took her hand and led her out of the tent. We walked toward the main building, greeting guests along the way. She soaked in the interactions, blushing at the compliments of her leading the dancers earlier and blushing more at the suggestive compliments on her attire.

Once we were inside the building, I led her upstairs to the bedroom areas so she could witness the coup de grace.

"What's up here, Daddy? i thought only the family would be staying in the main building?" shamise inquired, a bewildered look spreading across her face. I smiled as the answer to my question came in the muffled sounds of her brother, groaning and moaning behind one of the bedroom doors.

shamise stopped in her tracks.

"What's wrong, precious?"

"Is amani fucking my Goddess?"

I understood her hesitation.

Neferterri made it a habit of not having sex with our submissive bois in front of shamise and sajira. Her reasoning was simple: her girls should not see her in a position of submission, as it would mess with their training and psyche.

Not every Domina functioned the same way, and not every Domina would agree with her, either, but Neferterri was not any run-of-the-mill Domina.

Yeah, I was biased, sue me.

While I was well aware not to regress her training, or her sister's training, for that matter, I also knew what my Beloved was up to. In fact, it was something I knew shamise would want to see. I was so certain of it that I didn't bother answering her question and led her into the bedroom.

She looked as if she'd seen her favorite fantasy come true, and the smile across her lips couldn't be held in even if she tried.

Her Goddess and her brother submissive were intensely engaged all right, but not in the conventional manner she originally dreaded.

amani was on all fours between Neferterri and sajira, taking his Goddess's strap-on while orally servicing sajira. His arms were bound behind his back and he was in the "down dog" position, unable to move or much of anything else, honestly.

"Oh…my…God." shamise gasped in awe of the scene playing out in front of her. She took particular notice of the whip marks and trails of blood on amani's skin. She leaned against me to keep her balance. "He looks so…mmmm; damn, look at those cuts and marks."

The next thing she felt were sharp, stinging sensations against her skin.

Her breath caught in her throat, but it didn't stay there long. It might have had something to do with the fact that my fingers clasped around her neck to cut off her airway as I took the knife, concealed inside of the pendant around my neck, and began to cut across her chest.

sajira had been bound in chains with her legs spread wide and tied down to her arms. There was nothing for her to do but take whatever, or whoever, came her way, whether she wanted them to or not. Her eyes were shut tightly, her body convulsing with each orgasm that swept through her body.

The moans coming from amani and sajira combined with the nearly electric sensations of the blade cutting across her skin conspired to send her into the euphoric depths of her consciousness.

"Daddy...damn." Her eyes fluttered as she struggled to keep her eyes open, torn between being a voyeur or giving in completely to what her body wanted. "Hurt me, please, i'm begging you."

With my fingers still firmly clasped around her neck, I lifted her slightly enough so her feet barely touched the floor. I took the blade and sliced her hip, riding the blade along the curves like a Porsche on the Stelvio Pass.

"You better not come, pet," I warned as I consistently pushed the buttons I knew would send her over the edge, and releasing the pressure to bring her back. "Not until I tell you to."

She frantically nodded, refusing to speak to focus on the agonizing line between pain and pleasure she precariously tight-roped.

Out of the corner of my eye, I noticed my Beloved wearing our boi out, her nails gripping his ass to really get some work in. Watching sajira trying her best to keep from passing out from the consistent tongue action being performed on her by a skilled family member had me smiling wide. I didn't stare too long because I didn't want to cut my property too deeply, although she wouldn't have cared either way now that she was in a fully enraptured flight.

"Goddess, he's making me come again!" sajira screamed as her body quivered through another wave. "i can't take any more, please, Goddess, please, i can't—"

Neferterri was in a zone, ignoring our little one's impassioned pleas for relent. She continued to tear into amani, pushing off her own release until there was no other choice. She finally noticed shamise and I were in the room with her, bringing an evil smile to her face.

"you'd better take care of us, bitch!" she growled, slapping his ass for good measure. "There'll be hell to pay if you don't!"

I kept shamise flying high, whispering all the things I planned to do once I let her down, grinning at the incoherent rebuttal she attempted to convey, her body shuddering with each swipe of the blade across every erogenous zone I committed to memory.

"Fuck, I'm coming!" I heard Neferterri yell as she pushed as hard as she could into amani, collapsing to the side of where he and sajira lay. A trembling hand reached for the quick release on the binds around amani's arms, pulling them to free his arms. "Release your sister, amani."

Realizing the focus would now be on us, I whispered in shamise's ear, "It's showtime, baby. It's time to take you into the abyss."

I dropped the blade to the floor so I could get a better grip where I knew it would cause the quickest explosion, my fingers plunging deep into her sex. It was only a matter of time before I would hear the sweet sounds of my baby's waves crashing over her.

"Please, Daddy, I'm there, please, let me go!" shamise begged with what voice she had left straining against the pressure of my grip around her throat. "I've been a good girl, Daddy, please!"

I released my grip, waiting for the familiar tremors to announce themselves before she went into the throes of orgasmic bliss. I held her tightly across her chest, making sure she knew her flight and landing would be safe from harm.

"She looks so sensual when she's flying, Goddess," sajira commented as she watched her sister in my arms. "God, she's so sexy when she comes."

Neferterri's eyes sought mine, recognizing the familiar devious gleam that made her swoon when she wanted me to take over. "Yes she is, and your Daddy seems to be in rare form, too, baby. There must have been some displays going on out on the island."

I kept my focus on shamise, knowing her stay in the stratosphere could last but so long before I slowly, but surely, brought her back into her conscious state.

"shamise…precious…come back to Me," I whispered in her ear. I lowered us to the love seat near the bed, as I felt her body take its toll on my grip. I laid her head on my chest to hear my heartbeat, ensuring she had a secured entry point when she awoke from her trip.

amani sat up from his spot on the bed, shifting his focus to the aftermath of not only what happened to him, but realizing that shamise and I were in the room. "Is shamise okay? How long was i out?"

Neferterri giggled as she kissed his forehead. "Not long, baby, but your takeoff was quick and powerful. You're okay now. your Sir and sis came in as you were taking flight."

shamise finally opened her eyes, suddenly looking up to find mine before scanning the rest of the room as though she'd seen it for the first time. She buried her face in my neck to hide her blushing cheeks.

"you're okay, baby girl, there's no one in here but family," I re-assured as I lifted her face to show what I told her was true.

"i felt like i was floating away." shamise wiped the sweat from her forehead, sitting up while in my arms. She finally found sajira, who was smiling at her. Her hair was tousled and she tried her best to run her fingers through it to make herself look presentable.

"That's because you were floating away, sis. If it weren't for

Daddy doing what He usually does, you'd still be out of it." sajira giggled as she got up from the bed. "Sounds like another day in paradise to me."

Yeah, it was definitely another day in paradise. I found myself wondering if the morning would be as wonderful as what the night had been. It was a safe bet that it would be hard to beat, that much was for certain.

"We need to get some sleep; there's a lot to do in the next few hours." I looked over at Neferterri, sharing a knowing grin between us, realizing the week had only begun.

TWO ⚭ RAMESSES

"This is a beautiful island, Sir. How in the world did you pull this off?"

I walked with an early morning group on a tour of the grounds the next day, taking in the sights and enjoying the "oohs" and "ahhs" from the crowd every time we stopped to point out a landmark. We'd left the main building by golf cart caravan, moving through the landscape, which had taken some considerable time in putting together.

Let me tell you, taking on this project was more exhausting than the three compounds—*NEBU*, *Deshret*, and *Thebes*—combined. The logistics alone were daunting, with Dominic and I traveling extensively to oversee construction, excavation, and animal control and relocation. Thank the gods Neferterri and the girls were able to take care of things while I was away.

The initial business plan was to cater to the more affluent swingers who wanted the ultimate in privacy before expanding to the kink community to keep things viable. By the time we got word to the alternative community at large, Stateside and globally, things got so busy that we had to hire a full-time, year-round staff to keep up with demand.

It was a good problem to have, but it was still a problem.

The island was located close enough to Nassau's Lynden Pindling

International Airport to make it feasible to travel, and ironically enough, the original name of the island was Devil's Cay. After searching the Bahamas for the perfect private location, Neferterri and I were able to locate this prime piece of real estate: 170 acres of island paradise, ripe for the taking and renovating. The way we figured, it was easier to have patrons fly down to Nassau and then take the thirty-minute yacht ride up to the island. Dominic and I agreed it was the more efficient option to keep from paying for private jets and crews.

Sure, there were some hitches along the way, I will admit, but it wasn't supposed to be a walk in the park, either. Thankfully, everything came together when it needed to, especially when we brought in the personnel to get the purchase and zoning permits taken care of.

In the group touring with me were Amenhotep and Osiris, Blaze and Sin, and about six other people, including the persons who represented the answer to the question posed once we exited the carts to get a look at one of the fantasy and fetish locales.

"Ladies and gentlemen, I present to you, Mr. and Mrs. Jameson from London," I announced. Amenhotep's grin widened as He was finally able to place the names and the faces together. He'd only communicated with the Jamesons through the various phone conferences we'd had over the past few months once we were close to finalizing the deal. "They were instrumental in facilitating the purchase of this island."

After the applause died down, Amenhotep commented, "How did you and Ramesses hook up for this endeavor?"

"Well, our relationship began a couple of years ago, actually." Mrs. Jameson smiled at me as she recalled the events of that day. "One of his girls...Candy, I believe was her name...did some marketing work for a campaign my husband and I were doing for our novelty company. We kept in touch after she finished our campaign, and during one of our visits back to the States, Ramesses and Neferterri asked us out to dinner and told us about what they'd planned to do and wondered if we knew anyone that dealt in real estate in the Caribbean. Little did they know that one of our other ventures was in real estate. The rest was history. It was a grand opportunity we couldn't pass up."

"Well, I am glad everything turned out the way it did." Amenhotep clapped His hand against my shoulder. "I think this was a good investment, especially when the other properties are doing so well. I should have done this with You years ago, kid."

I laughed at that last comment. We'd known each other for almost twenty years and He still refers to me as "kid." I guess to Him, I always will be that youngster He trained so long ago.

We walked down to the area where I purposely stopped the tour, so everyone could see the crown jewel of the entire island.

"Here's the reason I stopped at this point in the tour, folks," I stated. I let the crowd take in the view and paused for dramatic effect. "Take a gander, and you can thank Me later."

I stood and looked for myself, smiling at the design of the space.

The area was surrounded by trees and brush, with the sand graded down and smoothed to look like carpet. Spread out in the midst of the clearing was gazebo-styled tents, complete with mesh screens that could be pulled back to allow air flow or left closed for semi-privacy. There was somewhere around twenty tents, spread out liberally throughout the clearing, with enough room for people to walk between the tents and not disturb the players as they engaged in their scenes, whatever the scene might be.

Bamboo lamps adorned the outside of each of the tents, providing the intimate lighting and lending to the sensual ambiance the tents were meant for. Knowing a lot of the clientele we were accepting into the island had a fetish for outdoor play, it became easy to see why most of the faces in the small contingent lit pup. The anticipation of this evening's activities would be further heightened by the disclosure of this locale to the rest of the patrons still resting from last night's events.

"Ramesses, You have outdone Yourself yet again." Osiris shook my hand as he marveled over the attention to detail. Everything from the scarab designs on the lamps that circled the perimeter of the clearing to the large Sekhmet statues, with the goddess Sekhmet being a revered lion-headed goddess who was rumored to have controlled the Tables of Destiny, providing the gateway to the space. "This makes the compounds in the States look like practice facilities. I'm scared to find out what You shelled out to make all this happen."

Hell, he was scared?

A man with lesser capital probably would have been once I disclosed the figures. I spared no expense to make sure the island was as decorated, if not more extravagant and detailed, than the properties in the States. I wanted to make sure these grand opening attendees would go home and brag and rave about the island.

Honestly speaking, why wouldn't they?

Nine million in cash for the island free and clear…

Another twenty million in construction and upgrades, not to mention another ten million for security and surveillance…

Yet another five million in underground advertising to screen the initial patrons that would represent at least six or seven different countries, spanning across Europe, Africa, Asia, North and South America, and even a small contingent from Down Under.

Yeah, this might have been initially set up for people of color, but I had bigger fish to fry, not to mention heavy profits to make.

Amenhotep asked me a couple of years ago if I wanted my own version of Hedonism.

Now that I looked at the way this place had developed, I shook my head at the comparison.

I wanted to leave Hedonism in the dust.

If I got my way, I would do exactly that.

"To put You out of Your misery, Bro…about forty million dollars, give or take a few hundred thousand." I waited for the long whistle to flow from Osiris after the figure sank in. "Thankfully, we were able to tap into some of the returns on investments Amenhotep and I were able to receive from some of our British connections, in addition to a few million extracted from former members who violated the clauses on their agreements over the past year."

"Damn, You mean someone was stupid enough to violate the clauses?" Osiris wanted to laugh, but I didn't think he would have felt completely comfortable doing it. After all, a million dollars is nothing to sneeze at, much less give away because your emotions got the best of you.

"So, what furniture have You installed out here?" Blaze inquired, shifting our attention to her. "And how have You prepared for the inclement weather that we all know comes through here?"

I grinned when I heard her question.

"It's funny you should mention that." I laughed as I took a remote from the base of one of the Sekhmet statues. As I pressed the button to start the sequence, I yelled out, "I guess you've forgotten who I am!"

The ground shook for a few moments as the bases of each of the tents slowly descended into the ground as though they were being swallowed by quicksand. Once the tents were completely out of sight, the enclosures moved over the tops of the tents, sealing them underground.

My satellite phone rang immediately.

"Dom...no, Sir, there is nothing on the radar; I checked before the demonstration...yes, Sir, it was needed, but we're good to go now."

I hung up the phone and almost laughed at the shocked faces surrounding me as the full weight of what they'd witnessed finally sank in.

Yeah, they were gonna learn today!

Not that I needed an answer to the question I was about to ask, but for the sake of a good chuckle, I went ahead and asked the rhetorical. "Are there any further questions?"

THREE ⊗ NEFERTERRI

"Welcome to the rules and protocol part of the program."

I was glad I decided to do this part of the resort itinerary. There was no way I was getting up to do the tour. He could have it.

I sat in the reception hall of the main building with shamise and sajira at my sides. I had amani assisting the medical staff in the first-aid building to ensure things were running smoothly. I didn't want to take any chances, even though the staff was kink-friendly.

We made sure the House had as much of its imprint on the island as possible. Ramesses made sure the overall operation of the island was as seamless as he could have it, while working with Dominic on the surveillance and security system, which was state-of-the-art. I was in awe of how intricate the system was, covering every square foot of the island. I took care of the travel arrangements for the entertainers and the servants, with shamise providing assistance. sajira put her accounting team together to take care of yet another arm of the ever-growing empire we'd built over the past few years.

It was definitely a sight to behold, and the hard work was definitely worth it.

I had the service slaves take care of serving the brunch trays to the audience while I moved around the front of where they sat, directing everyone's attention to the PowerPoint presentation being projected from the LCD monitor connected to my laptop. Thankfully, there would only be two of these presentations today, one this morning and one in the afternoon. I knew Ramesses would be touring all day and a part of me felt a little guilty. The tours had to be somewhat exhausting, but he was in his element, so I was not about to take away from his pleasure.

"If you take note of the protocol covering station cleanliness and safety, you will notice the standards are in line with the way we handle things at NEBU, Deshret, and Thebes." I continued my presentation, scanning the crowd to make sure anyone wasn't bored out of their skull.

As my eyes moved through the crowd, I noticed an intense pair of light-brown eyes begging for my undivided attention. Looking further, I realized those eyes were attached to a fine specimen of a man. I glanced at his facial features, including a thick pair of lips that spread into a smile to show his appreciation of what his eyes beheld.

He winked at me as he held my gaze for a few more seconds, trying to keep me engaged as best he could. I dismissed him as best as I could, but not before shamise caught the exchange between us. She looked up at me for a brief moment before returning her gaze to the audience. She knew better than to say anything at the moment, but the possessive shift in her kneeling position and body language let me know she might broach the subject later in the day.

I wasn't about to complain about what happened. The past few months, it had felt like there was a "no touch" policy when it came to any new men who might have wanted to approach me from a sexual perspective. Not that I minded too much because Ramesses and amani gave me all I could handle with the way they kept me in a constant state of arousal.

Still, it would have been nice to pick up a new "piece" to break in the island properly.

My mind briefly wondered what the mystery man, the one still staring at me, would feel like with his thick lips and tongue caressing my clit and licking my ass as I sat on his face. Hell, even our girls got slutted out from time to time to take the edge off; why shouldn't I?

Maybe I was getting bored because the men who threw themselves at me always made it easy to get it. Where's the fun in that?

I knew my Beloved had his moments where the thrill of the chase rose to the surface, but lately he'd been content with how things were. Between me, shamise, sajira, and his secretary, taliah, we spoiled that man rotten.

If it weren't for the light tapping of sajira's finger against my hip, I would have lost myself in my thoughts. I tried to regain my composure, taking my eyes off the stranger, so I could get through the rest of the presentation without another pause.

"Ladies and gentlemen, I hope you enjoy the island and partake in the delights while you're here. Have a great day, and if you happen to see me or my girls in passing, make sure you say hello." I stared at the mystery man as I finished my spiel, making sure he understood the not-so-subtle invitation to introduce himself as soon as fucking possible.

shamise was quiet for a few moments, and I could feel the tension on her body. sajira noticed it, too, although she might not have realized the reason why.

"shamise, baby, what's on your mind?" I asked her as the last of the guests left the reception hall. "you were stiff as a board during the last of the presentation."

"Yeah, sis, what happened, what did i miss?" sajira was still in "baby girl" mode, so her question came off more playful than showing concern.

shamise hesitated for a moment, her eyes looking in the direction of the mystery man, who was standing in the doorway. I couldn't suppress the smile that spread across my face, no matter how hard I tried. He returned my smile with one of his own before noticing the scowl on shamise's face. Realizing he wouldn't get a chance to speak with me alone, he stepped away and disappeared from the room, leaving the three of us alone in the hall.

shamise was not amused. "May i have permission to speak freely, my Goddess?"

"Yes, you may, precious."

"i'm a little disturbed that you openly flirted with another man in front of us, my Goddess," shamise remarked, struggling to maintain her protocol and training. I looked in her eyes and saw mild disappointment. "You've never done that before, my Goddess. You acted like a horny teenager, and i felt the heat rising on Your skin."

"Come on, sis, that man was gorgeous!" sajira giggled as she looked up at me, trying to take my side. "i mean, i know Daddy is fine and all, but our Goddess isn't dead, you know."

"This was different, sis." shamise turned toward sajira to explain herself. "If She could have cleared the room, dismissed us and fucked Him on the spot, She would have. i guess i'm used to Goddess being a little more disciplined, even in the audience of a man as fine as Him. Hell, i've seen Her keep Her composure around men finer than Him."

Damn, I hated when my Alpha slave knew me as well as shamise did. The unfortunate part was she was right.

I kissed shamise across her forehead and then across her lips. "shamise, you're right, I didn't carry myself in a manner that you are used to. But even you had to admit that man was gorgeous, baby girl."

shamise tried her best to keep from grinning before her lips parted and she had to fan herself for a moment. She looked up at me with a guilt written all over her face. "Okay, yes, He was fine as fuck, if You don't mind me saying so, my Goddess. To be honest, i tried to keep from staring at him the whole time, but He only had eyes for You."

sajira chimed, "Now that You mentioned it, my Goddess, He did seem like He was fixated on You, even though the other women around Him tried their best to get His attention."

Under normal circumstances, I would have taken that information as an immediate red flag, with the intent to dismiss him as a stalker. But I wanted to at least have a conversation with him to see if my suspicions were justified or if there might have been something more to discover.

One thing was for certain, whether I wanted to admit it or not.

He had my curiosity and my attention, but both were very hard to keep.

☥

The beauty of having a privately owned island was the ability to do whatever you wanted, and when it came to my Beloved and me and the things we tended to come up with, the word "whatever" could be one helluva feat.

I was grateful for the solitude for a couple of hours. shamise was coordinating things for the entertainers tonight, sajira was tied up taking care of some things for the other compounds in the States via video conferencing, and amani had to tend to a slight emergency involving heatstroke with the medical team. With Ramesses still caught up in tours for the remainder of the afternoon, I was alone to indulge and, to be blunt, I needed to come.

As I rubbed suntan lotion into my skin, thoughts of the mysterious stranger began to flood my mind. I preferred to tan nude, and since I didn't have to worry about whether or not it was illegal, I allowed my body to relax while I welcomed the lustful thoughts that invaded my mind. The sun was hot on my bronzed skin as I untied my bikini top and massaged suntan lotion into my breasts.

I lay back while enjoying the sounds of the ocean and felt the breeze caress my body, covering my face with my wide-brimmed sun hat and sunglasses to prevent a headache I knew would hit me if I didn't take precautions. I imagined the breeze was the stranger's hands, caressing and molesting me, and I moved my hips in flow with the wind, enjoying the burn from the sun's rays licking my flesh. My mind slipped into a deeper zone, imagining the sun's rays were my Beloved's hands, making my pussy moisten with desire.

I moaned, my sounds mingling with the crashing of the waves and the rustling of the trees, not wanting this pseudo-threesome to end any time soon. I grabbed for my two-headed bullet, slipping one egg-shaped node in my ass and the other inside my walls. The moment I turned the remote on, the familiar vibrations sent shockwaves through my clit, mercilessly coursing through my body, and I loved every minute of it.

"Damn, fuck My ass, Daddy," I whispered. I wasn't ready to shout because my body wasn't there yet. I reached out in my mind's eye to feel his dick inside of my anal tract, feeling so slick and wet that it could have felt like he was in my pussy. I rolled and grinded my hips, imagining he was under me, with my wetness exposed for anyone to come in and take my other hole.

I imagined the stranger coming in and sliding right in, envisioning his girth filling me up, pumping me from the top as my Beloved pumped me from underneath me, bringing me closer to an orgasm that would be so intense that I knew I would pass out.

"Oh fuck, give it to Me! I'm almost there!" My breathing shortened and my nipples were fully engorged. I almost pleaded with my body to let me enter into the blissful paradise, so I could completely release every ounce of energy into the air. "Oh fuck oh fuck oh fuck!"

A few moments later, I was in the throes of a full-body orgasm as my vibrator continued to prolong the trip, sending me deeper into a state of intemperate passion, my voice letting loose a sequence of unintelligible words and phrases I didn't care if anyone heard or could make sense of.

By the time my body expended its energy, I was completely spent with a slick grin on my face. I couldn't help myself. It had been so long since I'd had a fantasy that intense that I didn't notice the towel I lay on was soaked in blood. Damn! It must have snuck in on me this time around because I had been so sexually active the past few days with Ramesses before we got down here and then playing with the girls and amani.

I quickly gathered my things and rushed into the hut to clean myself up, pissed that the fun I knew I would have this week would be stunted by my period.

What a time for this bitch to show up!

FOUR ⊗ NEFERTERRI

"I'm so pissed I want to scream!"

I sat on the balcony of the family hut, which wasn't far from the main building, with sajira and shamise, venting my frustration over having to deal with my period a week earlier than expected. I had planned with Ramesses and the girls to make sure that we all were safe from dealing with that bitch while working through the grand opening week.

"Goddess, You know how it goes, if You don't mind me saying." sajira worked on my lower back while shamise worked on my thighs and lower legs, which I knew would be the first things hurting when my cycle started. "We planned it as best we could, and to be honest, I am spotting a little bit, and i'm not thrilled about it, either."

I didn't want to admit it out loud, but I took some solace that at least one of my girls might have been on the verge of going through the same thing as I was. shamise actually had her tubes tied years ago because she had no desires to have children of her own, which was why our children loved "Auntie 'mise" so much. Not that they didn't love "Auntie 'jira" as much, but shamise had been around the kids since they were toddlers.

From the energy I felt sajira putting into the massage she was giving me, I could tell something wasn't right with her, either.

"Okay, little one, speak. I know something's wrong because your energy has changed," I commanded. "And don't say 'it's nothing, Goddess,' either, or you'll put Me in a very bad mood. Considering I'm already going through it with My cycle, you might want to put some thought into your response."

sajira hesitated for a second before the emotions poured out of her. "It's the same conversation we've been having for the past year, Goddess, but i didn't want to burden You with it anymore. Ice is becoming more difficult by the month, especially now that shamise is living with us."

I exhaled. Ice had been becoming more difficult by the moment, and it seemed that no one could redirect his focus. He'd been especially disobedient and insubordinate toward Ramesses and me lately, to the point to where I had to break him down to his knees in front of his Mistress, Sinsual, to get him to calm down on the home front. His and Ramesses's relationship had deteriorated to where he no longer even came over on their traditional Poker nights to hang with Jay and the rest of the crew.

At the rate he was heading, he would find himself on the outside looking in if he wasn't careful. Sin's patience was at its limit, and she had privately confided in me that she was on the verge of releasing him if his behavior didn't improve. He even insisted on being called by his slave name, lynx, almost full time now, with the only exception being when we were in our swingers' circles, and he withdrew from that scene the moment Sin took him as her property.

I knew Sin, and she didn't take kindly to her submissives embarrassing her when they were not with her. tiger, her Alpha slave, understood that from the beginning, and even he was becoming disenchanted with lynx also. I secretly wondered if tiger were simply trying to figure out what he could get out of his interaction and training of his brother submissive, otherwise, he would have whispered in his Mistress's ear months ago to find a way to release him.

This entire situation began to wear on both of our girls, and while Ramesses and I offered to move them to our old house, sajira was insistent upon trying to work things out with her husband. shamise did not want to abandon her sister, as she had become accustomed to living with her, despite the negative energy resonating through the house. They even stopped having sex after sajira was collared last year, which seemed to concern sajira more than it did lynx. His only concern was pleasing his Mistress from then on, which was funny to me because his actions were definitely contrary to what pleased Sin.

As long as lynx wasn't verbally or physically abusive, Ramesses and I maintained our distance while keeping a close eye on his interactions whenever we were at NEBU or when we were at different functions in other parts of the city. In my heart, I'd hoped he came to his senses and realized he's hurting his wife, but at the same time, there was no other way to really make him see unless sajira left him.

The last thing either of us wanted to do was issue a directive, but enough was enough.

"sajira, you know your Daddy and I love you, but there's only so much we can take watching you go through this." I turned around and caressed her cheek, making sure she maintained eye contact with me. "Compromise takes two people, baby girl, and he's no longer willing to be the other party in this."

"Goddess, i know, but it's so hard to let him go." sajira fell to her knees, clutching my thigh as tears began to fall. "i still love him, but i also know he's being a bit ridiculous also. i want to strangle him sometimes because i know this is not the man i married."

"Sis, sometimes things run their course, you know?" shamise didn't want to put the possibility of divorce out in the universe for consumption. "i know it's not something you wanna think about, but the way he has been acting at home—"

shamise's thoughts were interrupted by a series of knocks that made us jump. The urgency of the knocking had us all on edge.

I walked toward the door, picking up my Glock 19 along the way as the knocking got louder and more intense by the moment.

I swung the door open and pointed the gun in the same motion, intent on scaring the person on the other side of the door. The barrel of the gun landed squarely between the eyes of lynx, whose angry scowl turned into trepidation quickly upon seeing the shiny piece of metal in my hand.

"I *know* your Mistress taught you better than this, slave." The irritation in my voice was not lost on him, and he immediately dropped to his knees, realizing I was not to be trifled with. "To what do we owe the honor of your, shall we say, visit?"

"i wish to see my wife." lynx's eyes continued to focus on the barrel. He never looked up in my direction, realizing that transgression would compound the issue that he had already placed himself in. I was irritated by the fact that he had to be reminded of his place and protocol.

"I assume you want to try that again, slave?" I cocked a bullet into the chamber to emphasize his need to repeat himself with the respect he was taught.

Watching the barrel trained between his eyes, lynx dropped to his knees and dropped his head. His eyes were cast downward. He opened his palms at his knees and asked again, "Lady Neferterri, this slave would respectfully request to see his wife, if You have finished with her at this time?"

"That's better, slave." I lowered my gun as shamise and sajira walked up behind me. sajira's face twisted when she saw her husband on the ground. I know she hated seeing him like that, but if he was gonna play games, he was gonna play by my rules, even if it killed him. "sajira, baby, go take care of business with your husband; we'll be in the main building taking care of tonight's entertainment."

"Yes, my Goddess, i shall meet you there in about an hour." She cut her eyes at lynx. The way her body stiffened, I didn't want to be a fly on the wall for that conversation. She turned her attention back to me, letting me know she had to make quick work of her husband before getting back to the tasks at hand. "This won't take long, i promise."

FIVE ✲ sajira

"Have you lost your damn mind?!?!?!"

I took my husband back to my private bedroom inside of the family hut since I knew we would have a slight bit of privacy to rip him a new asshole for embarrassing me in front of my D/s family.

"No, I haven't lost anything, at least I don't think I have." He had the nerve to try to sound pitiful. "As hard as this might sound to you, I miss my wife."

I didn't know whether I wanted to kick him or punch him after he made that statement.

For the past year, he had been an absolute jackass, doing everything in his power to try and make living with him as unbearable as he could. He'd moved into the spare bedroom in our home, all but stopped having sex with me six months later, and tried his best to make my sis feel like a piece of meat.

But now he missed his *wife*. Yeah, right.

"If you say you miss me, you have a fucked-up way of showing it, *Ice*." I refused to call him by his slave name. In my mind, he took the "only address me by my slave name" madness too far, and I wasn't about to feed into it anymore. "So, tell me, darling, when exactly did you start missing me? Was it before or after your Mistress stopped fucking you?"

His eyes widened, wondering how in the world I'd found out

that information. What he failed to realize was tiger, his so-called sub brother, had been feeding me information for months, which was how I was able to tolerate his bullshit. He was suffering more than I was, despite his attempts to ration out the dick he swore I couldn't get enough of.

If shamise wasn't living with us full time while he was being an asshole, he might have succeeded in that pitiful effort. Even if she wasn't, if I wanted to be a slut, I would have fucked every piece of prime male specimen my Goddess put in front of me, and she'd put some *quality* dick in my path, and dropped him like a bad habit.

"Yeah, that's what I thought." I huffed, eyeing him as I sat on the bed to get more comfortable. "You're lucky you're still cute, or I would have let my Goddess do you the way you should have been done for treating me like shit for the past year."

"I don't want to make this difficult any more than you want to go through it, Kitana—"

"My name is sajira now."

"Touché, I deserved that."

"You deserve to have your balls crushed, jackass."

"Why are you making this apology so hard?"

I crossed my legs and folded my arms over my breasts and gave him a look that could have burned through lead. "Is *that* what you're trying to do? You've done a helluva lot better than that in the past, so what gives with the half-hearted apology, huh? What, you couldn't take the yacht to Nassau to get me some flowers or something?"

Ice dropped to one knee, moving near my legs. I tried to avoid his eye contact, but I found myself connecting, whether I wanted to or not. There was still something in me that loved this man, and despite the madness, I still loved him.

"Well, I would have, but I wasn't sure you wanted to see me or not."

He moved his hands up and down my calves and my pussy twitched from the sensation. He still knew my spots, even though he hadn't tried to touch them in months.

I uncrossed my legs to let him feel the inside of my thighs. He tried to move closer to my bikini bottom, pulling at the strings to untie them, but I moved his hands away. I was gonna make him work for this, determined to turn this into a grudge fuck if I decided to let it get that far.

He moved between my legs, wrapping them around his waist as he kissed me the way he used to when he couldn't get enough of me. I was so wet I knew I soaked through my suit, and I couldn't have cared less because I wanted him to put this fire out.

"I forgot how good you feel," Ice whispered in my ear as he moved to bite down on my neck. "Damn, I can't wait to beat this pussy up again."

Shut the fuck up and fuck me, you idiot, I screamed in my head, trying to get him to realize he was talking himself out of some good pussy. I tried to coax him into taking me by slipping my fingers inside and letting him lick my fingers clean, which was what I used to do whenever we got in a quickie.

What he said next should have made me choke him to death. "If only we weren't in different D/s relationships, we could fuck like this again."

I heard the proverbial screeching brakes, drying me up quicker than a puddle of water in the Sahara.

"Get the fuck away from me *right now!*" I was so upset I was trembling.

"Kitana…look, hear me out, that's not what I meant—"

"What part of 'get away from me' did you not understand?" I repeated, shooting daggers through him with the piercing stare I gave him. "You…you don't get to hide behind your Mistress."

"Face it, Kitana, we had more fun when we were swinging." He tried to plead his case. "There were no boundaries and no bullshit rules and protocol to follow, and we got to connect at the end of the day once we were done. Tell me you don't miss that?"

This knee-grow got jokes!

"Please, spare me the whole 'we had more fun when we were swinging' bullshit," I retorted, grabbing a towel before I moved him out of my way as I headed to the bathroom. I felt a headache coming on, and I was pissed that I'd allowed myself to even have one. "As long as you were getting sucked and fucked, *we* were having a damn good time. I think about it now, and I'm really sorry I took one for the *team* all those years."

If I counted the number of times we were at swing parties and the men weren't half the man my husband was, both in their stroke game and their sex appeal, I would have stopped swinging a long time ago and let him do his thing solo. If it weren't for the fact that I was bi, and thanking God that either Neferterri or Ramesses was at the same parties a lot of the time, I would have been bored out of my skull while Ice fucked anything in a negligee.

"Wait a minute…you mean you faked it with all of those dudes you were with?" Ice asked.

"Don't look so surprised, babe." I laughed at my inside joke. His eyes narrowed, and I watched the wheels turning in his head, trying to go through all of the parties we'd attended. I did my best to help him along. "Keep thinking back, my love. Do you recall anything in particular?"

"Sonofabitch!" Ice yelled as the light switch came on. "You're serious? I mean, whenever we got home, you couldn't get enough of me."

"You're right, I needed to have you to regain my balance." I affirmed his suspicions, and I wasn't lying about that part. The sex was so awful, the only way I could get my nut and sleep in one piece was to fuck the shit out of the only dick I knew could get me off…my husband's.

"Look, I want you to leave the D/s world; I'm bored and sick of it now." Ice put the real reason for wanting to talk to me. "I'm pretty much done anyway because my Mistress is probably going to release me the minute we get back from this trip."

Now that was a piece of information that I was not aware of. He'd been messing up a lot lately, but I didn't think it had gotten that bad. Why else would Sinsual even think about bringing him along on this trip if she were seriously considering releasing him?

Something wasn't adding up, but one thing was for certain: I was not leaving my D/s family simply because he'd fucked himself up.

"That's not happening, Ice," I answered. "I'm happy within the dynamic I am a part of, especially when things are really beginning to take off for me professionally, too."

"So, you're willing to throw our marriage away for your dynamic?" Ice was incredulous. "We've been together for ten years. No one knows you as well as I do."

"You should have thought about that when you were busy trying to screw me over and screw my sis," I lashed back at him, willing the tears to keep from streaming down my face. I shook so bad it looked like the breeze was sending chills through me. "Or are you going to deny you've been trying to fuck her, too?"

"I see there's no talking to you when you're like this, so I'll let you think it over for a few days." Ice walked to the door. "Whether you realize it or not, or if you even care anymore, I do still love you, Kitana, but it's either them or me. The choice is yours."

He left the room, leaving me on my back, staring at the ceiling, feeling even more confused than ever…and in desperate need of my Daddy's touch.

SIX ❦ NEFERTERRI

"Do You think sajira is okay?"

shamise had reason to be concerned, and I had to admit, I was, too. She was at a precarious point with her husband, and I didn't envy her at all. lynx had completely lost his mind, and if I were a lesser woman, the medical staff would have been cleaning bullet fragments out of his shoulder and knees.

"I honestly don't know, baby; her body language was all over the place when she left us," I pointed out. "The only thing we can do is hope she's okay until we see her."

We walked to the main building from the family hut, leaving sajira to deal with her husband in private. Every fiber in my being told me to wait until I knew she was okay, but I also needed to trust my submissive to handle her business when the occasion called for it. I loved them both because they had that ability, and I wasn't about to stunt their growth.

As shamise and I greeted guests during our walk, I noticed the sun was surprisingly warm and inviting today, lending to a soothing atmosphere on the island. I felt it would be a perfect time to enjoy some down time, especially after I had to show steel to get a so-called submissive to stand down and follow protocol. I found a lounger while shamise found a chair nearby to sit in, but I didn't think she would need it for long.

"my Goddess, i would like to check in on my sis in a little while, if it pleases You?" shamise asked as she rubbed suntan lotion into my skin. Her fingers were amazing as she melted away the tension I unexpectedly built while dealing with lynx.

"Mmmm…yes, precious, you have My permission to leave as soon as you're done here."

I stretched out on the lounger, letting shamise's expert fingers massage every inch she could manage. I listened to her hum as she went about her task, smiling as devilish thoughts crept into my mind. I didn't care if I was flowing and it would stop her from pleasing me; I had an urge to take her back to the hut and enjoy every inch of her before taking a delicious nap.

The zone I was in was interrupted once her humming stopped and I heard her speaking to someone. "Good afternoon, Sir, is there something i can assist You with?"

"Yes, I was wondering if I could speak to your Ma'am." I heard a voice that could rival my Beloved's on the tone alone. I continued to enjoy shamise's fingers as she returned to what she was doing. I wanted to peek through my sunglasses to see who the voice belonged to, but it wasn't hard to figure out. He'd been trying to get me alone since he'd seen me.

shamise was obviously not as affected by the melodious tone in his voice, and if I didn't know any better, I would have sworn she was in a protective mode. She might be "Daddy's girl," but she was not about to let anybody into my space. "i'm sure You would, Sir, but at the current moment, She is a bit engaged. Please forgive me, Sir, i don't believe we have been formally introduced. my name is shamise, Alpha slave of the House of Kemet-Ka, and i believe You already know my Goddess, Lady Neferterri. May i respectfully ask Your name?"

"How rude of Me. My name is Sir Lyrical." He tried his best to keep the melody in his voice in an attempt to impress me, but his tone began to lose its sing-song tinge. He wasn't thrilled to have to speak to shamise so extensively. "I don't mind speaking with Her while you are attending to your tasks, shamise. It seems you're fully engaged, and I wouldn't want to interrupt a slave while she is taking care of her Mistress."

I felt shamise's fingers tense against my skin, her silent cue to alert me of her displeasure with someone. I knew she only had my best interests at heart and felt he might have ulterior motives, but I'd dealt with wannabe players trying to be Dominants in the past. Besides, I couldn't do anything if I wanted to, so there was no point in torturing myself.

"There's no need to worry about interrupting My shamise, Sir Lyrical, is it?" I chimed in, my eyes still closed behind my sunglasses. I pulled my sunglasses and propped them on top of my head as I opened my eyes to turn my attention to shamise. Gauging her facial expression, I realized quickly the depths of her displeasure. I caressed her face, bringing her lips to mine to give her a soothing kiss.

Lyrical seemed a bit put off by the display we were putting on. The look he gave me when I disengaged to focus on him amused me. I realized he wasn't much different from my Beloved, used to getting what he wanted.

shamise cracked a smile, realizing her part in his discomfort. Under normal circumstances, I would have spoken to her about her behavior, but I gave her some leeway, ensuring she understood that I would pull her leash if she went too far.

"No, I would not," Lyrical uttered, trying to find a way back into the conversation so he could have my full attention. "It seems the only time I can catch a chance to speak with You, You're with one of Your girls."

"Would You prefer Daddy be around You while you speak to my Goddess?" shamise's smirk was evident on her face as she stifled a giggle. "i would pay the price of admission to see how that would happen! Good luck, trying to get Her alone with You, Sir. It would take a tsunami to hit the island and separate us from Her for something like that to happen."

I saw the muscles in his jaw clench, and I felt it was time to slow my property down before she really began to take pleasure in his discomfort. As much as I enjoyed watching him squirm, I did want to see if he had what it took to go the distance.

"shamise, that's enough, baby girl." I placed my hand on her shoulder, calming her instantly. "There's no way that He would be able to be alone with Me unless I felt He was worth the effort. I don't believe this gentleman would make the mistake of crossing your Daddy by ignoring the rules of engagement, now would He, little one?"

She cut her eyes in Lyrical's direction, letting him know she was less than impressed with him, not caring that it might have looked like a disrespect of his station. I knew my girls, and neither of them showed their displeasure publicly unless there was a reason to. Her eyes finally turned to mine, her fingers interlacing through mine as she gave a soft smile. "Yes, my Goddess, i know He won't cross Daddy. No one is *that* stupid."

I giggled at her, remembering a time before the girls became a part of the House when someone was stupid enough to cross him.

He walks with a limp to this very day.

My Beloved had a temper, as quiet as it was kept, but he flashed it on very rare occasions.

shamise remained in her kneeling position, closing her eyes before she spoke again. "May i be excused now, my Goddesss?"

"Yes, you may, shamise. Check on your sis and make sure she is okay." I watched her hips sway as she moved in the direction of the family hut, where I assumed sajira might still be.

With her last parting shot, shamise looked back and addressed Lyrical. "Sir, please don't mistake my leaving as Your opportunity to be alone with my Goddess. It is only by Her command that i am leaving at all. Take this brief time to speak Your peace and understand that there are eyes everywhere."

Lyrical asked as he pulled up a chair next to my lounger, "Is she always like that? You would have thought I was trying to do harm or something."

"Our girls are very protective of us, Sir," I quipped, sliding my sunglasses over my eyes again. "You can only imagine how bad My boi is about Me."

"I have a feeling I might not want to find out." He smirked as his eyes roamed all over my body. Even though I was cramping horribly, I felt a twitch through my clit. I didn't want to show my arousal so soon, and I wanted to find a way to cover myself before my body betrayed me even further.

My nipples didn't quite get the memo as they perked up through my bikini top, making it known that his presence was doing something to me. He tried his best to keep from noticing, but they were sitting pretty enough for any man within a few feet of where we were sitting to realize I was in heat.

"Was it something I said?" he joked, crossing his muscular legs like he knew I was feeling him.

"No, it wasn't," I retorted, pulling my towel to cover my chest. "The breeze out here has Me a little cold, if You must know."

"The breeze...right...I can dig it." He chuckled to himself. I laughed along with him, realizing how paper-thin that excuse was. "So, would You like to find a place a little warmer for us to talk some more? I would love to get to know You better."

"That would be a negative, Sir." I lifted from the lounger to sit up a little bit. The heat rising from my skin made me uncomfortable, and being in a horizontal position where he could take advantage, and I would've wanted him to take advantage, was not a good look for a first encounter. I could be had, but only on my terms.

"Okay...so when can I see You? Perhaps we could have dinner together before the week is over?" He extended his hand to help me stand, and I had to smack his hand away from my ass when his fingers glanced across it. He grinned at the cat-and-mouse game he thought we were playing, but I was slowly getting bored with the amateur efforts.

"Honestly, I think I'll let You know if I feel like having dinner with You, Sir," I answered, moving to wrap the towel around my waist. "I don't think You're quite adept at the rules of engagement, but You're more than welcome to have dinner with Me, and the rest of My family, later on tonight, if You think You can hang."

The stunned look on his face let me know he was not used to being rejected very often, and it gave me a rush. Even if I did want to fuck him, and trust me, he was fine enough for me to want to fuck him, his actions put me off as though he had already sealed the deal, and it was only a matter of how quickly we could get to his hut and getting out of my swimsuit to do the damn thing.

There's only one man on this planet that had even come close. This one wasn't in the same galaxy as my Beloved.

"Fair enough, Lady Neferterri. As You wish."

I already knew he would show up for dinner later tonight; he was too curious not to show up and figure out why I wasn't as willing and anxious to let him have his way with me. I'd seen Female Dominants at times succumb to their urges and do what came naturally, and I didn't blame them for doing so as I'd done it in the past, too. But there was no way that Lyrical would be the beneficiary of that decision.

SEVEN ❧ RAMESSES

"The surveillance cameras are good to go, Dominic."

We were inside the main surveillance hub in the main building, doing the usual check of the systems and the range on the cameras in the different areas of the island. I spared no expense in getting a system that would make the casinos in Vegas jealous. Anything Dominic and I could find, we found it, and short of a dome to put over the top of the place, we had it installed and maintained as often as we could.

Because things were not always properly illuminated during the nighttime hours, we made sure the system had night vision technology needed to easily identify anyone within seconds, regardless of the time of day. Thankfully, most of the attendees traveled through Nassau to get to the yachts, which meant we could tap into the records at the airport and run facial recognition software without the attendees knowing it.

I took no chances...

"I think we might be good with making another sweep to make sure nothing has been tampered with," Dominic pointed out. "I think the cameras near the shoreline might need a closer look."

He wasn't fooling me. He saw some nice eye candy on the monitors and wanted to take a look at that. I wasn't mad at him. Neither of his girls, Natasha nor Niki, was able to make the trip because they were in the midst of the Christmas season. For law enforcement that meant it was the season to try to get away with stealing whatever from whomever.

"All right, Dom, let's make the sweep before nightfall. I have a feeling you might be right."

To be real, I knew he wasn't, but I wasn't about to deprive him of some pleasure.

We stepped out of the main building, working through the great room out to the front of the building, greeting guests and checking to make sure they were enjoying themselves. The walk did us both some good; it gave me a chance to check up on his progress with his submissives.

"So, talk to me, Dom. How goes it with Niki and Natasha?" I asked him as the candy passed us by.

"Ramesses, I can't complain with those two, especially after they went through the training with Your girls," Dominic answered. "Niki really took to the training, almost like she had been waiting to do it for a long time."

"Good deal, that's what I like to hear." I'd begun coaching the girls on training other new submissives, and Dom's girls were the guinea pig experiment to see if they had the skill to train others. "What about Natasha, is she taking to the training, too?"

"Natasha took a little time to wrap her head around the protocol, but once she equated it to the Academy training we went through as beat patrol, she finally came around," Dominic recounted.

"You know how it can be with aggressive women, My friend," I explained. "For the most part, they're trying to reconcile what submission really is versus the perception from all those romance books. Once they realize there is strength in submission, the mind calms down, and the body quickly follows."

"Don't I know it?" Dominic laughed for a moment as he enjoyed his inside joke. "I just hope I can keep it together. I'm not on Your level yet, but I'm learning quickly."

We continued to check on the surveillance cameras in the spots I knew were not an issue, but when we got to the beach area where the women usually sunbathed in the nude, I understood why he was in such a rush to get out there.

I couldn't stop staring, in awe at the beautiful bodies that were on display all over the area. Regardless of size, the hourglass shapes that assaulted my visual senses stopped me in my tracks and held me prisoner to the lustful thoughts in my mind. Dominic was right about needing to get a live feed instead of watching the cameras, but I wasn't about to give him the satisfaction of knowing he was right.

Dominic took one look at my facial expression and smirked. "Still think I was flexin'?"

"Fuck You, Dom." I laughed.

As I surveyed the field again, taking in the sights before we headed back to the main building to continue the sweep, a vision of exquisite sin came walking toward us. To say she had my attention was an understatement.

The bikini she wore was understated, almost boring by comparison to the pieces the other women wore on the beach, but there's something to be said for a body that makes anything look good.

Her eyes swept over the two of us, almost eyeing to figure out which one of us she wanted to deal with first. I was resigned to let her engage Dom instead of me, but with women, there's no telling what may happen. She locked eyes with me, never once looking away, which tripped my senses that she was a Dominant. Submissives usually didn't engage in eye contact, even when I requested that they do so.

"Good afternoon, gentlemen." She greeted us with an extended hand, turning in Dominic's direction. He shook her hand first, remaining indifferent despite the grin on his face in admiring her frame. I shook her hand after he disengaged with her, trying my best to keep my own composure as her body inspired some evil thoughts. There were a few things during our exchange that should have given me pause, but I was too enthralled with finding out more about her to listen to the warning bells sounding off in my mind.

She held my hand longer than I was comfortable with.

She held my eye contact longer than she needed to.

And she moved closer to me, ensuring I got a closer look at what I admired from a distance.

Dominic cleared his throat to break the connection between us. I could tell from his body language that he really wasn't about to stand around while I figured out if I wanted to say hello or not.

"Forgive Me, good afternoon to You." I finally got the words out of my mouth, confused as to why I was unable to speak. "I hope You have enjoyed the island so far?"

"Yes, I have, Ramesses," she remarked. "Although I have yet to experience the evil pleasures the island is developing the reputation for providing."

"You have Me at a disadvantage, My dear." I had to admit, she had me on my heels, and I wasn't sure if I liked the feeling or not. Usually it's my Beloved who put me on the defensive, so to have another do so without much effort was interesting. "You seem to know who I am, but neither I nor My associate do not so much as have Your name?"

"Well, let's correct that." Her smile widened as she continued to look at Dominic and me. Her facial expressions betrayed her, and her body language telegraphed exactly what was on her mind.

"My name is Domina Korina, but My friends call me DK, and yes, I do know who You and Dominic are."

"That's better, now that the pleasantries are out of the way, we have other business to attend to, Ramesses." Dominic's temper began to flare up. It was a matter of time before he cut loose and let his mouth tell what's going through his mind. "We have that fire play demo to prepare for You and sajira later tonight."

"I would love to learn fire play," DK chimed in, interrupting Dom's attempts at cutting the conversation short. "Watching Master Osiris last night was amazing. Do You think You could teach Me?"

Before I could answer, Dominic interjected, "I'm sorry, DK, but Master Ramesses's schedule is hectic over the next few days. It would be near impossible with the operations of the island during this critical grand opening to take the time needed to teach the basics."

"I'm sure I can find some time to instruct over the next day or so." I was contradicting myself, but I wasn't about to give up the opportunity to do some damage with my fire play skills. Dominic's jaw almost dropped as he watched the smile creep across DK's face and she subconsciously licked her lips. "You're more than welcome to watch the demo later on tonight, just to get an idea of how I do My thing."

"I think I would love to see You do Your thing." She moved closer to me for a brief second, an obvious attempt to trip my carnal senses. The mix of the ocean water on her skin and the scent of the suntan lotion should have been enough to make me want to take her right there on the beach, whether Dom was there or not.

Too bad for her. I did have business to attend to, and I wasn't about to deviate from my appointed rounds. Besides, there's no telling what may have happened later on after the demo.

"Well, I'll look forward to seeing You and the rest of the guests tonight in the main dungeon area, DK." I maneuvered around her, taking care not to touch her in any sensual manner. The last thing I wanted to convey was that I was interested in more than instruction for a demo. I wasn't that desperate for pussy. "Enjoy the rest of Your sun tanning. From the looks of it, You're doing a very good job of avoiding tan lines."

Dom and I walked away from her, and Dom couldn't resist looking back to get a last look. I didn't bother because if I played my cards right, she hadn't moved a muscle.

Dom cursed under his breath, prompting me to take a peek for myself. She not only hadn't moved from her spot, but she was grinning like a teenager admiring her first crush. Her eyes gave her away, letting me know I could get it when I felt like it.

Now, why did she want to go and do that for?

"Did You really have to go and get Her hopes up like that, Sir?" Dominic asked. "You know Your schedule is ridiculous right now; there's no way You will be able to give Her the attention needed."

"Dom, You'd be amazed at the time You can make when the occasion calls for it." I smirked as I thought about the exhibition I planned to put on with sajira later. "Besides, who's to say I won't be instructing tonight during the demo, playa?"

Dominic shrugged and shook his head. "We still have the rest of the island to sweep, Sir. It would be unfair for Me to tell You if you're playing with fire or not; I'm just Your protégé, remember?"

I cracked up at his attempts at passive-aggression, realizing he might be a little irritated because another woman chose to bypass him in my favor. I couldn't be mad at him about that, but I wasn't about to acquiesce to keep him happy, either. In a target-rich environment, it's dog-eat-dog, and the biggest dogs are the ones who eat the most sometimes.

Still, I felt the need to keep him satisfied and make the trip worth the time away from his girls, so I made a mental note to set things in balance later tonight. After all, he's my protégé, and I took care of my boys.

Even if they should be able to take care of themselves...

EIGHT ⚭ shamise

"i don't know what to do, sis. i'm so confused."

I finally caught up with sajira near the outdoor play area. She sat in a spot where she could watch the impact play, observing the submissives being punched, kicked, paddled, and everything in between.

I knew her well enough to know when she got like this, she had something to get off her chest.

"What happened with lynx?"

"What makes you think—"

"Have you forgotten who you're talking to?" I cut her off, moving in front of her field of vision. "i know how you get when you're in a mess, so don't try me."

Sajira lowered her eyes for a moment before meeting my gaze again. "lynx wants out, and he wants me to get out with him, leave my D/s family."

I exhaled.

Talk about déjà vu?

Memories of the phone call I dreaded making years ago because I *thought* I was in love with my ex-husband came rushing to the surface. Faced with the same prospect with my submissive sister, I became acutely aware of the emotions my Daddy and Goddess felt when they let me go my own path.

All of a sudden, I didn't want her to leave us.

"What?!?!"

"Relax, sis, i'm not going anywhere," sajira said, placing her hand on my arm. "I don't think i can go back to what i once was. i'm a spoiled, happy girl now."

"Yeah, i can understand what you mean by that." I smiled at the things we had done as a family in the past year, in and away from the BDSM world. The family trips with the kids, growing the businesses by leaps and bounds, and putting kinksters on notice that the House of Kemet-Ka was back to being the gold standard. She didn't want to leave all of that when we were really hitting our stride; I had to believe that. "i'm not gonna lie to you, sis. i was going to try to talk you out of leaving us if you really were thinking about it."

"That's the thing; i was tempted for a moment." sajira's eyes softened, and I caressed her cheek, tempted to kiss her in that moment. "The thing that changed my mind was the way he's treated me…the way he's treated you…the last few months. There's no way i could think he could flip the switch and be the man I married. We have both changed so much since we got into this."

This was where the comparisons stopped. She'd been married a lot longer than me, and there was no easy way to throw things away in the blink of an eye. I understood her temptation to stay with her husband, and no amount of convincing or cajoling would be able to sway her if that was where her heart lied. At the end of the day, it was still her decision, whether Daddy or Goddess were involved in the decision or not.

I secretly wished she wasn't thinking about it as much as I was. "Whatever you decide you want to do, i'm with you."

"Thanks, sis, that means a lot, considering you had to make the decision you made." sajira reached up to kiss my cheek. "For the longest, i'd hoped you would come back to us, but i knew you had to get some things out of your system, too. In my heart, i knew you would be back, regardless of the circumstances, because this is who we are. It's hard to go back to the vanilla world and think we can function like nothing ever happened."

I hated it when she was right. Hate it or love it, there are things in the kink community that trump the larger mainstream in ways that only those who have been around long enough could possibly understand. There's something about being surrounded by people who really "get" you, and that's something hard to find, even with all the kinky books that have come to light lately.

I was about to say something else to continue our conversation now that sajira was beginning to feel more like herself, when she looked over my shoulder and raised her eyebrow. "Someone's staring at us."

I quickly turned around and tried to quickly hide my facial expression. I was not in the mood to deal with this man, and my defenses were up immediately.

Sir Lyrical walked in our direction once he recognized my face.

I blew air as I found myself struggling to keep the Alpha in me behaved. sajira was confused at my rising anger as he drew closer to our personal space. "shamise, what's wrong? Do you know this guy walking toward us?"

"Yes, unfortunately, i do, sajira, but you're gonna have to trust me, there's something about this guy I'm not too happy with." I moved closer to her ear to whisper the rest of the information. "He pushed up on Goddess, trying to get some private time with Her."

sajira's eyes widened for a moment before she changed her expression, trying not to tip Lyrical that we might have been talking about him. Funny thing was, I had a suspicion he would think we were anyway, even if we weren't.

The smug look on his face and the smile that spread across his lips sent a wave of discomfort through me. "Good afternoon, shamise. I hope your day has been going well. And who might this lovely woman be sitting with you?"

sajira felt my fingers tighten their grip around her wrist, and almost as though she were taking a silent cue from me, she moved into protocol before she spoke. "Sir, my name is sajira, sister of sajira and amani, and princess of the House of Kemet-Ka. May i inquire as to whom You are, Sir?"

Lyrical's eyes roamed and lingered all over sajira's body, further angering me. After a few seconds of enjoying the view, he finally responded, "My name is Sir Lyrical, sajira. If you don't mind Me saying so, that is a beautiful slave name you have. your Master and Mistress must be very proud of you, too."

"Forgive me for correcting You, Sir, but the proper reference to Master Ramesses and Lady Neferterri in our presence would be our Daddy and Goddess." sajira's face remained expressionless as she spoke. I wanted to jump up and down and yell out, "Get him, sis!" "If our brother, amani, were involved in this conversation, then the reference You would use in front of us would be our Master and Goddess. i am appreciative of You liking my slave name, Sir; it was lovingly chosen for me, and i try to provide another source of pride to my family."

Lyrical's smile faded and his eyes darted in my direction, searching for anything that would give him a clue of whether or not I'd poisoned her against him. I gave him no satisfaction whatsoever. He turned to sajira to continue his conversation, such as it was. "Well, in that case, sajira, I should look forward to having dinner with you and the rest of your family later this evening. I am looking forward to it."

He walked away before either of us could answer to the dinner invitation he spoke of, and the looks we gave each other would probably have been a source of humor for anyone on the outside looking in, but we didn't know whether to be confused or pissed that we had to share space with this egotistical jerk.

"i know Daddy can be a bit over the top at times, but at least He's earned His arrogance." sajira was the first to break the uneasy silence between us. "What a jackass."

I laughed so hard I had to sit down next to her to catch my breath. "See, that's why i love you, sis."

"Where in the hell did He come from, and what did Goddess see in Him to invite Him to dinner?" sajira continued with the questions she hoped to ask Goddess when we all got together to prepare for dinner. "Daddy's gonna take one look at 'Sir Lyrical' and dismiss Him in a second."

"i don't know, sis, but She must have seen something because He got a rise out of Her; i felt it in Her body language," I explained from the interaction earlier in the day. "you and i both know how She can get when She has Her mind made up. Not even Daddy can change Her mind."

"So, what do we do if ol' boy tries to flirt on the sly?" sajira asked. "Daddy's got a temper, even if He doesn't show it, and it might get ugly. Do we take our concerns to them, or do we let the chips fall and watch for the fallout?"

We got up from the area we were sitting and walked toward the shoreline, and I pondered her question the entire way. The last time we'd collectively decided to hold something back from Daddy and Goddess, we nearly got caught up in a situation we couldn't control, and the consequences could have been more disastrous than the way it turned out. House protocol demanded that we request permission to speak freely so we could voice our concerns, but at the same time, this was our Masters' relationship, their marriage, and that was already tricky territory. One false step and things could fall apart in a hurry.

I didn't want to chance it unless we had proof that Sir Lyrical had ulterior motives for getting with Goddess. If it was just a fuck, then we could leave it alone because Daddy's never been opposed to it, with all of us still having roots in the swingers' community. But if this man had plans to split them up, they needed to be aware of it.

"For now, sis, we'll keep things under wraps, especially when amani isn't involved in the conversation," I advised. "We need to get Him in the loop, so He can keep an eye on Lyrical, too."

"All right, sis, if you think this is best." sajira shook her head. "i just hope we're doing the right thing."

NINE ⚭ amani

"Mistress Blaze, i would like for You to meet my good friend, Jelani."

I knew I was taking a real chance trying to play matchmaker with these two, but I had a feeling they would have a good chemistry, a vibe that would spark while out in this atmosphere. I wasn't completely convinced, but I was willing to see my boy enjoy himself.

Jelani was a good friend of mine from college, and we pledged the same fraternity. He was an accounting major while I switched from business to pre-med to pre-law because I couldn't make up my mind the first two years of college. I ended up becoming an EMT before I found my D/s family and settled in to taking care of the medical operations at all of the compounds.

Talk about a step up, huh?

Jelani and I were on the wrestling team together, too, and from sophomore year until graduation, we were like brothers on the mat and roommates off of it. We did some of the craziest and nastiest things during that time, running through women on campus like they were nothing more than ragdolls.

Senior year would change us both, when we discovered something about the other in one alcohol-fueled night at an orgy party off campus. That night, we got with a couple of women who dared us to kiss each other. Since we wanted them to make out, they felt it was only fair that we returned the favor.

The kiss was good…*really* good.

The sex that happened between us as we took turns fucking the women and then each other was mind-boggling. I didn't think that it would feel so erotic, so intense. The women we were with didn't bat an eyelash, either. In fact, it seemed to turn them on even more, and they were our steady pieces of ass because they kept their mouths shut in exchange for watching us go at it.

It sounded like a cop-out back then, but bisexuality wasn't the most talked about or accepted thing among black men. I couldn't exactly say things were much different now, but they definitely weren't as in the closet as they were.

We kept up with each other after graduation, and even though we were as wild as we were in college, we silently decided what happened in college stayed in college, and it was time to bury those urges and let the path take us where it took us.

That was, until my Goddess unlocked my sexuality and took me to heights I'd only fantasized about.

Whew, that woman… sorry, I had a moment, there.

We had plenty of conversations about being submissive back then, too, but until I joined my D/s family, I thought I had the concept figured out. He struck me as the more subdued type of submissive, but I was seriously mistaken. Jelani was more service-oriented than I was, and it took shamise and sajira to teach me the difference.

Blaze took one look at Jelani and tried her best to keep the smile from spreading across her face. "It's nice to meet you, Jelani. amani has told us good things about you."

My Goddess wasn't as cool and calm about her response. "I'd say it's more than nice to meet you, Jelani. You're gorgeous!"

I watched my friend blush at the compliment, but it wasn't like my Goddess was lying. Jelani's about six feet one and 200 pounds of lean, muscular, chocolate hotness! Hell, I had to keep from drooling as my mind flashed back in time.

"Thank You, Ma'am, i'm glad You both like what You see." Jelani's eyes were transfixed on Blaze. He was completely mesmerized by her appearance, and I didn't blame him one bit. Mistress Blaze was a strikingly beautiful woman, with a body that, at nearly forty-five years old, would put most twenty-year-olds to shame. "i do try to keep in decent shape."

Blaze finally grinned when she heard him make that comment. "So, Jelani, what made you come down to the islands unattended? I'm sure a beautiful man such as yourself would not have a problem with a traveling companion."

"Ma'am, that is kind of You to say, but the women i have dated over the past year haven't been all that accepting of who i am." Jelani's eyes never left Blaze's as he spoke. Under general protocol, I knew he wasn't supposed to consistently give a Dominant constant eye contact, but his body language gave him away. He was smitten with her. "Being a submissive black male is not the easiest thing for women to deal with."

"Well, women tend to be a lot more narrow-minded about a lot of things, but this is not the time for that conversation." Blaze tapped a spot next to her and then pointed at the floor near her feet—her subtle clue that she wanted him to be closer to her. "Perhaps we should speak on that later this evening at dinner?"

"It would be my honor, Ma'am." Jelani got up from his seat and walked toward the spot Blaze pointed to. He stopped short of sitting or kneeling, lowering his eyes and standing still.

Blaze raised her eyebrow, and my Goddess folded her arms across her chest from our spot in the room. She let him stand there for a few more moments before she asked the question to satisfy her curiosity.

"Are you seeking permission to sit, Jelani?"

"Yes, Ma'am, i am."

"Mmmm, good boi, amani has taught you well, for a newbie. you may sit."

As they continued their conversation separate from us, my Goddess began to lean forward, wincing as she grabbed her stomach. I reached for her, trying to find out if there was something I could do to help.

"I'm okay, baby, I'm going through cramps, and they're absolutely killing me," she responded to my concern. "I feel so damn icky right now it's not funny."

I felt a need to try and take the stress away, and I knew what would do the trick, but I needed her to trust me to perform the service for her. "Goddess, would You permit me to pamper You? I think I have a way to take Your mind off the cycle giving You so much hell right now."

"What are you up to, amani?"

"Goddess, please, may i perform this for You? i promise You won't regret it."

I spent the past year learning some of the finer aspects of service from tiger, and this service aspect would require a lot of trust from my Goddess, but I had a feeling she would agree to it because she knew everything I'd done had been with her pleasure and comfort at heart.

She smiled, resigning herself to the same conclusion I arrived at. "Okay, baby, I will allow it. I'm not sure what you have up your sleeve, but you've been a good boi all this time, there's no need for Me to think you can't do this for Me. Let's go."

☥

"Where in the world did you learn this?"

I smiled as I went about my task, purposely ignoring her question. I was taking a big chance on incurring her wrath for not answering, but I was willing to take the chance because once I was done, she'd forget I'd even ignored her in the first place.

At least, that's what tiger constantly told me when I was training.

When I'd first agreed to train under tiger to learn more advanced techniques to please my Goddess, menstrual service was the last thing I'd expected. Sure, I was an EMT, so the sight of blood didn't nauseate me. I had other things in mind, but tiger was talking about doing some things that would set me apart from the wannabes in a major way.

The first thing we did was sit down and go through all the angles to prepare for: the mood swings, the barking of commands, all of the other nuances that might surprise me during the service, doing whatever possible to make her comfortable, making sure if any conversation was being held, to keep the conversation light and sensual, but not overtly sexual unless I caught her in the moment where she wanted to be sexual.

It was like going to sex education class all over again.

I broke my silence after I ensured my setup was laid out the way I wanted it. "Goddess, may i offer You a drink to help You relax? Would You like some music to listen to while i work?"

"Not until you answer My question, amani." The tone in her voice caused my heart to flutter. Normally, that tone made me comply without hesitation, but I had to stand my ground and concentrate on the service.

"Goddess, please allow me to complete my task first. Once i am done, I will answer any questions You ask," I retorted. I worried I might anger her further, but this wouldn't work if she questioned everything every step of the way. "You entrusted me to learn advanced aspects of service, and i am asking You to allow me to show You what i have learned."

Her facial expression changed, which eased my tension. "you may proceed, baby boi."

Energized by her blessing, I moved to the bar and made her an Amaretto Sour to enjoy while I performed my task. Upon returning to her, I caught myself staring at her luscious body in her bikini, taking in every curve, my fantasies coming to life in my mind. I forced myself to focus, reminding myself that this was about her comfort and pleasure.

"Your drink, my Goddess." I watched her eyes as they moved from the drink in her hand to take stock of the inventory I had for the service I was to perform.

On the floor near the lounger she lay on were two towels, two washcloths, a basin sitting on top of an electric plate to keep the water warm, some scented soaps and lotions, sanitary wipes, two disposable razors, replacement tampons, a sheet of wax paper, a can of shaving gel, a small trash bag, and finally, a new bikini for her to wear.

"May i remove Your bikini bottom, my Goddess?"

"Yes, you may."

I pulled her bikini bottom down and over her knees, folding them and placing them out of view. I then carefully removed the tampon from inside her walls, taking care to use the sanitary wipes to catch any excess. I looked up and observed that her eyes were closed and her body was finally relaxing.

When the tampon was disposed of and out of view, I spoke again, snapping her out of her trance for a moment. "This next step is going to feel a little hot, my Goddess. Please bear with me."

"Mmmmhmmmm." She was in her zone, exactly where I wanted her.

I took the washcloth and the soap and lathered them in the basin. The water was at the temperature I wanted, warm enough to clean, but not hot enough to scorch her skin. I waited until the water was at the right heat level before I placed the cloth to begin cleaning. I started at her knees, undeterred by her flinching at the warm and soapy sensation on her skin. I moved up to her thighs, enjoying the scent of the soap and fighting through the arousal resulting from the aroma.

I moved up to her waistline, washing over her belly button, smiling as her body moved in rhythm with the pattern I created, not realizing the movements enhanced my arousal. I maintained my focus, determined to suppress my urges until later, so I could release. The way her hips moved, it became an increasingly arduous task.

By the time I took the washcloth to meticulously wash and massage her vaginal area, she was in heat. She lifted her head, her eyes moving to the source of her growing pleasure. I kept eye contact with her, breaking our connection only when I needed to wash the delicate folds of her labia.

"Mmmm, that feels good, baby." She never took her eyes off me, moving her hands to caress my face. I kept to my task despite her gestures, slipping the warm cloth over her clit before pointing the cloth, with my index finger wrapped around the cloth, deep inside her.

She gasped, instinctively grasping my forearm, trying her best to move my finger deeper inside. I resisted her attempts, grinning at her near desperation to have me make her come before my task was complete. Without another word, I gently took her hand and removed it from my arm, getting back to my task of washing and massaging her.

"Damn it, stop teasing Me!" I heard her demands and continued my work despite them, ensuring her labia and inner walls were thoroughly cleansed. She grew more irritated by the moment, trying to keep from screaming at me. "Didn't you hear Me, amani?!?! Stop teasing Me and make Me come!"

"i'm not teasing You, my Goddess." I lied, but I kept my composure even though my insides were shaking and I wanted desperately to give in to her impassioned demands. "Please, please allow me to finish my task."

Her eyes widened, no doubt surprised at my restraint. A smile crept across her lips as she lay back in the lounger, giving in to what her body felt without another complaint.

The next move would cause more of a stirring inside of her.

I took the shaving gel and began lathering. The coolness of the gel caused her to jump again, but she quickly adjusted, letting a moan escape her lips. I covered her nether region before I took the razor to shave her.

My Goddess already kept herself bare down there, but during her cycle she let it grow to keep the irritation to a minimum. I found that out from my sisters because they were bound by House protocol to do the same thing. Thankfully, shamise was willing to be my guinea pig while tiger walked me through shaving her. She was so impressed by my work she made sajira get shaved, too.

Those two were easy compared to our Goddess, and they knew it.

I took my time, keeping the blade warm and clear of hair as often as I could with the heated water in the basin. Long, slow, smooth strokes, wiping the blades clean, and repeat. I kept the steps in my head until her mound was as smooth as satin and clear of any hair.

I nearly wanted to take a picture and send it to tiger, but I decided against it. I was sure my Goddess would be gushing about this experience until she couldn't anymore. That alone was worth the effort.

The lotion would truly put my headspace to the test. Whenever I gave her a massage in the past, I immediately went into subspace, struggling to keep my head out of the stratosphere until the actual massage was complete. My body-worshipping fetish kicked into high gear the moment I took the lotion and massaged it into her skin. tiger had warned me about this part when I'd told him about my subspace triggers, and even had coached me to think about other things to delay the trip.

Easier said than done…

My fingers moved with the grace of a figure skater across her flesh, and I soon got lost watching glow from the sheen of the lotion. From her thighs, to her calves, then up and across her hips before finally moving across her pubic area, I found myself unable to delay the trip no matter what other thoughts I tried to use.

The aroma of her essence mixed with the lotion was enough to make me stop and beg her to let me make her come. Her body gave away her heightened sexual peak, and I wanted to put her out of her misery, but I had to finish.

"Goddess, i'm about to insert the fresh tampon now."

She sat up at my announcement. I noticed the slight trepidation at my next step before she lay back into the lounger again, closing her eyes to prepare for the insertion. "you may continue, baby boi."

Despite her want to simply feel for me to insert the tampon in, she lifted her head and met my eyes again as I took my thumb and index finger and spread her lips. Her eyes narrowed as I slid the tampon deep inside her womb. She moaned and gasped as it disappeared, leaving only the string.

I inhaled her scent again, tempting myself, torturing myself, as the aroma filled my lungs.

My defenses were weakened to the point to where she could have commanded anything and I would desperately succumb and comply without another moment's hesitation.

Goddess must have felt the desire on me. "Lick My pussy, baby."

"Yes, my Goddess." I was too far gone to care that I'd given in. Pleasing her was my only priority.

I concentrated on her clit, knowing that as sensitive as she was while on her cycle, she could come in seconds.

"Oh, fuck, baby! Damn, I'm coming already! Shit!!!" She grabbed the back of my head and buried my face deep against her freshly shaven mound as she shuddered from the orgasms sweeping through her body. I kept my tongue firmly against her clit, wrapping my arms around her hips and holding on tightly as she shook violently with each wave of pleasure.

Once her orgasms subsided, I retrieved the other swimsuit and kneeled by her side. "May i ask You to lift Your legs, my Goddess? i know You're weak from Your climax, but i want to make sure You have Your new swimsuit on before You rest."

She nodded as I moved her legs to slip the bikini bottom on. Then, I helped her lift from the back of the lounger to replace the old top with the new one. Goddess had a satisfied grin on her face, which warmed me inside. I grabbed one of the blankets on the bed and laid it over her body so she could nap in peace.

Before I excused myself to clean the mess and dispose of the trash elsewhere, I leaned down and whispered in her ear, "Thank You, my Goddess, i hope You enjoyed as much as i did. i will be back tomorrow to repeat the service. Enjoy Your nap."

TEN ⚭ RAMESSES

"Master Ramesses, it is a pleasure to finally meet You."

I wished I could have said the same thing about him.

When my Beloved told me we would be having someone else at dinner, I honestly was expecting someone I actually had some knowledge of. Sir Lyrical was not on anyone's radar that was in my circle, and that concerned me. I took a look at my girls and another look at amani and realized they were in as much bewilderment as I was.

The way the table was set up in the great dining hall, the chairs faced each other, and although the width of the table was enough to keep any touching from happening, it was obvious to me there was some chemistry between her and Lyrical. I wasn't worried about it because it was nothing more than physical, and we were on the island, so there would be some mystical encounters that would occur. Still, there was something to this gentleman that bore looking into a little deeper, just for the sake of sanity.

"Sir Lyrical, I'm glad You were able to join us tonight." I shook his hand and stared him down, awaiting his reaction. To his credit, he returned my stare with one of his own, giving my hand an extra squeeze, thinking he could crack a bone or something. "My Beloved tells Me that You are an acquaintance of Master Menes?"

His smile spread as he took a bite of the asparagus spears. "Yes,

Menes and I have been associates for a long time now. What is it, nearly ten years now?"

I grinned at his response. Menes, the former Lord Magnus, had been an elder in the Miami community for the better part of twenty years and I had nothing but the highest regard for him. I continued to dine on the New York Strip and rice pilaf as I listened to him rave about how Menes had taken a shine to him when he was younger and helped guide him as much as he could, considering his busy schedule.

Neferterri seemed to soak everything in. amani had more of her attention as he made sure her food was well prepared by the staff. I shared a glance with him for a brief second, and the territorial gleam in his eyes told me he couldn't trust him as far as he could throw him.

I took that under advisement, along with the fact that neither of my girls wanted to engage in conversation with him much. "sajira, baby, is everything okay? We don't want to be too rude to our dinner guest."

She smiled, realizing her poker face was not as convincing as her sister's. "Everything is fine, Daddy, and i don't mean to be rude at all, but i didn't want to interrupt Sir Lyrical as He was talking."

shamise interjected, taking up for her sister. "It's been a long day for us, Daddy. We had some snafus with a few of the payments from a few of the guests, and a couple of the entertainers took ill, so it had our attention."

"Sir, I don't believe they are being rude at all," Lyrical interjected, almost trying to keep things light and cordial. "I am enjoying the atmosphere and the wonderful company."

Not that I cared what he thought at the moment, but I noticed he was being a bit too accommodating. If my wife wanted to fuck him, it was her prerogative. I'd seen too many in the past try their best to pacify me in an attempt to get me to think there was no threat to my relationship.

Neferterri sensed the tension and sought to ease it in her own way…with misdirection. "Beloved, do You have everything ready for tonight's demo?"

"Yes, Beloved, I have things well in hand, except for the demo bottom," I replied. "I don't plan on using either of the girls because they won't be able to rest in enough time to deal with the demo. I had one of the entertainers taken off rotation so she would be rested up."

sajira gave a half-smile, and shamise tried her best to not look disappointed, but I knew they had gone through the ringer today. amani had not yet been through a fire play scene with Neferterri yet, otherwise, I would have used him. I wasn't willing to use anyone else because a lot of the submissive women on the island were looking to hook up, and there were enough Dominant men on the island to satisfy their whims.

"Daddy, You know we would do it in a heartbeat," the girls nearly said in unison. shamise giggled at their sync and stated, "We'll both be rested up enough to take care of You during the aftercare, promise. sajira and i both know how rigorous the fire play scene is when You play with us."

"Yes, Beloved, I'll make sure of it." Neferterri then looked at the girls and nodded. "Okay, you two need to head back to the hut and rest. amani, you, too. I'll expect to see you at our designated area in about two hours."

The girls excused themselves, kissed me before kissing Neferterri, and took their leave. amani kissed Neferterri before giving me pound and headed off.

"Well, I, for one, am looking forward to the spectacle You plan to put on, Master Ramesses." Lyrical inserted himself in the conversation again, and he was now beginning to threaten my calm demeanor. "I have heard You are quite adept at these types of scenes."

"I thank You for the endorsement, Sir, and I hate to be rude, but I do need to get prepared for the scene," I remarked as I got up from the table. I kissed my Beloved and excused myself to give them time to get better acquainted. "I will see You back at our hut in a few, yes?"

"Yes, Beloved, I will see You in a few." Neferterri's glance lingered a little longer than usual, and I felt the heat in her stare. The grin on my face let her know the feeling was mutual, despite the fact that I knew she'd hit her cycle. She was in heat, but she was plugged up.

I didn't want to ruin her fun, but it was limited, such as it was.

He didn't need to know that.

There was one thing that bothered me more than anything, though, and it was something I needed to make sure Dominic checked out to keep my Beloved out of harm's way.

I knew for a fact that his and Master Menes's paths had never crossed.

ELEVEN ✦ NEFERTERRI

"Your family is interesting, and that's putting it mildly."

The smirk on his face gave him away. He was glad we had some time alone to talk.

Maybe it was a good thing we did. I needed to know more about him before I made up my mind that anything would happen. I only hoped he wouldn't talk himself out of getting any later on in the week when I would be off my cycle and in need of a few good men.

I was a greedy bitch when I came off my period, so sue me.

"Yes, and as You saw, they tend to be wary of outside company who don't know how to let the conversation flow naturally." I took a sip of my wine, enjoying the buzz that would slowly turn into intoxication. Once that happened, my tact would definitely be gone, not that I really wanted any tact to begin with.

Lyrical smiled. "So, You saw I was trying to be a little too involved in things, huh?"

"Yeah, trying too hard, definitely," I stated. "They already know You wanna fuck; they just want to make sure You're not trying to pull any stupid shit."

Damn, I guessed I gave myself away with that one.

His smile eased my nerves a little bit, but the wine eased them more. "I honestly wasn't sure You were feeling Me or not. I mean, You kept putting family members in My way like You wanted Me to run through a gauntlet."

"Please, You're not special, bruh." I laughed at the look on his face. Did he really think I would be that easy? "You go through the same thing the other men who want to get at Me go through, just like the females that want a piece of the Great One have to go through. Family over everything."

"So, it's like that, huh?"

"Yes, Sir, it's like that."

"Then, since You already know I wanna fuck, why don't we try to get some in before Your husband's demo?" He looked at his watch. "We have at least an hour."

"Whoa, slow down, playa, all in due time." I wanted to enjoy the slow burn, but I wanted to give my body time to get through my cycle. I reached down toward his shorts and felt up his leg. He was already hard as hell, which excited the hell out of me. Oh yeah, this one's gonna be fun. "If You're a good boy, I might let You taste Me."

I unzipped his shorts and was surprised to see he'd gone commando. He must have thought he was gonna get a quickie in or something, and I smiled at his attempt to assume the conclusion between us. His manhood sprang to life in my hand, but he was more worried about the people around us.

"Oh, quit with the shy act, cutie," I slurred, the wine really taking my senses for a ride. "If I wanted You to, I would make You slide Me on this table and fuck Me…right…now."

"But what about all of these—"

"No sense of adventure, sexy? Aww, You're no fun," I teased while stroking his dick and watching him shrink in front of me. What is it about Dominant men? Once they get around me, all of the bravado and Alpha maleness flies out of the window. "I guess we need to wait a few days until we have some alone time."

I wanted to crack up at the disappointment in his eyes. He looked like a lost puppy or something, almost pleading with me to reconsider what I'd said.

"You know You want it as much as I do, so what's the holdup?" He tried to put the ball in my court, but he didn't understand I wouldn't be rushed. He thought he was in control, but he had another thing coming. "I wouldn't have let You take it out if I wasn't gonna use it."

"Yeah, but I can feel You pulsing in My hand. You're gonna come, no need in hiding it now." While he was busy trying to get back on top of the situation, I slipped some melted butter on my hand, making his dick slick enough to jack him off. "Mmmm, see, he feels so good in my hand. Imagine what it will feel like when my pussy is wrapped all around it in a couple of days."

"Mmmm, damn, but I…fuck…want it…shit, You got Me…now." He tried to sound impatient, but the other head was doing the talking now.

I was aroused from the power he gave me more than anything at this point. It would definitely be on my terms as to whether or not he would get a whiff of this pussy. I hated it when men gave in so easily, but when you boiled it down to its essence, men were still dogs chasing after pussy.

Damn…and he was sexy as fuck, too.

"Come on, bust one for Me." My language got more aggressive as I noticed people were staring at us. I wanted to put on a show now, to break him down to what he really was, and an Alpha male was not it. "Come all over my fingers so You can feel better."

I've always said that giving a blow job or a hand job was not as much of a submissive act as people assumed it was. I mean, who's the one in control of the dick when performing the act? I knew I had my days where if I wanted to put my Beloved to sleep, a good stroke and getting him to spurt so he could get the stress of the day off him was the perfect sleeping pill.

I kept talking dirty in his ear, giving him the impression that everyone around us couldn't get enough of the impromptu moment unraveling before their very eyes. If he had paid enough attention, he would have realized that most folks couldn't have cared less, but his eyes were focused either on me or they were closed tight trying to reach his climactic conclusion.

It was only a few more minutes before he would get that happy ending.

"Oh fuck…goddamn…shit, I'm coming!" He grabbed at my hand, trying his best to control the eruption that took him prisoner, but I shooed his efforts away and pressed my free hand against his chest, keeping his back against the chair. He was held captive to the pleasure his body needed, and the determined sneer on my face let anyone nosey enough to want to find out that I was gonna get what I wanted, come hell or high water.

His growls turned into pleas to stop, and I grinned when I realized he was multi-orgasmic. The second blast was as potent as the last, as the stream oozed from the head and over my fingers. I took my free hand to grab the napkins and wipe my fingers clean, ensuring nothing got onto the shorts so he could at least walk out of the area without evidence of his essence anywhere on his shorts.

At least, there wouldn't be any on the outside of his shorts.

His shallow breathing was proof of a job well done, but as I looked at my watch, I realized his aftercare would be short-lived. "Sorry, dear, I have to leave now; the demo starts in about forty-five minutes and I still have to go back to My hut and change. Thanks for the kinky time; I hope it was as good for You as it was for Me."

I got up from the table and walked out of the area before he had a chance to protest or respond. It wouldn't have done him much good, anyway. I had the upper hand on him now, and I had no intentions of giving up my advantage.

Why should I? He tried to play me like I was the one about to give it up, and he got the game flipped on him. Respect the power play and keep it moving.

I could only hope he would.

Men nowadays played by a different set of rules.

That's all right; if he got out of line, there would be two gentlemen that would see to it that he got back in his own lane. Like shamise said, no one's *that* stupid.

Or was he?

TWELVE ⚮ RAMESSES

"A word, if You're not too busy, Sir?"

I was in the midst of getting everything prepared for tonight's demo, and I was in a good zone while figuring out what I would use and when during the scene. Seeing Master Osiris walking through my door only served to enhance the zone I was in.

"Master Osiris, to what do I owe the honor of Your visit?" I asked. "I thought You would have been out with the audience by now."

"I was, but I wanted to find out who You were using as a demo bottom?" The genuine concern on his face gave me pause. "I understand You're using one of the girls on staff?"

"Yes, as a matter of fact, I was, Sir." I grew more concerned because this was already pre-arranged hours ago. With less than an hour to go before the demo began, my concern slowly turned to aggravation.

"I want Your demo to go off without a hitch, and I want it to be a success, so," he said as he tugged on a chain leash, revealing his Alpha slave, keket, who happened to be outside the door, "I'm giving You permission to use My keket for the evening."

Did he just say what I thought he said?

Rarely am I rendered speechless, but this gesture and the meaning behind it left me in that exact state. I'd only allowed shamise or sajira to be used in demos a couple of times, and those were to

Dominants I trusted beyond measure. I attempted to speak, but the words would not form and I felt like if they did, I would sound like a blithering idiot.

Noticing my distress, keket looked up at her Master, tapping her hand against his wrist three times. Upon his nod, she crawled to my side and kissed the back of my palm. "Master Ramesses, i have full trust in Your ability to take care of me during the demo. my Master taught You, and i would consider it an honor to be placed in Your care."

I looked down at keket, and then I glanced back at Osiris, before the ability to speak returned. "Big Brother, I would be honored to take keket tonight. I'm still in shock You would offer, but I would be a fool to reject."

"Little bro, I have to look out for My brethren, if it will help them shine more." Osiris grinned as he gave keket's leash to me. "But whatever burns or scratches she incurs by Your hand, You are responsible for the care. I know You already know the protocol, but it still bears expressing."

Yeah, talk about pressure?

"Consider it handled, Sir." I nodded, tapping keket to kneel while I finished my preparations. "I will treat her with the care I use with Our girls."

"I have no doubt You will, Sir." Osiris smiled as he made his exit. "Now, make sure You show out tonight. All eyes will be on You."

☥

"This is how I prepare for a fire play scene."

I knew I drew crowds, but to have the whole island watching my every move was humbling, and that was putting it mildly.

Not that I couldn't work a large crowd, of course, but I honestly thought there were other things the guests were doing tonight.

We were lucky the weather was favorable for tonight's festivities. It was warm enough to perform with keket naked and ensure she wasn't uncomfortable in the night air, while the winds stayed calm, allowing the demo to happen out in the open air instead of the confining space of one of the large tents. The crowd was able to form a semi-circle so that any sightline would be good to view from.

keket smiled like a Cheshire cat that swallowed a canary as I used everything from the fire gloves to the fire wands, saving my newest skill for last. I had only done it once before with shamise, so my nerves were a slight bit on edge. Having my mentor's slave on the Cross to perform it in front of a captive audience did nothing to help calm things in my mind.

I marveled at how radiant her skin shone against the firelight the torches provided, giving the area an intimate glow. I focused my attention to her breasts and nipples, moving up to her eyes to keep the connection strong between us. She was fast approaching subspace, and I did my best to slow down her ascension, keeping my voice in her ear and my hands on her body.

"Are you still with me, love?"

"Mmmm, yes, Sir, i'm still with You. Your hands feel so good."

"We're almost done, little one. I have one more trick to execute." I gave her fair warning before I reached in the bag for the powder I needed. "I'll take you off after I finish this last move."

"Mmmmm, yes, Sir, i'll be waiting," she purred.

I took the top off the cornstarch container, taking great care not to inhale the fumes once the canister was opened. The thing about cornstarch was, if inhaled, the damage to the lungs was not anything to be played with. Since I was a beginning fire breather, I didn't want to use the fuels that more experienced fire breathers used because I still cared about my lungs to a degree. But I knew enough to know to respect what I was about to do, and I needed as much concentration as possible.

"And now, ladies and gentlemen, for my final piece to this demo, I will breathe a fireball toward keket, and if I do this properly, the fireball will not burn her skin, as the compound I'm using evaporates once it is in contact with the fire," I explained to the crowd. The majority of them were completely awestruck, with some not believing I was doing all of this to keket and she didn't have a burn or scratch on her. I even invited different people in the crowd to feel for themselves that while her skin felt hot to the touch, she was unharmed.

DK did her best to volunteer when I asked for a few to do a quick how-to with the flash cotton. Once she was chosen, she got as close to me as she could as I showed her the way the flash cotton worked, eliciting whistles from the men in the crowd who had a feeling she was trying to arouse me while she was on stage. I cut my eyes in my girls' direction, and while sajira and shamise scowled in territorial defiance, my Beloved smirked at the desperation in DK's body language.

I remained oblivious to it all. I couldn't have been happier with the way things had turned out. Osiris looked like a proud teacher in the audience, and my Beloved and the girls were having giggle fits while high-fiving other guests around them. I even had the undivided attention of more than a few women in the crowd, including DK, who seemed to never take her eyes off me, despite the attention the men gave her during the demo.

The crown jewel of the evening would be a blast if I pulled it off.

"All right, here we go," I announced as I stood back a couple of feet to execute the maneuver. keket's eyes focused on the fire dancing on the end of the wand in my hand, hypnotized by its glow and entranced by the entire scene we'd performed. I took a spoonful of the cornstarch into my mouth, and a few seconds later, I sprayed the powder from my mouth, watching the particles explode upon contact with the wand and head toward keket.

The screams in the crowd were understandably in horror for a few seconds as they thought keket had been engulfed in flames. Those screams soon turned into applause as keket emerged from the flames completely unharmed, and I quickly moved to pick her up before she passed out. Master Osiris stepped from the crowd to help me with the quick releases on her wrists and ankles, and I carried her to the nearby beach towel, where I already had water and ice at the ready.

"Whew! Was that fun or what?!" I shouted toward the crowd as I continued to check on keket. She was floating, and her body let me know it the way it writhed and shook from the flight into subspace. "I'm absolutely thrilled you were able to join Me tonight, and I hope you enjoy the rest of your evening. Good night!"

Neferterri, shamise and sajira, and amani all converged on me. My Beloved kissed me deeply and whispered, "That last part made Me so fucking hot for You."

"Damn, Daddy, where'd You learn how to do that?!" sajira squealed as she watched Osiris continue a small burst of fire over keket. She sounded like a teenager with the way she beamed. "That was awesome! I want next!"

I gave amani pound and shared a nod between us as I continued to survey the crowd as they disbursed. DK stayed in my field of vision the entire time during the aftermath. With so many people trying to get my attention, there was no way she would get the intimacy she thought she would get.

She mouthed the words, "I'll see You later, sexy," before blowing a kiss and walking off in the other direction. I was in such a zone that I didn't worry myself about her subtle invitation to take care of the wetness between her legs and the lust in her heart.

That would have to happen another time.

Tonight, I was greedy for no one else...except my girls.

My senses were overloaded, and it felt like I'd developed an acute asthma attack.

Except, I didn't suffer from asthma.

Something was wrong, I felt it.

All I heard were muffled voices...some I recognized, others were slightly foreign to me. I tried to respond to them, but my throat was on fire. My arms felt heavy, causing me some alarm when I couldn't lift them to get someone's attention. I searched around me, finding shamise's face first, but I still heard muffled sounds coming out of her mouth.

I read her lips, recognizing the worry in her eyes. "You're going to be fine, Daddy, just keep breathing. You passed out."

I passed out? It didn't feel like I was that out of sorts a moment ago.

shamise took her hands and kept my eyes on her as I felt the bumps from the gurney rolling across the sand. I presumed that they were taking me to one of the medical tents. My ego kicked in, wanting my body to lift and prove that nothing was wrong with me. It was in that moment that I realized I was strapped down.

Panic set in. I didn't do well with being restrained for any reason, and my inability to speak thanks to the oxygen mask over my face only made matters worse.

I pleaded with shamise with my eyes to tell them to take the restraints off me. I read her lips as she continued to console me and try to keep me calm. "Daddy, try to relax, let the staff take care of You, please. You're no good to us if You continue to fight. Stop being stubborn."

I nodded, recognizing the situation was beyond my control. I focused on my breathing, fighting through the pain in my lungs as I continued to breathe deeply. I felt the gurney stop, looking up at the bright lights surrounding me, getting my bearings to realize I was in the medical tent. They lifted me from the gurney and onto the bed, and the next thing I felt was a sharp pain in my right arm.

"It's only a sedative, Daddy. They need to stabilize Your breathing, okay?" This time, I heard shamise clearly, giving up a weak smile to acknowledge her instructions. "sajira and i are here with You, and we'll be here when You wake up."

"Whe…where's…your—"

"Shhh, relax, Daddy, we're sending for Goddess now." Her tone was soothing, reassuring, lulling me sweetly as I descended into the darkness. "Get some rest, let us take care of the rest for now."

Despite me wanting to dispute what she was telling me, there was not much I could do to follow through with what my mind wanted to do when my body was in such distress and in need of rest. I succumbed to the medicine coursing through the blood in my veins, taking solace that our Alpha slave had things well in hand until I awoke.

THIRTEEN ✖ shamise

"You have ten seconds to get Your hands off my Daddy."

The nerve of this bitch...

Who in the hell did she think she was trying to be hugged up on him like that? And what was worse, he appeared to be receptive to it when I knew for a fact that he didn't know her like that.

I shouldn't have left him alone while trying to get the crowd to dissipate. One minute he was there, the next minute he was gone. He was already having trouble breathing after the fire play session with keket, and while the rest of the crowd couldn't tell, I knew my Daddy when he was in distress.

The aftereffects of the fire breathing portion of the scene could have been anything from mild smoke inhalation issues to full-on respiratory distress, depending on the health of the lungs of the person performing the fire breathing. I'd made it my business to learn every aspect of the art from keket while Daddy learned from Master Osiris. She'd cautioned me on some of the things to look for, including the possibility of him hallucinating from the fumes.

I glared at Domina Korina as she sat in his lap. She didn't flinch, returning my glare with a cold stare of her own. "Or you'll do what? He's with Me right now. you'll have to wait your turn."

One glance at Daddy alerted me that I had very little time to waste, and it was not about to be wasted arguing with this twit.

His eyes were glassy and he looked lethargic. He tried to speak, and it only served to concern me further. "baby girl…what…how did you…if you're here, then what—"

"Don't worry, Daddy, You'll be fine." I moved Korina from his lap, trying to figure out what the hell was on her mind. The look I gave her would have been a blatant violation of House protocol, but I didn't care at the moment. "I need to get You back to our hut so You can rest."

"Wait, I thought You were going with Me?" Korina actually pouted, trying to play on his sympathies. "I would have taken good care of You."

"Pop quiz, 'baby girl': what is Master Ramesses's choice of food and drink for bringing Him out of Domspace?" I snapped. "You have thirty seconds to answer, but i have a feeling You don't have a damned clue."

Korina stuttered, struggling to find the words to answer my question in the time frame I gave. I scoffed as I watched her try to take a cue from Daddy, forgetting that he was not in the frame of mind to know what he was doing. "You see, that's the problem with you new tricks. If you wanted Him so badly, you would have learned Him, not just what gets His dick hard. Thanks for playing, now move out the way so His real property can take care of Him properly."

I moved with him, walking past her while listening to his breathing to make sure he wasn't in distress. I cut my eyes at Korina, daring her to say another word.

sajira finally caught up with me with amani in tow. amani took one look at Daddy and shook his head. "Good thing you got to Him before He tried to do anything strenuous. We need to get some oxygen in his system ASAP."

"I'll…be…okay," Daddy finally said, sounding like he had run about thirty miles. It was obvious he was winded. "I just…need to…get My air."

"Sir, we need to get some oxygen in You, no exceptions," amani retorted, insisting he sat until we got one of the golf carts to pick us up and get us to the medical hut. "Try to relax, and don't do anything that might cause You more issues; do You understand me, Sir?"

Ramesses nodded, leaning back in the chair until the golf cart arrived.

"Where's Goddess?" sajira asked.

"She's one of the dungeon monitors tonight," amani answered as we laid Daddy onto the stretcher. "Once we have Him situated and breathing properly, we can go back and get Her."

I shook my head. Goddess needed to be involved regardless of whether it was something severe or not, and while we weren't at that point yet, she needed to be told. "All right, let's get Him somewhere to stabilize Him and we'll take it from there, but i will have security radio Dom and Goddess so they can meet us at the medical tent. She's not going to kill us for keeping Her out of the loop."

☥

"He'll be fine. He needs to rest."

Master Osiris understandably showed concern for his student, and I did my best to reassure him that Daddy was okay. Goddess and Dominic were on their way from their respective locations, and hopefully they would arrive soon.

He was hooked to the oxygen tank, and he was starting to breathe normally soon after we got him there, but true to his stubborn streak, he insisted he was okay and didn't want to be fawned over.

Between sajira and me, we had to coerce him to stay still so the treatment could work. "Daddy, quit fighting and let the staff take care of You." sajira cooed in his ear, and that seemed to get him to relax a little bit. I whispered in his other ear how much we couldn't wait to take *really* good care of him when he got out of there. Thankfully with our combined efforts, he was able to relax and let the oxygen do its work.

"I don't understand, He was fine during the scene; I kept a close eye on Him the entire time," Osiris explained. "Did something happen while we were taking keket down from the Cross?"

"Apparently so." The doctor joined in on the conversation. "The fumes were a bit much, and for Him to be a beginner, even with the precautions He took, His lungs are not used to handling that much smoke and fumes in such a short, concentrated burst. I'm surprised He didn't pass out the minute He was done with the fire breathing."

I smiled to myself, and sajira shared my smile with a grin of her own. "Doctor, have you ever been around Master Ramesses?" I asked.

"No ma'am, I would say I haven't before He screened us to be a part of the staff for the island," she replied. She looked confused, so sajira placed her hand on the doctor's shoulder to help clue her in on our Daddy.

"Then you might not understand the stubbornness of the Great One." sajira tried to contain her laughter, but the giggles caught up to her. "Saying no to Him is like saying no to President Obama. Not many have the guts to do it without incurring His wrath."

"Well, He seems to be stable, so it's best to let Him rest for a while." She looked down at him, trying to do a last check before leaving the room. "For now, we'll keep an eye on Him, but He should be fine in a couple of hours."

"I'll be more than fine, doctor." Ramesses spoke through the mask, but his words still sounded garbled. He coughed a little bit, which worried me, but amani grinned. I trusted his judgment.

amani kissed us on the cheek and said, "i'll be here, too. Goddess won't need me for a few hours, anyway. Just let Her know everything is fine with Sir and tell Her not to worry once She gets here."

"we will, bro," sajira said as we headed out of the tent. "If anything changes, you know where to find us."

Once outside, I wondered aloud whether or not we'd done the right thing.

"Goddess hasn't arrived yet, and neither has Dominic. Do you think the security officers got to them?" I asked sajira. The concern on my face was evident, and the look of anxiety on hers did nothing to help me.

"This island is pretty big, sis." sajira probably shared my concerns, but she actually tried to apply some reasoning. "Even if they radioed ahead, the carts can only move so fast. It's best to be patient and be here when they arrive."

I nodded. Without conventional cell phones, it could be difficult to really move without telling someone where we would be, and that would be reliant upon them staying put long enough to relay the message. The satellite phones were used for emergency contact to the mainland, and there weren't many of those to begin with. Even though there were landlines established inside of the huts and cabins, who would want to pay the exorbitant amount of money to make a call? The attendees enjoyed the quiet comforts without the hassle of modern conveniences. Otherwise, they would have simply gone to Hedonism in Jamaica instead.

I thought about the possibility of the phone system being able to make calls between the cabins and huts also. The problem with that was even if we were able to call ahead, someone would still have to make the trip to find Goddess inside the dungeon tents to alert her of what was going on.

sajira seemed to read my mind, placing a hand on my shoulder in comfort. We walked over to the lounge chairs near the front entrance of the medical tent and sat while recapping what occurred hours earlier to pass the time. "Look, sis, we're better off staying here and relaxing until Dominic and Goddess get here. No point in worrying ourselves over what-ifs unless you want us both to lose our minds. Once they're here, we can bring them up to speed and focus on Him getting better."

FOURTEEN ⚬ NEFERTERRI

"Are you sure this will work? I'm flowing a little heavily tonight."

I was in the medical tent talking with the nurse about something that I'd never heard of before because I didn't think I would ever have the need to use it. I wasn't exactly embarrassed or anything about wanting to use it, but I didn't realize that a company had made the product.

"Yes, m'Lady, it will work. i've used it myself, and once You get through the initial discomfort, You won't feel a thing, and You won't leak." anissa, my nurse, held the diaphragm-looking cup in her hand as she prepared to insert it inside of my walls.

I hated to sound like a teenager who didn't know anything about anything, but I was honestly curious because I'd never needed something like this before. Before I married my Beloved, whenever I was "on," I never bothered to want to have sex, and most of the men were too grossed out to attempt it. But Ramesses was nothing like the other men. On occasion, if I was horny enough like I was tonight, we just grabbed towels and did the damn thing. It wasn't like he was scared of blood or anything like that, or if we didn't do that, we simply went anal and kept fucking from there until "Aunt Flo" had left from her visit.

I was on the gynecological table with my feet in the stirrups, and I was amazed at how many other women on the island were suffering the way I was. All of these sexy-ass men and being completely plugged up was never fun, but it put my mind at ease to see other attendees having this thing inserted to get their fuck on.

If anything, it turned me on even more and intensified my desire to find him and fuck him into the mattress.

"So, how long would I be able to keep this thing in here?"

"About twelve hours, m'Lady," anissa answered. She had me lubricated pretty good, and I could have sworn she had my clit engorged because the moment she started slipping it in, I moaned and started shaking. "Don't worry, m'Lady, You're extremely sensitive during Your period, but i'm sure You don't need me to say that. i wouldn't be surprised if You came almost as soon as He slides in."

The devilish grin on my face inspired a similar one on hers as we looked like co-conspirators to the orgasmic death of my Beloved's primary weapon of ass destruction.

"If i may say so, m'Lady, You are able to be as rough as You want to be. It won't get lost or be hard to pull out when You're done." anissa looked as though she were having a flashback moment of her own as she explained things to me. "You'll even be able to get some in the morning before you come back to have it removed."

"I like you a lot. I see why My Beloved and My baby boi picked you as a part of this staff. you're a freaky little slut, aren't you?"

She blushed at my assessment and cast her eyes downward. "It is my desire to serve and please as i am directed, m'Lady," she whispered as she moved closer to me. She hesitated for a moment before she planted a soft kiss across my lips. She blushed again at her actions, trying to find the words while figuring out if I was upset or not. "i'm sorry, m'Lady, i couldn't help myself. It's been a long night and I've been trying to keep my lustful desires in check until I'm done in twenty minutes."

I placed my hands over hers to calm her before taking one hand to lift her chin to meet my gaze. "you are a lovely woman, and quite sexy, too. If I weren't already on My own mission, I would ravage you before you could clock out and leave this tent to get back to your hut. In fact, I want to give you a gift, especially when he has been a good boi also. I want you to present yourself to amani, and I want you to tell him you are a gift from his Goddess; do you understand?"

"Yes, m'Lady, i understand." Her grin had her glowing as I guessed the thoughts in her head. "he is a gorgeous-looking man, as is Your Beloved. All of the women on the island that have come here can't stop raving about Him."

I laughed quietly as to not disturb the others. She was a stunning woman, and her features gave me the idea she was recruited directly from the Bahamas. Her eyes gave her away the moment a naughty thought came to mind. She would be exactly what my boi needed for all the hard work he put in this week.

Once she finished with the insertion, I headed out with part of my mission completed. But I had one more stop to make before I went on the hunt for my Beloved.

He wouldn't know what hit him.

"I thought I might catch You here, gorgeous."

I managed to convince another person to cover for me as one of the dungeon monitors because I was so horny I couldn't see straight. I had to have my Beloved inside me by any means necessary. Thanks to the stop I'd made to the medical tent and the sleight of hand of anissa, I had an Instead Softcup® inserted and was stocked up on plenty of lubricant to make sure I put him to sleep.

The next stop I was in the process of making was to the main building to raid the kitchen of fruit and water. The way I felt, we were going to need it!

Seeing Lyrical standing there both startled and aroused me at the same time. I saw the way he kept his attention on me, and while the other men were doing the same thing, he was the first on my hit list. I didn't care if he simply shut the fuck up and let me get it, I was in blind heat and I needed it to be put out.

I didn't get greedy often, but I knew my Beloved would finish me off. That was a guarantee.

"So, now that You've caught Me, can You handle what I have for You?" I teased as I moved toward him and grabbed for his shorts.

The surprise on his face let me know he thought this was going to go a little slower, but I was already in third gear and needed him to get on my level ASAP.

He quickly adjusted, grinning at my anxiousness, thinking he was the reason I was wetter than Victoria Falls. "Oh, so You want it like that, huh? No warm-up, just straight, no chaser?"

"Quit acting like You don't want this pussy," I challenged him, pushing him against the island in the middle of the room. "Be a man and get this pussy!"

Out of the corner of my eye, I saw a figure watching us, but I dismissed it quickly, focusing on the prize in front of me.

Lyrical switched up, spinning us around and had me bent over the island before I knew what happened. Finally, I would get fucked properly by someone other than Ramesses. I purred as he whispered in my ear, "Okay, since You like it rough, bitch, I'm gonna give it to You rough." He gave my ass a hard swat for good measure, pulling his dick out and trying to slide in before I had the chance to figure out if he'd put on a condom or not.

I stopped dead in my tracks. *Bitch?*

And he's trying to enter me *raw?*

What the fuck was on his mind?

"Get off Me!" I tried to push away from the table and from him, but he had a full head of aggression and lust and wouldn't relent. That only served to piss me off more.

"Muthafucka, get off Me NOW!!!" I screamed louder. I only hoped someone at least heard me to get help and realize this was not some scene being played out. "You're hurting Me, You bastard!!!"

"Oh, no, You're gonna give Me this pussy now!" he growled, seemingly more aroused by my fear. He fought with my hands, trying to rip my bikini briefs off, with this wild look in his eyes. I didn't know who this jackass thought he was, but he was not about to get over on me. "All this teasing You been doing, who the fuck do You think I am, one of Your bitch bois or something?" He raised his hand in an attempt to slap me when his eyes darted away from me, focusing on a figure moving in his direction.

"I got Your bitch, *boy!*" I heard someone yelling from behind us. The next thing I knew, Lyrical's weight was off me in a flash, and I had a chance to breathe a little.

By the time I got my bearings, I saw amani on top of Lyrical, raining elbows and fists at his face and ribs. I thought he would beat the man senseless the way he continued his onslaught.

"amani, stop! That's enough!" I yelled in his direction. I wasn't sure to try to grab him when he was only protecting me, but I needed him to stop before things got out of control.

Before I made my move, Dominic and two security officers moved in. Dominic rushed amani, while the other two restrained Lyrical, who was yelling profanities in amani's direction along with threats to kill him for breaking his nose.

"Get them to the cage, immediately!" Dominic barked as the zip cuffs were applied to both men.

What a way to end a night.

But I would soon find out the morning was only beginning.

After Dominic checked me over to make sure I wasn't bruised or hurt, he dropped another bomb on me that I didn't see coming. "Ramesses is in one of the medical tents. Something went wrong after the demo scene. I need to get You there as soon as we get this mess sorted out."

FIFTEEN ❧ amani

"Let me out of this cage and i'll make sure i finish beating His ass!"

Lyrical picked the wrong one tonight!

I happened to hear the commotion while I was in the main building heading back to the medical tent. I was frustrated because no one was able to locate my Goddess, and I checked all of the locations I thought she might have been. To say it was luck I happened to be walking past the kitchen when I heard her screaming.

I rushed into the room and I couldn't believe my eyes.

Protective instincts took over, and I saw nothing but red. The next thing I knew, I'd tackled him to the ground, and the fists went flying.

He still had aggression on him because he was still trying to fuck my Goddess against her wishes, which only fueled my desires to rearrange the features on his face.

The first punch landed square across his jaw.

The second punch landed flush on his nose. I grinned when I saw blood gushing from it.

There would be no third punch because Dominic rushed me from the side, yelling at me the entire time.

"amani, chill!" he yelled in my ear, trying his best to restrain me. I felt more weight on my back before I felt the zip cuffs closing on my wrists behind me. "you're not doing yourself any good struggling!"

"Let me up!" I yelled back, straining against the cuffs as I saw them cuffing Lyrical. "He tried to rape my Goddess! Let me go!"

"amani, calm down!" Dominic tried again to get through to me, but I was still in a rage. He kept his knee to my neck, which would have put me in a different headspace under normal circumstances. He leaned in, putting more pressure against my neck to close off my airway. "I don't want to put you to sleep, but I will if I have to!"

"Dom, let him go!" I heard my Goddess yelling in our direction. "he didn't do anything; he was protecting Me!"

Dominic yelled out once more, "Enough! We're taking this to the cage so we can sort all this out!"

"Good! I want to press assault charges!" Lyrical tried his best to sound like he were the victim while being escorted out of the room. "We were having a private moment and he accosted Me for no reason!"

"I got Your no reason, jackass!" I shouted in his direction once Dominic got me on my feet. "You better hope they put us in separate cells, or I'll show You again how much reason I had to beat You to sleep!"

"That's enough, amani!" I heard my Goddess's voice, instantly shutting me down. "you've done what needed to be done; don't ruin it by talking shit!" The look in her eyes was hot enough to melt metal, and she forced me to stare at her, recognizing the intensity in her eyes. She knew I wouldn't refuse her, no matter how angry I got or how intent I might have been to rip Lyrical a new asshole.

"Yes, my Goddess." I relented immediately.

As Dominic walked me downstairs to the "Cage" and placed me in my holding cell, I cut my eyes in Lyrical's direction. He was holding a towel over his nose, and I couldn't help but sneak in a few jabs while she wasn't looking.

"Damn, that must really hurt, partner… i wonder how the other dude looked."

"you snuck Me from behind. There's no way you could take Me in a fair fight."

I couldn't contain my laughter. "Care to put that to the test? i would love to finish with Your ribs what i started with Your face."

"That's enough, gentlemen." Dominic interrupted my attempts to intimidate him further. "amani, according to Sir Lyrical, you assaulted Him in a fit of jealousy because He was intimately involved with your Goddess. Care to tell Me your account of the situation?"

"Well, well, well. Dude gets His ass whipped by a bitch boi—i believe was the term used to describe male submissives—and now He wants to play victim?" I rhetorically asked, looking in Lyrical's direction before returning my focus to Dominic. "my Goddess can fuck whomever She wants. i am Hers to command, and i will protect my Owner, period."

"So, you're saying that Sir Lyrical's account is incorrect?"

"Yes, it is."

"Would you like to give Me your account?"

"Yes," I flatly answered. "i was searching for my Goddess because there was a matter that She needed to be aware of, and She was not in the location we thought she would be. i went to a couple of different areas, hoping to find Her. I took the chance that She might have been in the main building."

"Go on." Dominic scribbled notes.

"i heard Her screaming, but i know Her tone when She's in the throes of passion and when She's in trouble, so i rushed toward the sounds." I continued to recount, feeling my anger rising again. "When i entered the kitchen, i saw my Goddess bent over the table, fighting off His attempts to take off her briefs. i distinctly heard Her yell out for Him to get off Her, and when He made the reference to being compared to one of Her bitch bois, i'd heard enough and rushed Him."

"You heard him! he admits to assaulting Me!" Lyrical shouted.

"And You just admitted to attempted rape and sodomy, Sir," Dominic replied as he opened the door to my holding cell. "Lady Neferterri has sought to file charges against You. You might want to call Your attorney; it doesn't look good for You."

"What the hell? She's been teasing Me this whole damn time!" Lyrical was beside himself with anger. He glared at me, yelling, "If You're going to charge Me with something, let Me out of this cell so I can beat him to sleep!"

"Kinda hard to do when You're still holding Your nose, playa," I quipped, still grinning at the site of blood in the towel. "You might wanna get some ice on that soon, too, before it swells up and have You looking like the Elephant Man."

We walked out of the Cage and back to the main level of the building, and Dominic gave me this look. "For a minute there, I hesitated."

"Why was that?" I inquired.

"I really never trusted that prick," Dominic confessed. "There were some complaints about Him from different women on the island, but we never could really pin anything on Him. I guess I saw you beating Him senseless as a sort of Karma. Once we get back to Nassau, we can report the incidents to the proper authorities."

Honestly, I didn't want him to suffer in the courts, at least not yet.

He needed to feel the wrath of a Pharaoh I served. That would be worth the price of admission once he found out what happened to his Beloved.

I couldn't wait.

SIXTEEN ⚬ RAMESSES

"I don't believe My Beloved would betray Me like that."

I didn't want to believe the images I saw in the video playing in front of me.

I wanted to believe they were untrue, but my Beloved was nowhere to be found to explain her side of things. In fact, none of my girls were anywhere near me, and that bothered me more than I wanted to admit.

The meds had me a little disoriented and the lateness of the hour found me a little sleep deprived, but my eyes could not tear away from the scene that unfolded.

There was no way this could have happened.

"Sir, the video doesn't lie, and I would have no reason to lie to You." Korina sat next to my bed, looking as though she didn't want to show me what she'd captured. I couldn't understand why she felt the need to, but my reasoning and logic were being overridden by anger.

I closed my eyes. "She would never do this to me."

"I know You love Her, Sir, but the allure of the island can turn even the most faithful into something they don't recognize." She touched my hand for effect. I didn't pull my hand away. I was in too much shock. "No one is immune to seduction, Master Ramesses… not even You."

"So, is that why You wanted to show Me this video, Korina?" I got up from my prone position and grabbed her by her throat. I didn't pay attention to the fact that she didn't budge or move her hands to try and remove my grip. My rage was building by the second. "You already knew the attraction between us was evident. You didn't need to show Me this to get Me to fuck You."

I squeezed tighter, watching her eyes glaze over, but she never broke eye contact with me. If I were a little more lucid, I would have sworn she were in a euphoric status, on the verge of orgasm from the touch of my hand alone.

"I...wanted...You to see...You're choking Me, Sir." Korina began to see her original plan wasn't working, and she moved her hands to try to get me to loosen my grip.

I released her without further incident. She gasped for air, her chest heaving to get as much into her lungs as possible. "Sir...I... this was not meant as some ploy to get You into bed. I ...I wanted to give Myself to You before this incident with Your Beloved happened. You have to believe Me. I only had Your best interests at heart."

I placed my hands over my eyes in a desperate attempt to remove the images now etched in the recesses of my memory. Lyrical would pay dearly for his part, but my Beloved would not escape my wrath, either. I was irate that neither of our girls were here when I awoke to be here with me, and I thought at least amani would be nearby to keep abreast of my situation.

I slowly suspected that maybe Korina was right.

No one was immune to seduction...not even me.

"You will leave Me now and wait for Me in Your cabin. I'll claim You when I get out of here." My stare penetrated the windows to her soul, causing her to tremble. This wasn't about what she wanted anymore. This was about using her to erase the hurt in my heart that my entire family was elsewhere. There would be time to deal with the pain later, but right now I was going to get this out of my system so I could deal with them all. "You will be at My mercy and My control until I deem otherwise."

A mixture of genuine fear and unbridled arousal spread across her face. I didn't care if she was ready or not; if she wasn't ready, she wouldn't ever be ready. She awoke the beast within me, and as its prey, she had no choice but to absorb the brewing storm, and the tempestuous and carnal nature that came with it.

"Yes, Sir, I will do as You ask." Korina got up from her chair and left the room without another word. She was smart not to ask questions or offer any rebuttal, lest she find out the depths of which I could derive my sadistic nature.

The nurse walked in moments later, taken aback by the fact that I'd gotten dressed and was heading toward the door. "Sir, You cannot leave in Your condition."

"And what condition might that be, nurse?" I moved my arm around her waist, physically removing her from the doorway. She tried to grab my arm, holding me in place for a moment or two. The icy glare that greeted her when I turned my head in her direction scared her into releasing her grip. "As you can see, I am fine now. When My *family* comes by to check on My condition, tell them I have recovered and I will see them after I have taken care of a pressing issue. Am I understood?"

"Yes, Master Ramesses, You are understood." There was nothing else she could say that would appease me. I was sure she would radio to security to alert them of what I'd done, but by the time they would be able to respond to confront me, I would be where I needed to be. "Sir, there is something You should know. It's about Lady Neferterri—"

I was out the door and down the hall before she could finish her statement. I'd deal with her later.

Right now, a wanton slut awaited my arrival.

☥

"Hurt Me! Oh, God, it hurts so good!"

She was on all fours, wide open, and taking every inch of my girth inside of her other pussy.

She never had a chance to offer resistance. Not that she wanted to.

"This is how You wanted it, whore, so take it like a good slut."

"Yes, baby, give it to Me! Make Me Yours! Take it all out on Me!" A flash of understanding washed over her, and she knew she would never have the chance to take control of the situation. Her body made it clear she didn't want to be in control, and I was going to pound her into submission whether she wanted me to or not. "I want to be a good slut for You!"

I noticed the developing redness on her right cheek from my hand slapping her ass incessantly, grinning at the palm print shaping quite nicely on her skin. There would be no doubts who took her on this day, and I would not deny it if anyone asked.

"Shut the fuck up!" I growled as I pulled her up to place my hand over her mouth. I didn't want to hear her talk dirty to me. All I wanted was to exorcise the demons that threatened to spread through my mind like a cancer, poisoning any good thoughts I might have had before she brought my world into chaos.

Her body exploded with each thrust inside of her ass, my shaft resembling a piston inside of her hole, each stroke attempting to open her further without a care of whether I was causing any damage. I was going to make her pay for the pain she caused me, all so she could be fucked.

Her pussy, her ass, and her mouth would remember me for weeks to come; I was going to make sure of that.

I smelled the heat of her sex and needed to get back into her pussy, so I pulled out of her ass and slid inside of her pussy in one smooth stroke, sliding my thumb inside her ass again to feel my dick sliding inside her pussy. I took my thumb out quickly, sliding two fingers inside, listening to her scream out as I continued pounding her into the floor.

Her dirty talk was reduced to nothing more than grunts and moans now, her body taking over and getting what it wanted. I took my fingers out of her ass and grabbed for her arms, pulling them behind her back to finish her off. I felt my own climax on the horizon, and I wanted her to do nothing to disturb the tsunami that awaited to consume and wash away everything in my mind.

"Oh, God, I can't take any more!" she begged as her body convulsed and twisted, trying to get away from me. "It's too much! Please, I beg You! You're making Me come again!"

I had her tuned out, concentrating on my own pleasure, gritting my teeth as tunnel vision took over. I ignored her pleas to stop, neglecting her cries that her orgasms had turned into multiple streams of pleasure, rendering her speechless. All I cared about was releasing everything I had into the universe, praying to the gods that the hurt would leave with it.

I pushed her head down into the floor, pressing her face against the hard floor, feeling it coming on strong. I pulled out, taking the condom off my pulsing manhood and flipped her onto her back, holding off from shooting until I leaned over her mouth.

"Open wide, bitch!" I sneered as I jacked off and felt my explosion heading into her waiting mouth. I grabbed the back of her head and forced my length deep inside, shaking as I felt the back of her throat taking all I had to give down her throat. "You better not spill a drop, either!"

She took it all, licking around the head, trying to suckle me back in while I was still hard. I didn't want her to try to turn this into some sort of pseudo-romantic moment where sucking my dick became a sensual experience where I would want to cuddle afterward. I pulled away, leaving her writhing and quivering on the floor, trying desperately to have me close to her again. "Please, I want to suck You…I need it in me, I don't care where! Don't leave Me!"

I was done with her and bored with the routine. I felt like a new man as I gathered my clothes and walked out the door as I heard Korina whimpering and trying her best to crawl after me. Before I did, I took the video camera with the information I needed to handle the situation in front of me.

Korina continued to crawl toward me, screaming out her desire for me and her need to be devoted to me. I never bothered to look back, satisfied that I'd taken her ability to walk away from her. I dressed in the doorway and walked into the warm morning sunlight.

The sun felt good on my skin, but inside I felt hollow, without the ability to feel anything other than quelling my desire for answers. Once that was done, maybe there might have been room to heal and figure out the next step.

It was a damn shame the day would be so bright and sunny.

A storm was on the horizon. A tempest no one would ever see coming.

SEVENTEEN ⚯ NEFERTERRI

"What do you mean, you can't find Him???"

Dominic was angry, and I couldn't blame him.

How do you lose track of the owner of the island without any idea of where he might have been located?

I wanted to strangle the security officers myself, but Dominic was doing a good job of that without any help from me.

The whole island was frenzied with the news of Ramesses's disappearance. The nurse on duty was inconsolable, wondering if she'd simply called security before he left the medical tent rather than after she'd tried to stop him. This wasn't like my Beloved at all to have acted in such a threatening manner, but the way the nurse recounted how he'd behaved, something had gone wrong. I felt it.

"Sir, we got here as fast as we could when the nurse called us to the medical tent, but He was nowhere to be found, and He covered His tracks well." The officer who had enough guts to talk to Dominic tried to explain the aftermath of Ramesses's absence, but it wasn't enough to pacify me.

"Find My husband or there will be hell to pay!" I yelled as the other officers scrambled in different directions, interviewing anyone in sight that might have seen which direction he could have traveled in.

shamise, sajira, and amani were in shock. The cryptic tone of his message meant for all of us to hear had them all shaken up. In their haste to make sure I was okay, they didn't check with the medical staff to find out how long Ramesses would be sedated, or if he might come out of it quicker than expected. My emotions were split between worrying about his safety and dealing with the attempted rape hours earlier. I prayed he would turn up soon so I could find out what happened to him.

"Is He that upset with us, Goddess?" sajira's eyes were soft and needy. This was the first time she'd dealt with his anger, and it left her distraught. "He wouldn't leave us like this, would He?"

shamise tried to calm her as best she could, but she had her own reservations about this recent chain of events. Yes, her Daddy's temper was legendary, but it had never been directed at any of us, including me. "Let's just hope the officers are able to find Him in one piece. We can work on what to do afterward once that happens."

amani focused on making sure I was stable, ensuring the incident didn't overtake my emotions. "Goddess, they will find Him. He can't go too many places without someone seeing Him."

Dominic nodded. "He might think He knows all the security protocols to avoid being seen, but He has another thing coming."

"Don't be too sure about that, Dom." Our attention immediately shot in the direction of Ramesses walking up behind Dominic. The expression on his face was stoic, as though it were made of stone and couldn't be shattered.

Now I was really worried.

I was the first to approach him, and when I tried to hug him to connect with him again, he pushed me away. I tried to blink the shock away because he'd never refused me. "Beloved, what happened? The nurse said You just walked out of the tent without Your detail."

"Don't *Beloved* Me, Mercedes." His curt and emotionless reply chilled me to the bone. I knew he was angry because he never called me Mercedes unless we were at home and away from any of the compounds. "I needed away from You, all of you, so I could think a little bit. Now that I see things a little more clearly, I can deal with the fact that you abandoned Me to deal with whatever the fuck you wanted to deal with."

My eyes widened, trying to make sense of what the hell he was talking about.

shamise rushed to my side, with sajira in tow. "Daddy, we're so glad You're okay." sajira tried to move toward Ramesses, but she was rebuffed also.

His eyes were still transfixed on mine, searching them for something. I was more confused than ever. "Beloved, please tell Me what's going on?"

The answer to my question came in the form of a small video camera. He clicked the machine on, and played the footage. I looked in horror as the events of what happened between Lyrical and me played out on the screen, triggering my trauma, unbeknownst to him. "Care to explain this?" he asked.

I was speechless. I couldn't mouth a word. I was reliving the event in my mind all over again. Tears began to fall from my eyes; I didn't have the strength to answer his question.

"Sir, it's not what You think," amani interjected for me. "Goddess was—"

"Fucking another man while I was laid up in the medical tent, right?" Ramesses's fury rose to the surface, threatening to destroy anyone in its path. "Save it, amani; Domina Korina took the footage. Besides, none of you were around to at least let Me know *something*, were you?"

I was still reeling, my eyes glued to the screen as it finally went black at the moment before all hell broke loose and Lyrical turned the tables on me and tried to rape me. It was then I realized that Korina had played him, and my despondence turned to anger.

By the time I could reason with him, he was at the point of no return. "Baby, listen to Me. I didn't do what You're accusing Me of doing. You have to believe Me." I pleaded as best I could, but his eyes were cold and there was no way to get through to him.

"I'll be at the main building for the remainder of the week." He turned and walked away, leaving us in further confusion and hurt. "Until I can figure out what the fuck is going on, I don't want to see any of you."

The girls were devastated, and I wasn't able to process what he'd said because I didn't want to believe it. The anger in amani's eyes was evident because he knew the truth, and Ramesses shut him down before he could get it out.

Dominic didn't flinch. He radioed to one of his officers. "Call off the search; Ramesses has been located. Get a message to His cabin, there's something He needs to help with. He may be the only one who can get through to Ramesses." He turned to me and offered a consoling shoulder. "He's hurting right now. He doesn't know what happened, and You know how He gets when He doesn't allow anyone to get a word in edgewise."

"Yes, I know, but it still hurts." I buried my face in his chest, trying to find some refuge in his arms. "None of this works without Him. Bring Him back to Me, Dom, please? He needs to know the truth."

"Consider it done, My Lady." Dominic took a hand towel from amani and wiped the tears from my eyes. "I called in the heavy artillery for this, but we'll get it done."

EIGHTEEN ⚮ RAMESSES

"There's nothing You can say, so, save Your breath."

I guess I should have known Dominic would call Amenhotep to try to talk me off the ledge, but this is something even He couldn't fix. My wife had breached the trust between us, and that's not something you can get over in a few hours' time.

I had already downed half a bottle of whiskey by the time they got to me, and my inebriated state would be another obstacle for them to overcome, not that it would matter much. I mean, what could they say? *It's not what You think, Ramesses?*

"You know, I remember a couple of years ago when a youngster, a man who I regard as a son to Me, did something I never thought He would do." Amenhotep sat down next to me and poured a shot of whiskey, downing it in one gulp. "He got Me to remember that regardless of the situation, You should do no harm to those in Your charge."

I was incredulous and irritated beyond measure. "My wife was caught *on tape* committing a sex act while I was out of it in the medical tent, basically cheating on Me, and You want me to remember, 'Do no harm'? Get the fuck out of here with that, Sir," I slurred.

Dominic commented, "Is that what Korina told You?"

"She didn't *have* to tell Me shit, Dom! It was right there on tape, dammit!" I yelled.

Amenhotep grabbed my shoulder and turned toward me. "And You believed a total stranger over a woman who has been devoted to You for over a decade? Do You really hear Yourself right now, youngster?"

"Fuck You!" I tried to take a swing at Amenhotep, but Dominic caught my arm before I connected. Amenhotep never moved a muscle, confident I would have never made contact in my diminished state. "I don't need to make sense right now! The cameras don't lie!"

"Oh, You mean like this camera?" Dominic pulled out his tablet and raised the surveillance cameras that were in the kitchen area. I tried to look away, dismissing it as something I'd already seen. Dominic forced my head in front of the camera. "Oh, no, You're going to watch this…all of it. The truth never lies, either."

I watched as the scene moved past the point where Korina stopped taping and saw what happened after. My eyes narrowed as I saw Lyrical force himself on my Beloved, calling her a whore for teasing him. I turned my eyes away, tears flowing freely, as I realized the mistake I'd made in drawing the wrong conclusion.

I wanted to scream.

"We interviewed Lyrical after we peeled amani off of Him," Dominic said. "It seems He and Korina had designs on splitting You two up so He could have Her, and Korina could have You. The only thing that went wrong was when She turned the tables on Him after He began trying to humiliate Her during the encounter. If amani hadn't gotten there—"

"He's a dead man before He'll ever get the chance to tell a jury anything." I threw the shot glass against the wall, shattering it into pieces. "Where is He now, and don't tell Me I can't see Him, either, Dominic."

Amenhotep kept His hand on my shoulder the entire time I

ranted. "Kid, listen to Me. I know You want to handle this and protect Your Beloved's honor, but all things in due time, understood?" He waited for me to nod my head before He continued. "You need to make things right with Your Beloved, first, and then the rest of Your family. They are hurting because You didn't give them a chance to explain things to help You to understand what happened."

Tears still flowing, I dropped my head. "I fucked another woman without My Beloved's consent based on a lie, Sir. How in the hell do I reconcile that? She wasn't the one who betrayed Us, I was."

"You two are the closest thing to family I have left on this planet, and I've seen You both go through ups and downs and survive a lot to get where You are right now." Amenhotep grinned for the first time during our conversation. "You will find a way to reconcile; I have faith in that. You two aren't done yet. In life, everyone is going to hurt You; I have been around long enough to know this for a fact. The key is to figure out who You are willing to suffer through the hurt for. I think You know the answer in Your heart by now."

I took comfort in His words. He was always a balancing influence on me, and having Dom there to beat me over the head with the cold facts was sobering enough to make me put down the bottle and shot glass and look for a pot of coffee. "You're right, both of You. I need to set things right before My family thinks I don't want them anymore."

"Now that we've gotten that out of the way, Sir, what do we do about Korina?" Dominic asked, trying to get me back into business mode. "She's basically an accessory to the crime, but it really won't stick in court because She didn't know Lyrical would take things to the extreme."

"I don't want Her in anyone's court, Dom." The anger rose as I thought about the turmoil she'd caused and how stupid I'd allowed myself to be. "I need for You to do some digging on our little co-conspirators. I want to know everything there is to know before we make the next move."

"Sounds like an extraction is in the works." Dominic tried his best to hide the smile on his face. "Are we talking temporary extraction or permanent extraction?"

"That would depend on the information You are able to come up with, Bro," I answered, looking at my Mentor and stroking my beard as I thought about the next moves to make. "If there are no ties, as I suspect there aren't, I believe a permanent extraction would be necessary, with extreme prejudice."

"Consider it done, Bro," Dominic stated before leaving the room. That left the two of us alone with our thoughts for a few moments.

"You know that bitch has to pay, right?" Amenhotep stated in a tone that made me do a double-take.

"What happened to priorities, Sir?"

"I know what I said, youngster, but I also know that what She tried to do...what they both tried to do...is worthy of a punishment that should send a message to never fuck with a union when it's strong." Amenhotep started to sound all fire-and-brimstone, which scared and amused me at the same time.

"I didn't know You cared so much."

"I always look out for My family, kid," He stated. "You've always been the closest thing to a son I'll ever get the chance to have. I make it My business to make sure You and the rest of the House are safe and taken care of."

"So, what do You suggest, Sir? Death is messy and complicated, and too good a fate for them, for what they've done."

"There are worse fates than death, youngster." Amenhotep's grin bordered on the sinister, but this time, I didn't care what he was contemplating because I was already there. "We'll get with the rest of the Society, put our heads together. If Dominic finds out there are no loose ends in the States to tie up, then God help them where they're about to go."

NINETEEN ⚙ amani

"So, how are things going with Mistress Blaze?"

With all the drama surrounding my Goddess and Sir, I had no chance to catch up with my boy, Jelani, to find out if his weekend had gone as well as I'd hoped. We were in the family cabin, out on the balcony enjoying a beautiful, tropical day. The sun was shining, but I felt like the storm within my D/s family overshadowed the weather.

The grin on his face was worth the trouble it took to get him down there.

"Man, D, She's everything i'd dreamed about and then some," he said, gingerly sitting in the chair next to me. I wanted to laugh because I knew how much of a sadist Blaze was, but he didn't need to know that information ahead of time. "Serving Her over the past couple of days has been bliss, but did She have to blister my ass to where i can't sit down for long periods of time?"

I nearly fell out of my chair laughing. I tried to keep from laughing at him, but he couldn't stop adjusting in his seat to find a good spot. "Sorry, dawg, but you see taking an ass whooping on line and taking a scene from one of the baddest in the kink world are two different things."

"Yeah, you're the one to talk." Jelani glared at me as he studied the bruises on his body. "I don't remember you being all that bad-ass when we were on line, either, bruh."

"That's easy; i figured out how to process pain, bruh." I glanced at him for a moment, feeling the need to school my frat on a couple of things. "my Goddess and my Sir helped me to understand the mental aspects of pain. If you think of it in one way, that's the way your body will react to it. After a really intense scene with them one night last year, at one point i couldn't feel a thing, at least, it wasn't a bad pain. Once i came down from subspace, i felt every-thing, but by then i'd already applied what they taught me."

"So, that's why you were looking all high that night when you came to my fight party?" Jelani gave me the side-eye for a minute before memories began flooding his mind. He shook those images for the moment to try and finish his thought. "That must have been why i was so trippy last night, huh?"

"Yes, felt like you'd gotten ahold of some MJ, right?"

"Yeah, i wasn't that high, but it was close enough." He laughed as he thought about the comparison of the sensations. "i caught the munchies like hell, though."

"That's why i usually keep something nearby after a scene. The endorphin rush burns calories and then some, and if you don't have something to eat or drink to make up for that, you can wind up sick."

"So, let me ask you something, dawg." Jelani found a sweet spot to sit to keep from hurting so badly. I tried again to keep my laughter to myself as best I could, but he wasn't making it easy. "Has your Goddess ever given you some? i mean, have you two had sex?"

"Yeah, why?"

"Because when we were in our scene, She kept saying how She needed to get some dick as soon as She was done with me," Jelani recounted. "you know i'm down for the cause because She's fine as fuck for a woman in her late forties, but as soon as She was done, it was lights out for me and She headed to take care of what She said She needed. What's up with that?"

"Okay, bruh, first rule of serving a Female Dominant: it ain't about you," I explained. "The minute you try to make it sound like you're getting your rocks off without first thinking about Her is the minute you find yourself *persona non grata* in Her life."

"But, i'm saying, bruh, She's been talking about how fine i am, how She would love to find out how well i can please Her, shit like that." Jelani sounded frustrated, and it wasn't as though I could blame him. Goddess put me through the same paces when we were first together.

"Bruh, listen to me, and this is the most important piece of advice you'll ever get from me," I advised. I leaned back in my chair, feeling like I was looking at a reflection of my former self a year ago. "Don't expect Her to fulfill your sexual fantasies, and don't expect to handle all of Hers. Just be thankful when She chooses you to fulfill them, and when She does choose you, you make Her want to choose you over and over again."

A knock on the door startled us. I turned toward the front door and then back toward Jelani and asked, "Were you expecting someone?"

"I was about to ask you the same question, bruh."

Not knowing who would be at the door, I cautiously walked and asked the person through the door, "Who is it?"

"amani, your Sir requests your presence," the young woman answered through the door. "He says it is of utmost importance and requests that i escort you to Him personally."

☥

"I need answers, and I need them yesterday."

Stepping into the interrogation room with my Sir while not knowing the nature of his sudden need to see me had me on edge on a few levels. I kept my guard up, even while the slave who escorted me to the room remained in the room until he dismissed her. I had a feeling it would concern the events surrounding my Goddess, and more importantly, his Beloved, but I was not about to be summoned like some mongrel who was dying to have his master's attention, either.

"You requested my presence, my Sir?" I began as I kneeled beside the chair facing him at the table.

"Yes, amani, I summoned you here because I need to know what happened, and I need to hear the truth, because for some reason everyone wants to give me versions of what happened." Ramesses's demeanor was businesslike, stoic and cold. This was the side of him I knew most people feared, and I understood why. Callous. Cruel. Unfeeling. I didn't recognize him. "I know you won't lie to Me, so give it to Me straight: did My Beloved cheat on Me or did you keep Her from being raped?"

"With all due respect, my Sir, but why are You asking this question?" I was incredulous. I'd only known them to be upfront about everything, and I'd witnessed their unwavering belief and faith in each other. "You know the answer to this question, why on Earth would You need my answer?"

"There are demons that unfortunately have not been exorcised that you might have a hand in eradicating once and for all with the answer to My question, amani." Ramesses's face showed no emotion, but I wasn't about to show any fear. His eyes penetrated deeper as he moved closer to my face, making me rethink my original stance to not show any fear. "you are more than welcome to try and debate the methods of My madness when I'm in a better mood to entertain, but right now, a simple answer to My question will suffice."

"If You want an answer, then i will show You my answer," I retorted. I stood from my kneeling position, taking off my shirt. His eyes widened as he observed the bruises, which had turned black from the reddened shade a few hours ago. The most glaring ones were around my ribcage where we'd taken the fall before I'd turned his face and torso into my personal punching bag. In a tone I wasn't sure I meant to have or not, I stated, "Does this answer Your question, my Sir?"

He never answered me, at least to say yes or no. He got up from the table, took one last look at my bruises, and said before walking out of the room, "Thank you, amani. you have given Me every-thing I need to know."

TWENTY ⚮ shamise

"That doesn't sound like the Mercedes I know and love."

I relaxed in the cabin with Jay and Candy, finding myself in need of a break from the intensity of the day's events. I'd never seen my Daddy that upset before, and there was nothing any of us could do to calm him down. I didn't know how to deal with that, and it scared the hell out of me for the first time since I'd been with them.

I lounged on the couch, enjoying the feeling of letting my body relax for a few moments while I tried to make some sense of things, and maybe finding a solution to set things right between my Daddy and my Goddess. I was their Alpha slave, and whether they wanted me to or not, I had a duty to help keep the House intact.

Candy leaned against Jay on the bed, enjoying the teasing on her skin, cooing every so often when he placed his lips on her skin. I felt a twinge of envy, wanting to find my own pleasure and solace, if only for a few moments until my mind cleared. Jay looked up at me and said, "Scarlett, you know how Kane can get when he's pissed off about something. You have to give him some time to process things. He doesn't stay angry for long; he's too measured and controlled to allow that emotion to take over."

"I understand that, baby, but it's rare that the focus of his anger is Mercedes," Candy chimed in, sinking deeper into Jay's chest to get more comfortable. "This might last a little longer than usual; it's never been this crazy, not since—" Her voice trailed off.

"Not since what, Candy?" Jay and I were both at a loss, confused over her cryptic reference to the past.

"Not since Kane cheated on Mercedes a long time ago." Candy sighed as she thought about the situation. "That was a bad patch… a really bad patch. It was a miracle they survived and got things back on track."

Jay sat up from his spot and looked at Candy as though she'd revealed that she'd cheated on him. I had a similar "what the fuck" look on my face, too, trying to get an idea of what Candy really knew that I felt I should have known.

Candy felt the eyes on her, and she exhaled and sat up on the bed to begin the story. "Kane wasn't always the man you both know now. He was a selfish man, a player of the nth degree. He thought he was God's gift to women, and had no problems telling anyone exactly that. I guess it was his overbearing arrogance that attracted us to him."

"Okay, so what's so different? He's still an arrogant man," I quipped. My body reacted, and I cursed under my breath to calm down. Even when speaking about him in anecdotal, he got me wet.

"Yeah, but he was a train wreck waiting to happen back then," Candy soberly explained. "Between his arrogance, his narrow-minded outlook on women, and the mistake in the form of a woman by the name of Imani Taylor…I think back on it now and I really wonder if it was by the grace of God that things worked out the way they did."

"Okay, you're being cryptic again, baby." Jay was irritated, and I couldn't blame him. I needed her to get to the point, too, but I forgot how much of my Daddy's influence could be had on other people. "Get to the part where this makes sense to us, okay?"

"Okay, okay." Candy looked perturbed that she was being rushed, so she settled in again and recounted the incident. "Mercedes, Kane, and I were a threesome couple at one point in our lives, and Imani threatened to split us all up because she wanted Kane all to herself. She hatched a plan that nearly worked because he wasn't as strong-willed or as sharp mentally as he is now, playing us and making it look like we were just another couple of tricks, saying that we had been fucking other dudes behind his back between parties."

"Wait, so, he wasn't playing when he said you belonged to him and he allowed us to date?" I saw Jay's ego deflate in the blink of an eye with that revelation. He tried to recover by focusing on the story at hand. "So, did Kane believe her over both of you?"

"Yes, he did." Candy wiped away a tear. "There was this other dude that wanted what Kane had, and at every party, he would find a way to sex one of us and then brag about how it was all our idea and one of us would come after him. He laid it on thick, telling anyone who would listen that either Mercedes or I would make humiliating comments about Kane, and his lack of skills while fucking him."

"But that's crazy!" I yelled before realizing I never met the man when he was single. All I'd ever known of my Daddy was when he was married to my Goddess. "Okay, I have to remind myself that he was what he was before I met him."

"We were young and dumb back then, but we both loved him. Mercedes was the one who married him, but they kept me close the entire time." Candy kept rattling off the details. "Imani had him convinced that his wife and his girlfriend were with him for the wrong reasons and that she was the one for him. He left us at a party to sleep with her at her house and then came back acting strange and accusatory."

It was all I could do to keep from tearing up. Whether she realized it or not, Candy was slowly tearing down the man that I worshipped. I knew he had faults, I wasn't entirely naïve, but it hurt my heart to realize that he could be so cruel toward the women he loved.

Candy trembled for a moment as the memories of that night threatened to overtake her own emotions. I wanted to comfort her; this couldn't have been easy for her to do, and despite her strong feelings for Jay, her heart belonged to my Daddy. I couldn't blame her; I was cursed with the same affliction, and sajira was only a nudge away from the all-consuming abyss, too.

Hopelessly hooked…and I wouldn't trade it for anything in the world.

Jay felt like he was the odd man out for a moment. Fighting his way back into the conversation, he said, "Look, Kane is not that man anymore. He's my boy, and we've been deep for a long time. He'll get through this without a problem, and he will make things right."

Candy kissed Jay across his lips. "I know he will, baby. He has his moments when he loses his way sometimes, but that's what makes him…well, him. We never gave up on him back then, and we won't give up on him now, right, Scarlett?"

I smiled for the first time since this conversation began. Yes, my Daddy had his faults. He could be stubborn, cruel, and that temper of his could make the devil himself quake in his skin. But there's the side of him that only those closest to him are privileged to see, and I wasn't about to give that up for anything. He was worth suffering for because the bliss that came after the suffering was so delicious, so decadent, one would think we were addicts who couldn't get enough.

"Yes, Candy, you're right. He's going to find his way back, I feel it deep down in my soul." I sat up on the couch, feeling the storm clouds lifting. There was a shift in my attitude, like I had the energy to go for the next twenty-four hours without sleep. I felt my Daddy's presence surrounding me again, and the peace of understanding that everything would be okay pushed me into a different zone.

God, the things that man did to me even when he's not around me should be considered illegal.

I unconsciously touched my shoulder, welcoming the flood of fond memories of the things we'd done over the course of the week, and the fantasies of what I wanted him to do to me before we left the island, including a replication of that hot fire scene he did with keket. My legs instinctively parted, and soon nothing and no one else mattered except reconnecting with him in my own way. I mouthed the words, "Daddy, come back to me, please," as I gyrated my hips and touched my skin as though every nerve was on fire.

I forgot Candy and Jay were there, and I could only imagine what they could have been thinking in that moment. I looked straight through them and saw his image behind them, his eyes locking with mine, giving me the motivation I needed to stay right there with him in this space.

I heard his voice in my ear, "I might be out of sight, baby girl, but I'm never out of your mind." Soon, my mind delved deeper into my subconscious, placing me right where I wanted to be… kneeling at his feet.

"Daddy, don't leave us, please."

"I haven't gone anywhere, baby girl. your Goddess and your sis, your brother…I won't be going anywhere unless He deems it necessary."

"But the way You pushed us away, how were we supposed to help You?"

"There are some things that even you are not able to fix, My precious

shamise. Know that I am returning to you, and those that tried to take Me away from you will pay dearly for their treachery."

"What happened? Can't You tell me anything to help the others ease the anxiety?"

"I know you want to help, baby girl, but this is something that Daddy needs to put to an end, so that it doesn't happen to anyone else again."

"i love it when You're like this, Daddy...it turns me on when You're aggressive like this."

"I'm just getting started, My darling. I'm sorry I wasn't strong enough to deal with this properly. I know I might have done some damage... that you might think a little less of Me."

"i am Yours, Daddy...i belong to You and my Goddess...we belong to You. Nothing will change that, ever. i love You."

"I love you, too. Now, let Daddy go and take care of some trash so I can come home and make things right. I promise I won't be long."

"i'll be waiting, Daddy."

By the time I came out of my trance, I returned to stares as though I'd lost my mind.

"Where in the world were you?" Jay asked. "The way you moved—"

I blushed. "i was with my Daddy."

Jay shook his head. "He and I need to have a long talk one day so I can figure out how in the hell he managed to...never mind, I don't know if I'd ever understand."

Candy and I giggled, sharing a knowing glance before I got up from the couch and walked toward the door. I blew a kiss at them and commented to Jay, "You never know what you might understand unless you open your mind to the possibilities. You'll come around sooner than you think, especially if she has anything to do with it."

I walked out of their cabin and made my way to the family cabin. I felt lighter, especially after feeling my Daddy's presence around me again. I wasn't completely convinced that the rest of the day would be peaches and cream, but I had a feeling things would be set in their proper balance.

By the time I got to the cabin, I would realize how right I was.

TWENTY-ONE ⚥ sajira

"What the fuck are you doing???"

My worst nightmare had come true and he had the nerve to act like there was nothing wrong.

I had intended to have a serious talk with my husband. I felt there was a way to find a compromise because I was still in love with him, despite the craziness that had happened, and I thought there was a way to work things through. I happened to walk by Mistress Sinsual's cabin where I knew lynx was staying for the week, and the sounds I heard coming from the balcony stopped me in my tracks.

The sounds were purely orgasmic, but that wasn't what stopped me cold.

Not hearing a woman among the sounds was what forced my feet to move a little faster and figure out if I heard what I thought I heard.

I rushed up to the balcony area where the sounds came from, doing my best not to disturb the participants until I felt I couldn't hold it in any longer. I could hear the familiar sounds of my husband, but the other man in the amatory affair were foreign to my senses.

I finally reached the point to where my eyes and ears could focus their attention simultaneously, and the shock to my primary senses was cataclysmic.

I felt like I was having an out-of-body experience as I watched lynx and tiger having an unbridled fuck in the open space, with the setting sun as the backdrop of their pending climax.

I couldn't take my eyes away, no matter how much my mind wanted to.

But it was so fucking sexy.

lynx's left hand dropped down to tiger's right thigh, making it spread wider, their thighs pressing against each other. The skin contact seemed to add to the growing wave of pure lust flooding through both of them. lynx moved his right hand, reached for tiger's midsection, its final goal more direct. I watched as he slipped his hand over tiger's engorged manhood, stroking it as he pumped slowly inside of his chocolate passageway. As he stroked deeper, he continued to masturbate tiger, sending waves of pleasure through his body. tiger spread his legs wider, giving me a good view of what was happening between them.

A haze slipped over my mind, thoughts being replaced by direct sensation, looking down as my hand began to slide slowly along my lips, mimicking the motion of my husband's hand over tiger's shaft, cursing as my body betrayed me despite my mind's protestations that it was my husband in the middle of a homo-erotic encounter— an encounter that would have caused multiple orgasms if I had been watching someone other than the man I loved while in the throes of passion.

My fingers began playing with my nipples as I continued to watch them. I wasn't sure I was supposed to be enjoying this, the war between my mind and body escalated with each passing moment. In the midst of my inner conflict, I neglected to notice my heart breaking at the blatant act of betrayal that my eyes saw and my ears heard.

They were consumed by their lust for each other, tiger's screams of his lover's name echoing in my ears and bouncing against the walls and into the dusk that began to surround us. It would be night soon, and there would be nothing but darkness for the next few hours to come. I shed tears as I came hard against my fingers while my emotions began to make their presence known, over-taking my lustful thoughts and feelings.

Finally, my mind took notice of the pain in my heart and shouted for me to cease my self-indulgence and take notice of the pain that would soon arrive, no matter how hard my orgasms washed over my body. My body ignored my pleas, relentless in its intent to push further past the point of no return, greedy in its pursuit of higher heights to reach its personal meaning of the pleasure principle.

"That's it, boi, make me cum!" I heard tiger screaming out. "Make me shoot all over your chest, dammit!"

That was when my mind snapped back into reality.

"Didn't you hear me?!?! What the fuck do you think you're do-ing?!?!"

"i'm…getting…fucked, that's what…i'm doing!" tiger shouted between strokes.

lynx was in a zone, and from the looks of it, he never heard a word I yelled. It wasn't until I slapped the back of his head to snap him out of his blissful state did he recognize his wife was in his space.

"Owwww! What the…oh, it's you." He scowled like I'd inter-rupted a moment that he wouldn't get back again. "I thought you were off somewhere on the island getting yours, too."

He never budged an inch, still inside tiger's ass, hand firmly on his length, looking up at me like I needed to excuse myself so they could finish what they started.

I was so pissed I could have spat nails.

"Oh, i'm sorry, did i interrupt your little rendezvous? i guess the shoe's on the other foot now, huh?" I avoided the tears because there was no way I would give him the satisfaction of thinking he had the upper hand on me. "i actually was here to reconsider your proposal and maybe negotiate a few changes so we could both be happy, but on second thought, never mind."

I began to walk down the stairs to make my way toward the main building with the hopes of collecting myself before I looked for shamise, but lynx quickly dismounted from tiger and rushed after me. He blocked my walkway at the foot of the stairs, surprising me with this look of confusion on his face.

"you really wanted to…I mean, you really thought about it?" His face really showed what I thought was genuine interest in what I had to say. "you'd leave your family to try and be together again?"

"Come on, lynx, quit acting; she doesn't even know the truth about you," tiger shouted down after grabbing a towel to wrap himself and walked to the top of the stairs. "If you're going to do this, you need to tell her the whole truth, and don't leave shit out."

My eyes turned from tiger before focusing back on my husband, who now couldn't match my gaze. "What is he talking about, Ice? What haven't you told me?"

He looked like a teenager who'd been caught breaking curfew and couldn't come up with a quick lie to cover the truth. He rubbed the back of his neck, which was my tell-tale sign that he wanted to tell me, but he didn't want to hurt me. "Goddamn it, Ice, tell me!" I shouted.

"i…i have been fucking tiger ever since the night of your collaring a year ago." He finally dropped the bombshell that I should have seen coming. "i'm in love with him."

If he could have slit my throat, it wouldn't have hurt as much as this revelation did. I couldn't breathe, and I struggled to stand while on the stairs. "How could you? you're in love with him? So, what was the proposal about yesterday?"

tiger's ears perked up at the end of my last statement. "Proposal, what proposal? Oh my God, don't tell me you're trying to claim you're bi? Are you serious?"

"i still love my wife, tiger." lynx tried to sound sincere, but I didn't possess the ability to believe anything else that came out of his mouth. "Yes, i have fallen for you, but i still want her, if she'll still have me."

"No, i don't want you." I heard the words come from my lips, but I didn't think I was the one who said them. The whole situation was surreal. "As a matter of fact, when we get back to the States, i'll be moving out of the house, and shamise will be leaving with me."

"No!" lynx pawed at me as I tried to push past him. "Don't leave me, please!"

tiger had his arms folded over his chest. The smirk on his face was infuriating, and I wanted to run up the stairs and smack it off his face. He had the nerve to act smug about the whole thing. His smirk soon turned to abject fear when he saw someone he didn't expect to see walking toward the cabin.

"Bois, sajira, what are you doing here?" Sinsual surveyed the scene, immediately noticing my distress. She moved toward me to study my face, her frown evident when I tried to hide my tears from her. "Is everything okay, sajira, and tell Me the truth, baby doll."

I looked up at tiger, who looked like he was about to pass out based on my answer, before I looked down at lynx, his face reflecting his own distress, like his future hinged on whatever was about to come out of my mouth.

I looked up at Sinsual, offering up a half-smile, and I replied,

"Ma'am, everything is okay; i was congratulating the bois; it seems You are looking to take things to the next level with lynx. my tears were those of joy because things will be changing for the better."

Before Sinsual could ask another question, I left the three of them to their conversation. I felt better knowing that I was rid of my husband. He was no longer in my circle of concern, as my Goddess loved to say. I still felt the pang of sorrow in my heart, but eventually that would pass, and I had a few things in mind of exactly how to numb the pain.

First things first, though…I needed to get with my bro and sis to figure out how to help fix things within my own House before it was too late.

TWENTY-TWO ⚯ shamise

"i can't believe it. Are you sure that's what happened?"

amani and I found sajira staring off into space, barely acknowledging our presence around her. She didn't bother saying a word, which was particularly disturbing because she's usually the most hyper of the three of us.

Something was wrong, I felt it.

"my husband has decided that he is in love with another man." sajira tossed out the statement like she was trying to come to grips with it herself. "No remorse, no hesitation, just came out and said it like the last decade meant nothing."

"i still don't believe it. he's always been into you, sis. At least, that was the impression I got whenever I saw him around you," amani commented. He picked her up and brought her inside to lie on her bed while I grabbed something for her to drink to settle her nerves. "he wouldn't be stupid enough to throw all of that away over someone he's barely known a year, right?"

"i almost did," I confessed, noticing one of my choices manifested itself in someone else's choice to harm someone I loved. I couldn't bear the thought of my sis suffering from such a selfish choice, but I had to face facts. "i nearly left the House for good because of some flight of fancy, and i was lucky they accepted me back."

"Don't beat yourself up, sis. This is not about that." sajira took the drink and downed it in one swallow. I saw her face contort for a moment as her palette adjusted to the burn. "i nearly made the same decision, remember? Hell, i was even willing to negotiate with him to figure out how to stay in both worlds. he even had the nerve to still claim he wanted me, but how the hell was i going to accept being with him when he wants dick as much as i do? That's not what i signed up for. It would have been one thing if i knew he was at least bisexual, but he didn't give me any way to at least make up my mind. God, how could i have been so stupid?"

"you weren't being stupid, sis, you were in love with your husband." amani wrapped his arms around her waist and kissed her on the cheek. "Love can be a crazy thing sometimes, and we've all done stupid things in the name of love, so what makes you think you're immune to it?"

"amani's right, baby, there's no need in dwelling on what has been done, the only thing we can do is focus on moving forward, figuring out what needs to be done and getting there," I told her. "Once we get back to the States, we can figure out where to go from there."

"Already a step ahead of you, sis." sajira seemed to come around, using her analytical mind to start calculating her next moves. "Things are already in motion on that front, but i know what i plan to ask for at the party tomorrow night, and i'm hoping Daddy allows it once we've gotten Him and Goddess back together and in sync."

"Speaking of which, is there really anything that we can do?" amani asked. "i mean, they are husband and wife, and while we have a little influence as their property, wouldn't they need to work this out on their own?"

I grinned at the questions. He was right, but I'd been with them the longest, and I'd been through a lot with them, too. "Daddy has a tendency to let His temper get the best of Him, but once He calms down, His cerebral side takes over, working through all the possibilities and resolutions before making His final moves. He knows we want to help, so we simply have to be in a position to help."

"What exactly does that mean, sis?" sajira looked confused, as though she couldn't figure out what I already realized. "you saw the way Daddy pushed us all away, even Goddess. He's never done that, as long as i've known Him."

"Well, i guess i should put this part in, too," amani interjected, causing us to look in his direction. He shook his head like the words I said clicked from something that happened earlier.

"He had me in the interrogation room with Him earlier today. All He did was ask questions, and when I answered them, He said thank you and left without another word."

"That's the Daddy we know." I beamed. He was already in head-hunter mode, and it was going to get really interesting really fast. "Don't be surprised if He asks you to help Him with something else."

"Great, at least you gave me the heads-up." amani sighed. I didn't think he'd gotten used to how Daddy and Goddess operated. When they had a command that needed to be followed at that moment, you couldn't hesitate. "So, what do we do about Goddess? She has to be reeling from all of this, too."

"Actually, i've taken care of that, too," I answered as I heard a knock on the door. Anticipating that the island slaves were able to accomplish their objective, I asked my brother and sister submissives a rhetorical question: "Are you ready to serve your Goddess?"

☥

"Good evening, Goddess, it is our pleasure to pamper You tonight."

The surprised look on her face was a strong indication that the slaves did as they were

told, explaining to her that we were in distress and were in need of her presence immediately. Her expression turned to relief when she realized there was no distress and everything was as it should have been. I knew it was a risk in having them tell her a lie, but it was the only way to shock her out of her doldrums.

"What is this all about, shamise? sajira, I assume you and amani were in on this also?" Neferterri asked as she looked in their direction.

"No, Goddess, they were not involved in getting You here; that was my doing." I took her by the hand and led her to the bathroom. "But they will be helping me with getting You back to Yourself, and the best way to do that is to pamper and please You."

"I won't be able to get back to Myself until I know for a fact that your Daddy is okay," she insisted, offering slight resistance to me guiding her as her rebuttal.

"Daddy is okay, my Goddess," I reassured. "In fact, amani said He is in the midst of resolving part of the problem as we speak."

"Yes, my Goddess, shamise is correct," amani offered as he drew the bath water. "Things will come back into balance quickly."

"I still don't believe you three, but I do need to take My mind off things." She relented, allowing me to take her into the bathroom. sajira came in soon after with the fragrances, the soaps, and the bag that housed her wipes and other essentials for changing out her tampons. "I've needed this, badly, but with everything that has been happening—"

I kissed her across her lips to quiet her before she got on a rant. "we are here to serve You and pamper You, Goddess. No more words are necessary for now, unless You are giving a directive."

Neferterri smiled at my passive-aggressive nature in getting her to relax while giving her the option to command when the need arose. Years of training under keket was time well spent, and I planned on showcasing the full repertoire before tonight was over.

"amani, come," she ordered as sajira and I helped her into the oversized tub.

He walked over to the side of the tub, kneeling once he stopped. "Yes, my Goddess, how may I serve You?"

"I want you to perform the menstrual service you performed the other day when I get out of the tub," she stated. "I'll need to release. It has been a rough couple of days."

A slick smile spread across amani's face, and I was curious as to why. "Yes, my Goddess, i will gather what i need and await Your arrival in the bedroom once my sisters are done."

I focused on the task in front of us while he left to attend to whatever it was he was supposed to be doing. I was clueless to the menstrual service he and Goddess referred to, but I concluded that both sajira and I would find out after we were done.

Neferterri must have sensed a need for the three of us to be alone, because she silently beckoned us to the side of the tub. "I have a surprise for tomorrow night, and I'm going to need your help with that. We will revisit that once you're done pampering Me, so let's get to it. I have another pressing appointment that I'll need energy for."

TWENTY-THREE ☒ RAMESSES

"Aaaaaaaaaaaaaaaarrrrrrrrrggggggggggghhhhhhhh!!!!!"

Carl Jung once said, "The healthy man does not torture…generally it's the tortured who turn into the torturers."

If I was a tortured soul, it was because the culmination of events turned me into one. By Jung's phrasing, I had become a torturer because of the circumstances that turned me into the tortured.

Death was too good for what he tried to do to my Beloved, but torturing him to within an inch of it would have to suffice.

I had Lyrical tied down to an inverted St. Andrews Cross, giving me the ability to lay him in a supine position and to give me full range of his body. I planned to abuse every inch until I got tired, and I was wide awake with plenty of energy.

I was beyond the point of sadism now. Some would argue that there is no difference between sadism and intolerable cruelty, but I was not in the mood to argue the point. The only thing that mattered to me was to quiet the storm, the unbridled tempest within me. He needed to suffer, and he needed to suffer by my hand, and no force on this planet was going to stop me.

Not even Amenhotep…

I would leave Korina to my Beloved to deal with as she wanted, but I had plans for Lyrical. Those plans included watching him bleed until I had no choice but to see him to a medical facility in Nassau.

I took a knife to the inside of his thigh, careful not to pierce the femoral artery. I didn't want him to bleed out, at least not yet, anyway. Hearing his screams meant nothing to my desires to watch him flirt with the edges of consciousness, fading in and out like the flicker of a flame.

"Mercy!" Lyrical screamed out, his voice doing nothing more than reverberating against the walls of one of the underground panic rooms, built in the event of a hurricane. I slid another knife through his hand, watching it protrude through the muscle and bone, inducing another blood-curdling scream.

"It's funny how the guilty scream out for mercy when they become the victim." I leaned down over his face as I twisted the blade in his hand. "Did You hear my Beloved when She screamed out?!?!?! Did You hear Her when She screamed for You to let Her go?!?!!?"

"Ahhhhhhhhhhhhhh!!!!!!!! Noooooooooooooooooooo!!!!!" The bass in his voice was leaving him, sounding more like a child than a man. The volume increased as I took the knife out of his thigh and plunged it in his abdomen, just below his ribcage. He whimpered once I took my hand off the hilt. "Why are You doing this to Me?!?! You could've sent Me to the police?!?!"

"Oh, I'm sorry? You have Me confused with someone who actually believes You will get the proper justice." I stared into his eyes, satisfied with the genuine fear I saw in them. "We're not in the States, partner, and we're not in anyone's criminal jurisdiction, which means, I *could* turn You over to the proper authorities in Nassau, but that means at least another six months until a trial comes around, and that also means I would have to endure You trying to come up with some bullshit defense strategy and watch My Beloved take the stand. That, Sir, I cannot allow."

Through clenched teeth, Lyrical tried to sound like we were in some sort of bad crime show. "You won't get away with this, Ramesses! I have friends who will ruin You if You kill Me!"

"I'd love to see them try it, especially since we've already had You checked out, Travis Prater." I was crossing the line by using his legal name, but he had to know that I was serious about my threats. "Besides, You sound like death is the end of this journey. You'll die, but not anytime soon. There are fates worse than death."

Lyrical's eyes focused on me, and as I returned his glare, he noticed the lack of fear in my eyes. I, however, recognized the terror in his. The unknown of what I was capable of doing to him became evident as his body language contradicted the bravado he tried to portray.

"Do I need to prove that Your threats mean nothing to Me? Or do I need to explain to You that the friends that You claim will ruin Me are in debt to a few friends of Master Osiris's in Moscow?" I asked. "I'm not bluffing, and You know I'm not, either, don't You?"

The recognition of the Moscow connection shook him to the core. He strained against his bonds with more fervor this time around, almost dislocating his shoulder in the process. "Please, I'll do whatever You want to make this right! Please, let Me make things right!"

"We're a little late in the game for that, Lyrical." I turned around as I heard a voice from behind me. I wasn't sure to smile or not because I needed to keep my edge and advantage over him. Master Osiris entered the room, his face showing the disdain for both Lyrical and the circumstances under which we were here. "You've pushed a fellow brother into a position that He did not need to be in had You simply followed one simple rule: 'Master Thyself.' Now, You have not only enraged Ramesses; You've enraged the Society. There are ways that we deal with Your transgressions."

"What...what do You...mean?" Lyrical asked, coughing up blood from his mouth, alerting me that he needed to be sent to the medical tent to be patched up. "You're doing all this for a woman? Are You serious?"

That statement brought a right fist clean across his jaw, hearing the bone-crushing sound of its breakage. "Then I guess You won't mind if we have done to You what You tried to do to a woman, since You seem to think it's not a big deal."

Lyrical gurgled and moaned from the sharp pains rushing to the broken area. I reared back for another strike when Osiris held my arm, keeping it from a second arrival at the same destination. He kept me there until I relented, finally releasing his grip when I stepped away from the vicinity of the Cross.

"You seem to have a bit of a problem moving Your mouth now that it's been popped out of socket, so all You need to do is listen," Osiris spoke, not caring one way or the other whether Lyrical answered or not. He cut Lyrical's wrists loose before he said another word. "In about ten minutes, Dominic and his sweeper team will come in, gather what's left of You, and take You to the yacht. Once there, the medical team that is in place will patch up Your wounds, make sure You're able to travel, and escort You to the private airport in Nassau. Once on the plane, You will be blindfolded, as to keep You from realizing where You're being flown to, and upon reaching Your destination, You will be sedated and placed in Your new locale, along with the corresponding information with regard to Your new home, occupation, and citizenship within Your new country. You will never set foot on U.S. soil again."

Holding his jaw in place to try and talk, Lyrical's protests sounded more like desperation than demands. It was almost comical to hear him talk and not move his jaw at the same time. We could barely make out the words he said because he grimaced every time he spoke. "You can't do this! You just said we weren't in the States! What You're doing is illegal!"

"No it isn't, and to be honest, we're doing You a favor," I chimed in, trying to convey to Lyrical the gravity of the situation. "In fact, the Russians are interested in extracting You to help Your friends settle a debt. You know, the same 'friends' that were supposed to ruin Me if I killed You?"

"What…what do they want?" Lyrical asked. The nervousness in his voice was palpable as he awaited my answer.

"Well, as I understand the situation, they've already 'disappeared' because they were unable to pay off the debt, which I've found out is somewhere around seven figures. They gave You up the first chance they got to try and avoid disappearing. Needless to say, it didn't work." I recounted from the conversations while digging into his past.

"So, it sounds to Me like You have an easy choice, Sir, and I'm only going to offer this once." Osiris leaned in close so Lyrical could hear his words clearly. "You can either take our offer of mercy, or You can take Your chances when we turn You over to the Russians. The choice is Yours. You have three minutes to make a decision. When You do, knock three times on the Cross You're on to let us know You've decided to live. If You don't, we'll send Dominic and there won't be another word to be said."

We left the room, heading outside to meet up with Dominic, who happened to be sitting outside with the sweeper team in question. "Do You think He's stupid enough to not take the deal?"

"We'll know in about ninety seconds." I checked my watch, looking toward the room for a decision one way or the other. "Hopefully He isn't that stupid. He's playing a high-stakes game of roulette thinking He'll get out of this scot-free."

A few seconds later, we heard three knocks against the wood of the Cross, followed by yelling to make sure we heard him.

"I guess He wants to live." Osiris chuckled. "Too bad the alternative isn't as desirable."

Dominic looked at Osiris, confused as to what he'd missed out on. "I don't get it, Sir.

What was his alternative?"

"Colombia, Sir," Osiris replied. "He'll be living in the slums while working for the Marquez Cartel. He won't last a month before they kill Him."

"Damn, remind Me never to piss off any member of the Society, okay?" Dominic shook his head. The Colombian drug cartels had a reputation for abusing outsiders if they didn't get with the program right out of the gate. "I knew You had a temper when we were younger, but damn, I thought old age would have mellowed You out. And what happened to 'Master Thyself,' huh?"

"We're Masters, not Saints, Dom." I laughed. He might not have found it so funny, but I thought it was hilarious. "It might sound cruel, but sometimes things have to be done in order to make an example of what not to do. Consider this merciful, for the most part."

The yelling continued along with the knocking, drawing our attention back to Lyrical. Dominic looked at me and stated, "Well, don't just stand there, Gentlemen, You have a magic trick to execute: making a Dominant disappear without the authorities being the wiser."

"That's not the only trick we have to execute tonight, Dom." I winked at him as Osiris and I head toward the door. "There's one more piece of trash that needs to be removed before I make things right with My family."

TWENTY-FOUR ⊗ NEFERTERRI

"I didn't mean for...He was only supposed to seduce You!"

Thanks to amani and the girls, I felt like a new woman.

I was so elated when amani told me during the menstrual service that my cycle had completed that I fucked him on the spot the minute he was done. After we'd finished, I sent him on another task while the girls and I prepared for a special undertaking.

Now that I had my faculties again, this bitch was going to pay dearly for what she did, and my girls would play an integral part in this particular sequence of events.

The funniest thing was she could have had him if she'd simply respected my position as the Lady of the House.

I really did hate women who didn't know their place. *Hate* is a strong word to use, but I hated her.

No, I didn't hate her. If I hated her, that would have meant I wanted to be like her, and nothing could be further from the truth. So, maybe *hate* was a strong term to use.

I wasn't about to invite the bitch to high tea, either, that's for damn sure.

I had her "escorted" to where I was because we needed to have a woman-to-woman chat about a few things. She wasn't exactly escorted, to be honest. Actually, she was abducted from her cabin after being drugged. She had to know her time was coming once rumors around the island ran rampant that Lyrical couldn't be found. Considering I knew her partner in crime was being dealt with by Dominic, and I had a feeling my Beloved would be involved, too, that meant the woman in the equation needed to be dealt with by me.

Oh, she was about to get dealt with, all right.

I was incensed when Dominic told me of the scheme between them to separate my Beloved and me. I'd heard of some low-down, ignorant shit to do, but to conspire to break a couple up, especially in a sex-positive atmosphere that we lived in, was beyond reprehensible. Once I told shamise and sajira what had occurred, they were more than happy to oblige my desires to work Korina over before disposing of her.

She needed to be taught a lesson for trying to put asunder what no woman had cause to do.

The look in Korina's eyes conveyed her fear of what I might do.

The look in my eyes confirmed her fears were more than justified.

"So, instead of being a real woman, and a so-called Dominant at that, and coming to Me to say You wanted to sex My Beloved, You decided to be a little girl and play childish games with the intent of trying to replace Me. Does that about cover it?" I wanted to get the gist of what she thought she wanted. I needed to see if she had the guts to be real with me.

"Neferterri, please, it wasn't supposed to go down like that." Korina tried to plead her case, and given the predicament she was in, she had reason to try.

Being suspended upside down against a metallic spider web when she finally regained consciousness while at the mercy of a "Black Widow" and her henchwomen might make a person a little nervous.

"So, how *exactly* was it supposed to go down, Korina?" I asked.

I nodded in shamise's direction, giving her silent permission to use the instrument in her hand.

Korina's eyes shot over to her left, where shamise had an attachment of the violent wand shaped like a devil's pitchfork. shamise moved the attachment closer to her skin, watching the purple-hued electrical current begin to surge from the attachment onto her flesh.

Korina's screams were music to my ears. shamise kept the attachment near her skin, watching the current course through her body. For the first pass, she took care to avoid the sensitive areas that might cause arrest, keeping the current in her lower extremities. She did, however, keep the setting at maximum. That meant no matter where she put the attachment, Korina would be in for the shock of a lifetime.

A few seconds later, shamise took the attachment off.

"You were saying about something not going down the way it was supposed to go, right?" I reiterated her words. "Before You answer, let Me alert You to something: You are suspended on a metallic apparatus while being shocked by an electrical device that, if I commanded My baby girl to do so, can be placed over Your heart and cause You to go into cardiac arrest."

"You wouldn't dare."

"I assure You, Korina, I'm not bluffing." I raked my fingers through sajira's hair, stroking her like the kitten she was. "You see, You threatened Our submissives' peace of mind by trying to split apart their Daddy and Goddess. Now, they know We have Our moments where We might fight and be angry with each other, but they also know that We will always make things right and get back to what We do best. You have threatened that balance, and for that, You must suffer."

"You can't do this!" She screamed.

"Is that Your final statement? My baby girl is getting a little itchy to follow through on My command."

Korina thought it over for a few moments, looking into shamise's wild eyes and realizing she was in an untenable situation.

"Time's up, Korina."

"Noooooooooo!!!! Okay, okay!!!! It was My idea, all right? I wanted Your husband for Myself, dammit! Are You fucking happy now?!?!" She screamed. shamise acted like she didn't hear the confession and continued moving closer to Korina with the attachment aimed right for her heart. "I told You what You wanted to know! Get her to stop, please!!!"

"See, now that wasn't so hard, now, was it?" I teased as I shook my head in shamise's direction. She stepped away from Korina and turned off the violent wand, the look on her face giving away her disappointment in not inflicting any more pain.

I swear she had her sadistic moments. She'd been paying more attention to me than I'd realized.

Korina tried to control her breathing, but she realized how close she came to closing her eyes for the final time in her life. Her naked chest heaved as she tried to get the words out in a feigned defiance. "You're...lucky I'm...chained...up like...this!"

"And You're lucky I'm in a merciful mood," I retorted, ready to completely lose my sense of decorum around her. "I don't want to see You, or even hear about You, being around anyone or anything connected to Me, or so help Me I'll have You brought up on charges of conspiracy to commit rape and make sure Your life is a living hell."

Korina scoffed. "I'll do whatever I damn well please, and I'll make sure You pay for what You and Your girls have done to Me. You think You're the only one who has friends in low places? This won't be the last time You see Me, bitch!"

Before sajira could catch me and before shamise could step in the way, I moved to where she was suspended and landed a sweeping kick to the side of her face, knocking her out cold. I continued to knee and punch into her abdomen before the girls caught my arms in midflight and pulled me away from her limp body.

"Goddess, we'll handle it!" I heard shamise scream. "i'm calling the sweeper team to take her away now!"

sajira loudly echoed her sister's sentiment. "She won't be found where She's going, and that's a promise!"

The next thing I heard was shamise's voice on the radio calling in the sweeper team. Minutes later, Dominic showed up with the rest of his team, and the only question he asked was, "Mercy or no mercy?"

"No mercy," I spat, still angered by Korina's defiance after I'd spared her. The more I thought about it, the more I realized death was too good a price for her to pay. Dead women cannot show remorse. Tortured women, however, could sing a dozen tales, and I knew exactly where she could sing, too. "Does Seti still have His connections in North Africa?"

"Yes, m'Lady, He does," Dominic responded.

"I want full discretion, Dominic. No mess, no tracks."

"Consider it done, m'Lady. They'll know exactly what to do with Her the moment She touches down."

The rest of the team immediately unshackled her and took her away from the room. It would be the last time I would see Domina Korina, and for the first time in a long while, I truly didn't care what would happen to her.

I had my family to worry about.

TWENTY-FIVE ⊗ RAMESSES

SMACK!!!

"That's for fucking Her!!!"

The sting of her hand against my cheek didn't deter me from kissing her harder.

"You sonofabitch…fuck, don't stop…fuck You, I'm still…shit, fuck Me!"

She had every right to be pissed, but her body needed to be fucked at that moment.

I was more than happy to oblige.

I growled in her ear as I pulled her legs over my shoulders, acting as though this encounter would be the last thing I'd ever do on this earth. She continued to claw and scratch at my face as I drilled into her, going deeper by the stroke, trying my best to erase the pain of the past forty-eight hours.

I was intent on reclaiming what I knew already belonged to me, no matter how pissed off she was.

She was intent on making sure I had plenty of battle scars to show for it, despite her body calling for me to take the pain away.

"You had to have Him, too, huh? Before He tried to turn the tables on You." I tried to rush the words out of my mouth as each stroke brought us closer to the brink of climax.

"But…You…fucked…Her!" She wasn't about to let my transgression fall by the wayside, but her body had other ideas about her continuing the conversation in a coherent manner. Her tears streamed down her face as orgasmic waves rushed through her with no remorse or hesitation, turning her body into a conduit for the pulses I sent through her, enhancing her flight into the stratosphere.

"I…was…tricked…into…it!" I grabbed for her throat as she raked across my face, scratching my neck in the process. "I…love… You…fuck…give it to Me!"

Angry, white-hot, make-up sex was some of the most intense sex anyone could have. I wanted her, needed her, to take out her wrath on me, to unleash the storm that built inside of her ever since word got back to her about the encounter between Korina and me.

I knew once I weathered the hurricane, things would go back to the way they were.

Too many things got in the way and too much miscommunication clouded things beyond the point of no return.

"You…didn't…have to… fuck Her!" She wailed as another wave of pleasure took hold of her. "You fucking bastard!"

My patience snapped as I screamed, "I…thought…You fucked… Him! Dammit!"

She struggled against my grip, pinned against the floor as her legs wrapped around my waist, squeezing me harder with every thrust inside of her sex. "Let Me go! Let…Me…GO!!!"

As strong as she was in trying to push me away, I was stronger, fueled by my desire to get us through the hurt we were both going through. We loved each other more than life itself, and no one would break the bond we'd forged, no matter how hard they tried.

This would not be how the story would end; I was convinced of that.

"Your body's telling Me different, Beloved." Her eyes betrayed her, even in her fiery resistance. She wanted what I wanted, and we both wanted to put this ugly episode behind us. I gripped her hips tighter, stroking her so hard the impact sounded off, echoing against the walls. "Give it to Me, baby! Give Me everything!"

Time and space meant nothing. All that mattered was this moment, releasing every ounce of negative energy, with no hopes of a reprisal.

"I'm coming, Daddy!!!!" She yelled, beating her hands against my chest with the remaining strength she had left. "Don't…stop… fucking…ME!"

I pulled out of her and muscled her on all fours, entering her while grabbing for her arms to pin them behind her back. She screamed out, her mind and body syncing together for her temporary objective of squeezing out every drop of pleasure from her body as quickly as possible. Before long, she gave in to her desires and screamed out to me to keep fucking her, shouting to the gods that her flight was the most pleasurable it had ever been.

"Damn You!!!" She kept throwing it back at me, her body completely taking over from her mind and taking full control over what needed to be done. "Oh fuck…just like that, Daddy, please!!!!"

I slammed into her, releasing her arms and grabbing her hips, losing myself in my own pleasure and the visual of her ass bouncing against me as I stroked her with everything I had. My body tensed, letting me know I was mere seconds away from my eruption. I wasn't ready to let off in my Beloved, but my body had other plans.

I barely pulled out of her before the juices flowed. I saw stars the force was so intense, holding on for dear life as wave after wave crashed over me, threatening to drown me as I struggled to keep from blacking out. My body shook as I expended the last of my climax over her back and ass.

She collapsed onto her stomach as I collapsed on top of her, neither of us unable to speak for several minutes as the afterglow of the encounter began to set in. I reached for the pillows and the throw nearby to cover us before the cool breeze made its presence known.

"I'm sorry," I whispered.

"I'm sorry," She whispered as she kissed me.

"Forgive Me?"

"Nothing to forgive, Beloved…We both made mistakes; it's time to move on from them."

"Did You take care of Your loose end?" I asked, finally able to form a complete sentence.

She grinned as she kissed me again. "I hope She enjoys being the whore She tried to be for You."

"No more than I hope He enjoys paying the ultimate price for the sins He committed against You and a few other people He and His people wronged." I felt her hand moving toward my shaft again, trying to get me rejuvenated before I was ready. "If You keep this up, You're gonna get fucked again."

"Good, because You're going to fuck Me again." She smirked as she continued her hand job under the covers. "Except this time, I won't try to kill You while You fuck Me."

TWENTY-SIX ❧ amani

"Well, this is a nice surprise. Did you come to help with my tan?"

I truly wasn't here on a social call, but from the moment I walked up on lynx on the beach, he thought it would be some sort of flirting session.

Nothing could be further from the truth.

"lynx, i think we need to talk about your wife."

I sat down next to the beach towel he lay on while one of the island masseurs worked him over. "i don't think you realize the damage you've done. There has to be another way to resolve this rift between you."

"Man, why are you trying to kill my vibe talking about my wife?" lynx's eyes never opened as he succumbed to the masseur's skills, letting moans escape to let him know how much he enjoyed the session. "i'd rather talk about more pleasurable things, like you and me getting together later tonight."

"To do what, exactly?" I wasn't trying to play coy, but at the same time I knew there was a vibe between us that, under normal circumstances, I would have acted on in a heartbeat, with my Goddess's permission, of course.

My sis being in pain over this split between them took priority over my carnal urges.

"Quit playing like you're not feeling me." He turned his head to face me before he spoke again. "What goes on between us does not have to be broadcast. It can be our secret time together while everything else is going on at the main building."

I wanted to ignore what he proposed. Sure, I'd known about lynx's bisexuality since sajira's collaring ceremony, but I had no intentions of really acting on those urges back then because I was too busy trying to get in the good graces of my Sir and Goddess. Now that things were flowing well with them and my sisters, the initial plan was to use this time on the island to fulfill some of my more homoerotic desires, and tiger and lynx were at the top of the list.

He would have to go and screw all that up.

My mind made it clear this wasn't the right move to make, but my body was filled with lustful desires that were strong enough to make me consider the possibilities of doing something off the grid. My eyes glanced over his skin, bronzing in the sun as the masseur continued to knead and squeeze his muscles, eliciting more moans from lynx and turning me on even more.

My body betrayed me before I could adjust to keep from making it obvious I wanted him as much as he wanted me. I tried to hide the ever-growing bulge in my shorts, but lynx's grin let me know my efforts were in vain.

"Why are you torturing yourself, amani?" he asked, turning over on his back to allow the masseur to work. "you know you want to give in to what you want. That's what this whole trip to the islands was supposed to be about, right? What my wife doesn't know won't hurt her."

In that instant, my mind won the battle.

"i am not about to betray my family." I snapped out of the haze and focused on the reason I was there. "Look, lynx, there's no reason why you and sajira can't have the best of both worlds. Sinsual has never been cruel to you in that aspect, so why not explore it?"

"Because fish is no longer on the menu, that's why." lynx was so matter-of-fact with his response I would have sworn the temperature dropped a few degrees. "i've been in denial for years, even while i was married to her. Why do you think we never had kids? i wasn't about to put innocent children through something like that. Trust me, it's best for everyone involved to do exactly what i did."

That statement stopped me cold. "What???"

"Yeah, i didn't think she told you that part of it." lynx chuckled to himself for a moment. "Things haven't been exactly peaches and cream between us for the past few years, as quiet as it is kept, and while i'm sure her Daddy and Goddess know the full story, she probably kept certain details from you and shamise because she knew one of you would do exactly what you're here doing now."

I was stunned by his admission. How in the hell do you keep that type of thing away from your spouse for so long? I looked at lynx, who by now had encouraged the masseur to engage in a happy ending to his massage, and I shook my head, not knowing if there was anything else more to say to him to convince him otherwise. He truly was no longer in love or lust with his wife.

The thought sickened me. Yes, I was bisexual, and I had my moments where I wanted men as much, if not more, than women, but my sister submissives had the ability to turn me on with a word or a kiss on my neck.

If he wanted to play for the other team completely, who was I to criticize? Still, I wanted to slap some sense into him for letting his relationship go without so much as a half of a fight.

"It's probably not a good idea for the two of us to get together… ever," I finally concluded. There was no point in entertaining it, or even leaving the door open for him to even think there was a chance in hell of things happening sexually between us. "Being cordial, yeah, i'm fine doing that, but nothing more will happen."

"No sweat off my back, bro. It's not like i don't have my fun with tiger, anyway," he concurred, indulging further into the blowjob the masseur was now performing on him. "Hell, this sexy-ass right here might be my willing victim for the night."

He really didn't get it. It was more about the connections than the sex, but it was a matter of understand the phrase, "to each his own," and he hopefully would understand that before it was too late. Even among those in the swinger community, eventually you got sick of sport fucking.

I stood up from my spot, walking off to get away from the weird vibe lynx was giving off. After I dusted off my shorts of the sand on them, I turned around to say goodbye, but he was too engulfed in his own pleasure to recognize it.

Instead of directing my final words toward him, I simply said them into the air as I walked away. "Enjoy yourself, bro, and i hope you get what you think you want."

"I never got a chance to say thank you, amani."

My mood changed tremendously as I sat in front of Jelani and Mistress Blaze. This was just what I needed to go into the party tonight.

He sat like a content puppy as Blaze caressed his head, playing in his hair. He had learned the kneeling position I'd taught him on the fly pretty well, adjusting it to his own style and in the manner that Blaze liked. I wasn't sure if things would gain any kind of traction once we all got back Stateside, but it did my heart good to know someone had been enjoying themselves during this trip.

I was a bit taken aback by Blaze's thank-you, though. "What are You thanking me for, Ma'am? i honestly didn't do anything."

"Ma'am, he's being modest, just like when we were in college." Jelani smiled up at Blaze, trying to deflect some of the attention from me. "he had a feeling that You and I would be a good match, and he was right."

I chuckled quietly as to not disturb the groove they had going on. "Ma'am, it was my pleasure to place you two in each other's paths. Jelani is right; i didn't know if it would have worked out between you, but seeing you both now, it's easy to see things couldn't have gone any better."

"I'm glad you did, My dear." Blaze continued to fawn over Jelani. "I almost took Sin up on Her invitation to take lynx from Her had you not intervened. That would have been disastrous, to say the least."

"Oh?" I queried, interested in how the plot thickened before my eyes. "Tell me more, Ma'am."

"Oh, I think I've said too much already." Blaze placed her hand over her lips as though she were trying to keep anything else from escaping them. "But since I've somewhat let the cat out of the bag, I guess I can reveal the rest…at your discretion, yes?"

"But, of course, Ma'am." I lied through my teeth, knowing I would be telling my sisters the moment I had a chance to. "You have my word another soul will not be told."

"you're a cutie, and a horrible liar, but I think this will get out sooner or later anyway." Blaze sat up in her chair and leaned forward in a mock conspiratorial position. "Sin was fed up with lynx during this trip."

"Wow, You don't say, Ma'am?" I got into gossip mode, asking only the questions needed to keep feeding the answers along. I leaned forward, encouraging her to keep the information coming. "i had just left lynx a few minutes ago before i came over here to visit with You."

"Well, I hope he's enjoyed himself thoroughly while he's been over here," Blaze said. "If She can't pawn him off on another Domina soon. She's following through on Her original threat to release him."

"But, why would She, Ma'am? i thought She was happy with him?"

Blaze shook her head and laughed. She knew I wasn't the least bit interested in lynx's well-being, and she was right, especially after what he revealed not an hour before. But she read my body language, and she knew I wanted the dirt. "lynx won't follow House protocol, and he's failed on several occasions to correct his behavior. She's gone so far as to put tiger up to sabotaging him, setting him up to fail at every turn. he's been so swept up in thinking he was getting what he wanted that he hasn't realized he's screwed himself."

"Well, Ma'am, i'm not about to sit here and say i feel sorry for him, after the way he's treated sajira this week." I dished out my own bit of gossip to put a smile on her face. "i would say i hope this will make him realize how good he had it, but he needs to lose everything to appreciate people more."

"Sad to say, I agree with you, My dear." She exhaled. "That boi has been acting like he's hot shit almost from the moment Sin placed him under consideration."

My mood was improving by the minute. sajira was coming out of this on top, and it would be a matter of time before lynx realized it. I hoped she would take as much comfort in hearing it from me as I had hearing it from Blaze.

"Enough of that, Ma'am, or else we'll really put Jelani out of the loop," I said, watching the doelike expression on my friend's face and taking the hint to move the conversation to something he could contribute to. "What are Your plans for my boy right here? Do You think he's worth the effort to train him to Your liking?"

She looked down at Jelani, who returned her gaze. They stayed that way for a couple of minutes before I had to clear my throat to interrupt them before they sank deeper into each other. Blaze finally composed herself long enough to utter, "Yes...yes, I think he'll do just fine, amani."

I checked my watch and realized I had only an hour before it was time to meet my sisters to prepare the tents for the festivities on the last event night on the island. Thankfully, it wouldn't be until tomorrow night, but I knew shamise wanted to make sure everything was ready ahead of time to keep from dealing with any last-minute problems.

"Forgive me, Ma'am, but with Your permission, i would like to be excused so i can help prepare the tents for tomorrow night," I asked. She nodded, and I walked toward the door to head to the family cabin. "Thank You, Ma'am, i have a feeling it's going to be an all-timer."

TWENTY-SEVEN ⚇ shamise

"Good, you're both here; we can get started."

As the House submissives, the responsibility fell on us to make sure the dungeon spaces were ready to be used on event evenings. Thankfully, we had the help of over twenty staffers to quickly turn things around after last night's activities.

Yes, I knew the event wasn't until the following evening, but I believed in being prepared, and there was no way I was going to get caught on the biggest night of the week.

Unlike the other compounds where the dungeon was one large space, the *Isle ne Bin-bener* spanned beyond the main dungeon, out into the front area near the beach before going deeper into the island to the other tents that were more intimate, but more cumbersome to maintain. It was a challenge to try to figure out all the logistics, but it was also a lot of fun.

It had turned into a labor of love for the three of us, and sajira enjoyed it as much as I did. Well, once she got the hang of it, anyway. amani took to it like a duck to water, flowing right along with us when we were first charged with setting up *NEBU* for a big event we'd had there last year. The look on Daddy's face when everything was complete that night was priceless!

From that point forward, he left the dungeon preparations to us.

The main dungeon didn't take too long to prepare. We only

needed to rearrange some of the furniture a bit to open up more space in the middle of the floor for the more advanced whip throwers. Also, since we didn't need to remove any of the larger pieces from the dungeon, I had some extra pieces shipped in from Nassau for the night to ensure there would be enough to go around. Daddy and a few of the other Dominants invited some of the locals to partake in the festivities, and after talking it over with amani and sajira, we concluded it was necessary to get the extras.

I love it when a plan comes together!

From the way the island slaves drooled over the apparatus being brought in, it was safe to say that a good time would be had by all, and then some!

We moved from the main dungeon out to the tents in the space in front of the main building. While they were being erected, I took a quick look at the forecast via the sling box on my tablet computer. Tonight would be cool, according to the weather report, but not to the point to where we would need the portable heaters to keep things comfortable. To be safe, sajira suggested the heaters be placed anyway, quoting Goddess's favorite sayings, "Better to have it and not need it, than need it and not have it."

The tents would take some time due to their size, so it gave amani and me a moment to check up on our sis to make sure she was okay now that she was a day removed from the events of a day ago.

"So, we couldn't help but notice your mood has improved, sis." I nudged into the conversation to test the waters. "Are you feeling better about things now?"

Her mood had improved, there was no doubt about that, but I wondered if she was overcompensating to get through the rest of the week. She was aggressive around the male slaves, openly flirting and kissing on a couple of them. She couldn't keep her hands off amani all day, and while he enjoyed the special attention she gave him due to his attraction to the both of us, it tripped warning sensors in my head.

"sis, i'm better than okay. In fact, it feels like a weight has been lifted off my shoulders."

sajira beamed as though she had been released from a long-term prison sentence. "Hindsight is twenty/twenty, and if i'd paid more attention to the signs, i wouldn't have reacted the way i did."

"What warning signs?" amani was confused, but now that I thought about it, he didn't live with us, either. "i thought lynx was really into you. At least, that's how it looked whenever we were out together."

"That's what he wanted you to see, amani." I thought back on some of the incidents and red flags that I'd neglected to pay attention to. "There was the time when he came on to me because sajira supposedly didn't want to have sex with him one night about six months ago."

"And there was the night we caught him watching gay porn flicks he said he got from tiger, only to find out he bought them himself because he was too stupid to use cash instead of a credit card." sajira shook her head when she dug that one up from her memory. "That was around the same time we stopped having sex, but i didn't worry about it because we were too busy fucking you and Daddy, amani."

"Like i'm complaining?" amani laughed, causing us to giggle along with him at the quick joke. Hell, I wasn't complaining, either, because between amani and Daddy, who had time for outside dick? "If anything, i'm benefiting from all of the attention, seriously speaking."

"Good, because i plan on giving you a *lot* of attention, little brother."

sajira slipped her arms around his waist, kissing him on the neck. She turned back in my direction and winked. "Do you think Daddy and Goddess will permit us to fuck him tonight?"

Yeah, my sis was definitely in a zone hours before an event of this size. I had the feeling she was in the mood for a bit of exhibitionist activity. "What else did you have in mind, baby?"

"i want Goddess to direct an all-girl gangbang for me." She licked her lips at the visual in her head. "you haven't fucked me in almost a month, shamise. i was beginning to wonder if you didn't want me anymore."

I grinned at the sexy pout on her face, poking her lip out for dramatic effect, and I couldn't resist melting at the way she looked at me. The desire radiated around her, and it made me wet.

sajira jumped and giggled when amani grabbed her ass and squeezed. "Mmmm, naughty boy, do you plan on squeezing that later while you fuck me?"

"Well, you know me, sis, i have no problems doing what comes naturally." He returned the favor of kissing her on her neck. I watched her shiver as he bit her before lifting from her skin.

"Okay, we need to focus, you two," I said. "There'll be plenty of time for that later."

"Awww, come on, sis, don't be like that?" amani was feeling the heat, and I couldn't blame him for wanting to keep the heat going. "i haven't fucked you in almost two months. i don't know about you, but i've been craving some of you."

Damn it, I didn't want them to distract me from the purpose of talking to sajira, but all this flirting was making it difficult to be mad at them right now. I tried my best to find a way to redirect the conversation, mainly because we would be back home in two or three days, and sajira and I needed to figure out what needed to be done.

"Okay, we'll have to present these requests to Daddy and Goddess and let the chips fall where they may," I stated, trying to sound calm when underneath, all I wanted to do was shirk our responsibilities and find the first open bedroom. "First things first, sajira, baby, are you sure about this thing with lynx? i mean, i don't want you going through all of this half-cocked without thinking this through."

"Yes, i have thought this through, baby," sajira said. By now, she'd turned her back to amani and leaned against him with her ass grinding against his crotch. She wrapped his arms around her waist, and leaned her head against his chest. "lynx is out of sight, out of mind, and out of my heart, period. The minute we get back to the States, it's only a matter of moving crews to get the furniture i want, and we're moving into the spare house Daddy and Goddess have before figuring out the next move. Divorce is inevitable now."

I didn't argue, and I wasn't about to, either. I took my ex-husband for half of his inheritance and property for basically doing the same thing, so who was I to argue against her doing the same thing? After all, he fucked up, and he was definitely going to pay, even with our lifestyle convoluting matters, the right attorney, especially a kink aware attorney, could tip the scales in her favor once it was all said and done.

"Well, you know me, sis, i'm with you," I concluded as I moved toward them to give her a kiss. I reached up to kiss amani before I separated them. "Now, we have a task to complete. The tents are up now, so we need to get the pieces moved in so we can rest before tonight."

My request to get back on the work grind was interrupted by one of the male slaves walking toward us. "slave shamise, forgive the intrusion, but Master Ramesses and Lady Neferterri request your presence, and that of sajira and amani also. They sent word for me to escort you to your family cabin at once."

I mumbled under my breath. Sometimes they had horrible timing, but luckily it didn't happen very often. "Is the meeting urgent?"

"Yes, slave shamise, i am certain it is, and Lady Neferterri mentioned that you might ask that question." He tried to hide his grin over Goddess knowing me so well. "She has already sent word for another of the staff to complete your task. Now, if you will follow me, i want to get you to your Masters before they think it's taking too long."

TWENTY-EIGHT ☿ NEFERTERRI

"I'm sure you three have been wondering if everything is okay. I assure you that we are."

Watching their faces, even in their kneeling positions, as we explained to them that all is well within the House was a pleasure to observe.

shamise, although she tried to be the strong one as our Alpha slave, let the relief show in her facial expression. Ramesses and I knew this was hardest on her because she was the most in tune with us. I took pleasure in watching her try to keep from smiling, careful not to break protocol until we gave the word.

sajira tried to follow in her sister's footsteps, but she's too much of a baby girl to hold out for too long. As usual when she received good news, she subtly rocked back and forth, trying to contain her happy energy until we released them from protocol. I felt her energy, although I was curious as to why it wasn't as boundless as usual.

amani took the news to heart, although as a male submissive, he wasn't as openly expressive as the girls. Still, I saw the smirk across his face. I needed to do something for him for saving me from a horrible fate at the hands of Lyrical, and hopefully, the surprise we had for him later tonight would be a start.

Ramesses finally chimed in, rather than let me monopolize the conversation. "I want to apologize to you for My behavior through all this madness. I have My quirks at times, and they come up at the oddest of times. Thankfully the storms have passed, and things are as they once were, and in some ways, a little stronger between your Goddess and Me."

"So, what we're saying is, we will try to at least let one of you know what's going on, even if all hell is breaking loose." I followed up Ramesses's thoughts with those of my own before releasing them from protocol so he and I could catch up with what was going on with our submissives. "Okay, now that we've gotten that out of the way, what has been happening with you three? sajira, I'm feeling some aggression on you right now; is there something your Daddy and I need to know?"

The smile almost faded from her face when I asked the question. Her eyes were sad, which concerned me. Finally, after what seemed as though she were mustering the energy to blurt out the words, she looked up at us and uttered, "my husband and i are about to go through a divorce, Goddess. i confronted him at Mistress Sin's cabin after watching him fucking tiger, after which he told me he was in love with him."

shamise quickly placed her hand on sajira's shoulder. "It's okay, sis, there's nothing he can do to hurt you now."

"Wait, I'm a little confused here." Ramesses's protective instincts took over. "your husband…my shotgun partner when we roll out on the bikes…is in love with another man? And he had the *nerve* to express this to you like it was supposed to be old news?"

"Daddy, looking back on it now, it honestly wasn't exactly breaking news," sajira explained. "i ignored him after a series of events that resulted in us no longer having sex with each other about six months ago. The truth is, he should have told me this a while back, it would have saved us the trouble, but he honestly did me a favor because now i can use his infidelity against him in court. he knew i would have never allowed him to be with another man sexually."

"I'll kill him," Ramesses bellowed.

"Daddy, for my sake, leave it alone, please?" sajira's eyes pleaded with him. "i'm not exactly innocent in this, either."

"she has a point, Beloved." I wrapped my arms around his waist to keep him calm. "Besides, from her demeanor, it looks like she's got everything well under control."

"Especially when he won't be Mistress Sin's property after tonight." amani dropped that tidbit out of the blue, refocusing all of our attention in his direction.

"I'm sorry, would you mind running that by us again?" I hadn't even talked to Sin yet, and the incident with Lyrical kind of sidetracked that discussion, too. Hearing my boi rattle off information that neither I nor Ramesses knew about was interesting, to say the least. "Who did you hear that from, amani?"

"Goddess, Mistress Blaze informed me after i spent time with Her and my friend, Jelani," amani mentioned. He straightened up in his kneeling position, continuing to spill what he knew to his captive audience. "She said Sin was fed up, and this trip was going to be his final as a member of Her House. It seems he's been misrepresenting the House on several occasions when he was not under Her watchful eye, and tiger had been charged with setting him up to give cause for release."

"Damn!" The collective response from the four of us was enough to cause him to laugh.

He looked over toward sajira and kissed her on the cheek. "i had been saving that information to tell you privately, but under the circumstances, i couldn't help myself. shamise and i told you he would get what was coming to him."

"Yeah, he said he wanted out of the lifestyle," shamise confirmed. "This was a helluva way to do it!"

I didn't know what to think at that moment, it was all coming so fast. Our submissives had already dealt with all of this while Ramesses and I put things back together so the House would be intact. I sat back and took notice of the blessing that those three were. Lesser submissives might have stood by, meek and acting helpless, waiting for their Dominant to "save the day," but they handled things beautifully while chaos ensued.

I couldn't have been prouder of them.

"Okay, since there isn't anything that we need to take care of, your Daddy and I have are going to relax for a change and send you back to the task at hand." I looked in the girls' direction and nodded. "Once you're done, we want you to do the same thing, which means you have all day to rest, relax, and enjoy the island to do whatever you want to do without us around. Tomorrow night is going to be extremely interesting, and you're doing to need your rest."

TWENTY-NINE ❦ sajira

"Daddy, i need to talk to You."

I didn't realize I needed him so badly until our eyes connected.

We'd been friends longer than we'd been in this D/s relationship, and whenever I needed to talk to him as a friend, he always dropped protocol so we could. I think that's how I allowed my husband to do whatever he wanted when things went sour. I replaced him with the other men in my life.

Life took you on some interesting journeys and in directions you never thought possible. I couldn't say monogamy was for my husband and me; it was one of the reasons we started swinging in the first place. I didn't care who he fucked because his heart belonged to me, and he felt the same way about me.

By the time we'd hooked up with them—at the time it was Kane and Mercedes—before the D/s part showed itself, we were in a natural progression. The sex was amazing, the friendships we made with him and Jay while I got closer to her and Candy; things just felt good. Not perfect, but good.

Then, a couple of years ago, things began changing.

When we got curious about D/s, I thought it would be the same as it was when we were swinging, for me and for him. I was sorely mistaken. While I enjoyed how things flowed with Daddy and Goddess, he plunged headfirst into all things Sinsual.

His personality changed, and not for the better...

The sex drive and his appetite, not just for me, but for women in our swinger circles, diminished to the point to where I wondered if he was thirty-five or fifty-five.

When he did have the urge to fuck me, it was absolutely horrible! We went from the adventurous positions and locations to missionary, doggie-style on rare occasions, and nowhere else but in bed.

I tried to call him on his shit. When shamise moved in with us, she and I tried to seduce him into a threesome. He turned us both down, saying it was against Sin's wishes unless she set it up.

I was nearly at my wit's end, and it started to affect my ability to be appealing to Daddy and Goddess. That's how I'd ended up doing the phone sex line as a part of my slut training, as a way to snap me out of my haze. Thank God it had worked because my husband wasn't helping at all.

The straw that broke the camel's back was catching him with the gay porn videos. I hit the roof I was so angry! He tried to explain it away, trying to use my fetish for watching male-on-male sex as his reason for trying to find something to get "us" in the mood to have sex. He even called himself proving it by fucking my brains out while watching the video.

I'll admit, that was one of the hottest nights of sex we'd ever had, but my intuition kept tingling as though something wasn't right.

Watching him and tiger together was a surreal moment. While it did turn me on, it sickened me because it was "my" husband who was involved. I simply wasn't mentally evolved enough to deal with it, as hypocritical as that may sound. By then, we were more like roommates than husband-and-wife, and I shouldn't have cared, but I did. We were together for ten years, and you simply don't throw that away overnight.

Hearing him say he was in love with tiger would have ripped my heart out, if I were still in love with him. Yes, I loved him…I always will…but everything he did to stay in Sin's good graces pushed me further away from him and into the arms of my D/s family.

"What's wrong, baby girl?" He saw the look in my eyes and instinctively knew something was wrong. My heart smiled when I saw the concern in his eyes. "I thought you were going to take the yacht to Nassau to enjoy the city?"

He sat down on the couch and I straddled his lap in moments, kissing him before he could adjust and figure out what was going on with me.

"sajira…precious…wait…stop." He tried to slow me down, but I didn't want to stop. I wanted the negative thoughts in my head to be erased. "Stop, baby…stop…talk to Me."

He finally managed to get a tight grip on my arms, holding me in place. It took everything within me to keep the tears at bay, but the moment he forced me to look at him, I completely lost it. I couldn't hide my true emotions or thoughts from him, or from Goddess, for that matter, because they'd trained me so intensely that it became second nature to be an open book.

He let my arms go and I wrapped them around his neck as his arms locked around my waist to keep me from moving. I wasn't going anywhere, and I didn't *want* to go anywhere. If I could've stayed within the safety of his arms for the rest of the day, I would've been content.

He waited for the tears to subside before he asked his first question. "What's this about, sajira? you've never been so desperate."

"i want these evil thoughts in my head to go away, Daddy." I couldn't stop sounding like a teenager around him, but I didn't care. I wanted *him* to make it all better. "i'm all out of sorts, and i'm losing focus."

"Listen to Me, baby." He caressed my face, knowing from past experience it would calm me down and have my attention focused on him. "This storm will pass, and we will be there to help you through it. lynx will be dealt with, wait and see."

"But i want these feelings to go away now!"

"I know you do, baby, and I have just the thing to help with that." His smirk had me wet already.

My ears perked up when I heard that. My body took notice of his manhood rising between my legs, straining against the fabric of his shorts. He was turned on, but he needed to know if I was okay first.

I would be, as soon as I took the Chairman out and proceeded to give him my latest oral presentation.

"What do You have planned for me, Daddy?" I cooed in his ear. I was in full-blown, teenage baby-girl mode now, and there was nothing either of us could do to stop it. "Is it something tasty for me to suck on?"

He laughed as he slid my hand to feel the answer to my question. My eyes widened and I licked my lips in anticipation of his next command. "you'd like that, wouldn't you, baby girl?"

"Yes, Daddy." I slipped off his lap, tugging at the waistline of his shorts, trying my best to keep from looking like I was rushing to give my presentation. "I haven't had him all week and i'm already wet with thoughts of having him enjoy my oral presentation."

"Mmmmm, damn, baby, you have Me weak." He leaned back against the cushions, lacing his fingers in my hair. I had him where I wanted him, and I didn't want him to say or do anything. All he needed to do was lie back and let me do all the work. "If you keep this up, you're gonna put Me to sleep."

"You know i wouldn't have it any other way, Daddy," I purred as I slipped his shorts off. His shaft sprang to life once freed, and I didn't know whether I wanted to suck him or ride him, I was so horny I didn't care which one I did first! "Your wish is my command; my body is Yours to control and enjoy."

The next thing I knew, he lifted me off my knees and I was on top of his lap again, my pussy inches away from being completely engorged with his girth. "your body will be pleasing to a few tonight, My sexy girl."

"A few?" I asked, gritting my teeth as I slid down on top of him. God, he felt so full inside me, and I hadn't hit the base of his shaft yet. *Fuck*. "As long as I get You at the end, I don't care, Daddy."

He took control of my hips, moving me up and down slowly, making me feel every single inch of him, my body trembling with each downward stroke to feel him deep inside of me. His hands were so damn strong, for a moment, it felt like he had total control of my body, moving me the way he saw fit.

"I'll be there, precious, I promise." He groaned as I squeezed tightly around his dick, determined to make him lose control and let me do the work. The grip on my hips began to loosen, enough for me to move his hands to my ass so I could really go to work.

His eyes narrowed. It was his usual tendency to alert me he knew what I was trying to do, but he never stopped me. I wasn't about to stop, not until I got what I wanted. I grinned as I felt the negativity slipping away from the recesses of my mind, replacing them with all kinds of delectable, deviant and evil thoughts of what he might command of me later tonight.

My mind was ablaze with any and all possibilities, and I secretly wished a few of my darker fantasies would be realized while in this tropical paradise. I wanted to be used and abused in every way possible, with my skin kissed by more than a few dragon tails and bull whips being at the top of the list. I wanted to feel the stinging sensation, the near burning that came with the skin being broken as I submitted to several whips being thrown at me at once.

I was so entranced in my own thoughts I didn't realize Daddy had picked me up and had me pinned under him on the couch. The plush pillows and his drilling deep inside of me with no hesitation awoke me from the fantasies I enjoyed to realize I was still in the middle of one with him!

"Daddy, shit!" I screamed, every nerve ending at its most sensitive, begging to be released into a symphonic cascade of orgasmic waves that would threaten to take me at least twenty-thousand leagues deep. "Daddy, i'm coming!!!!"

He was in his zone, and it didn't matter what I said to him, he was not going to hear me, so I grabbed and clawed at his back, screaming in octaves I didn't know I had, losing myself in the release that I needed and that only he could take me through. My body convulsed, trying to brace itself for the multiorgasmic torrent that was soon to come as he continued to piston in and out of my sex until he reached his own crescendo.

His primal growl in my ear made me come again, knowing it would be mere seconds before the eruption I awaited would arrive.

"Give it to me, Daddy...come on, i want it all!" I cheered him on from my vantage point, ready for him to pull out and stream his essence all over my chest and stomach. The intensity of his strokes gave me a clue that he'd been so built up that I might expect a river by the time he'd released.

"Fuck, baby, I'm coming!" He pulled out of me and barely had enough time to get close to my chest when the explosion gripped him. I grabbed his shaft and continued to stroke him, delighting in the stream of his essence as it landed on my stomach, my chest,

and my face. "Ohhhhhhh fuuuuucccckkkkkk, you got Me....
shittttt!!!!!"

He slumped once his orgasm relented, barely able to breathe as
I kissed all over his face to keep him grounded there with me. Any
negative thoughts that I thought I had were a distant memory, and
there would be no worry about whether they would return, even
if I happened to see the source of those negative thoughts at the
party tomorrow night. With any luck, I would be so engrossed in
whatever Daddy and Goddess put me through that he wouldn't
be able to get a word in edgewise.

He finally lifted up slightly, pulling me into his lap to kiss me
some more. I relished this chance to simply be in the moment with
him, the same way when I was with Goddess or shamise. Once I
realized I would have that type of connection with amani, my
pussy tingled again, ready for another round.

"Okay…what were we…talking about again?" He tried to breathe
through the questions in his mind as he struggled to remember
the conversation we had before lust took over and brought us to
where we were right now.

I kissed his lips before settling back into his chest. I wasn't about
to ruin a perfectly wonderful afternoon with idle chatter that we
could have tomorrow. "Don't worry, Daddy, i'm sure it will come
to You sometime tomorrow, and we can talk about it then."

THIRTY ❦ amani

"She's amazing, bruh, absolutely amazing."

I spent my "free" day on the island chilling out with my frat, catching up on how things were going with Mistress Blaze since the last time I visited with them. I wanted things to work out between them for my own selfish reasons. Let's face it, being a submissive male, a black submissive male, for that matter, was not a bed of roses. As it was, being a submissive male came with its own brand of madness.

Of course, there were the stereotypical views society had: we were spineless; we had no real backbone and didn't know how to stand up for ourselves; we were dismissed as not being "real men," or we were only "acting" submissive because it was an easier way to get pussy.

The last time I checked, the above assumptions that women had about submissives made it harder to get some, not easier. But what did I know?

Hell, being a six-three, 200-pound young, black male who was in good shape had its own issues. Jelani would catch some of the same heat for having relatively the same build. tiger was slight of build by comparison, about five feet eight inches and about 160 pounds on a good day. lynx wasn't much better: maybe around five feet eleven inches and 180 pounds, so they didn't get the issues we get in terms of women assuming we're dominant or we "should" be dominant.

What had been the most irritating insinuation of all was the ideal from the male Dominants that we could be pushed around and we wouldn't push back.

Sir Lyrical found out how untrue that assumption was. He was still nursing that broken nose and sore ribs, the last time I asked about him. I should have put him to sleep for even breathing hard in my Goddess's direction. Oh well, I guess I could've gained some measure of satisfaction that he was going to get what was coming to him.

Combine those frustrations with the "do-me" submissives that made shit difficult for those of us who truly wanted to serve and you had daily fights that had to be won or lost, depending on the day. I think that was why I wanted Jelani on board as a lifestyle submissive. If anything, I'd be able to have someone to help me understand myself even better, and it would be with someone I could trust not to out me, too.

"So, since She's so amazing, bruh, why don't you see if things can be taken to the next level?" I asked.

He thought about it for a moment, and the answer he gave was, in my opinion, a complete copout, but he might have honestly been feeling that way. "Bruh, the other relationships i have had with other women, once i told them about the things i am into, the relationship goes south quickly." He found himself trying to figure out what the real holdup was, almost trying to measure his words. "i don't want to put myself out there and then She turns into those same women who swore that my submissiveness wasn't a deterrent, but the exact opposite is true later on down the line."

"And you honestly believe She doesn't feel the same way about what you might be, frat?" I rebutted, trying to give him the "shoe-on-the-other-foot" argument. "i have been around Mistress Blaze for a while now, and She is as genuine as they come. She wouldn't be a part of the Society if She were less than genuine, trust me on that. If i told you about the countless wannabe submissive males that She's met, it would make your head spin, especially the ones coming from the foot-fetish sect. It sounds like you both are a little gun-shy, and that's okay, too."

"So, what do you suggest, bruh? i mean, really, because i am extremely attracted to Her, and after the night we had last night, i know the feeling is mutual, but i'm not about to get my hopes up again." Jelani's eyes searched mine to get some idea of how to proceed.

The smirk on my face confused him as I felt like I was looking at myself about a year and a half ago, at the same crossroads with my Goddess and Sir. I loved him like a brother...hell, he was a brother, he was my frat...so I decided to explain some things to him.

"i'm going to let you in on a little secret, bruh." I leaned in close as though I were letting him in on some conspiracy. "i have had you two followed the entire time you've been on the island."

"What the fuck, bruh?" Jelani protested.

"Not like that, bruh, they haven't been taping you or spying in on whatever you have been doing behind closed doors, but they have been observing the both of you, when you're with each other and when you're away from each other." I tried to keep him calm to make sure my words sank in. He needed to get the gist of what I was trying to do for him; no one really did that for me, at least not another submissive male, anyway. "Those persons let me know what i already suspected: you two are more than compatible to each other. During the time you two were away from each other, neither of you bothered to partake of some of the indulgences of the island, and you know what i mean by that."

He blushed when I mentioned the last part. I purposely tried to set him up with the masseuse, including arranging for a happy ending, and he summarily declined the offer without as much as a double-take. He was into her, and she was her type, but his nose was wide open thinking about Mistress Blaze.

"Quit playing like this opportunity will come again in another week or something; we both know that it won't," I stated, staring him down. "i almost made that same mistake with my Goddess, and if it weren't for my Sir dropping the hammer on me to help me see the truth of what i was doing, i guarantee you i would not be with the House i am with now. They have no tolerance for submissives who try to fake their way into getting what they want."

It wasn't the easiest thing to admit, and I hadn't thought about that uncomfortable ride in the car with Ramesses in quite some time. I believed that things happened for a reason, and truthfully speaking, if he hadn't been the one to screw my head on straight, I probably would have been on the outside looking in. I shuddered to think what might have happened if Goddess were single instead of part of a Dominant Couple and I pulled the stunts that I pulled.

I guess my words had some effect, as I observed Jelani in deep thought. His eyes were closed, and I imagined he was trying to weigh the pros and cons of what he was about to consider doing. It wouldn't be easy, but hell, if it was easy, everyone else would be doing it. As I'd learned in my own lessons, those that truly want to serve, it was a calling, not simply some passing fancy, and I believed Jelani was one of those. With a little coaching and help from my sisters and me, he could have been a diamond in the rough. I wanted to be to him what tiger tried to be to me, a mentor, but he screwed it up because he was too busy worried about fucking me on top of teaching me.

I wasn't sure if I was ready to do that, but you have to start somewhere, right?

After keeping his eyes closed for a few more brief moments, he opened them, took a deep breath and exhaled, and declared, "Okay, bruh, tell me what i have to do to get Mistress's attention and keep Her attention. Nothing ventured, nothing gained, right?"

THIRTY-ONE & shamise

"you're interrupting my morning massage."

I had a routine I followed on event days.

First, I had my morning massage, followed by a long, hot bath.

Next, after breakfast, I checked, and then double-checked, to make sure everything was in place for the event.

Finally, I got with sajira and amani to make sure Daddy's and Goddess's attire was taken care of and ready for the event.

There were other things I either did or delegated in order to prepare during a day like today, but I wouldn't bore you too much more with the details. Let's say I was extremely thorough and we'll leave it at that.

My morning massages were meant to clear my mind and put me in the right headspace to handle the tasks ahead of me. As sexy as my masseur for the morning was and the permission from my Goddess to enjoy more than a simple "happy ending," I was looking forward to a morning glory of delicious proportions.

lynx threatened to kill my high by his mere presence alone.

I guess it was my fault for wanting my massage outside of the family cabin instead of inside where I could have enjoyed my peace and quiet, not to mention the potential for some quality long stroking, but he didn't have to be here, either.

"i was hoping we could talk," he said.

"There's nothing to talk about, lynx, and as you can see, i'm a little busy right now," I purred as my masseur started to reach my problem areas in my lower back. All I needed was another few minutes and I would be back in heaven right now, ready to let the orgasmic waves take me.

I felt lynx's eyes on my body as I continued to enjoy the heaven my masseur created. I'd hoped that the more I ignored him and concentrated on my bliss, the more he would get the point and simply move on.

Anyone want to bet what he decided to do?

"Well, you don't have to talk; you can lay there and listen," he said, sitting down on the sand next to where I was getting worked over. I rolled my eyes and focused more on the magic fingers kneading my flesh. "i want to find a way to get my wife back, and i was hoping you could help me with that."

Really???

My masseur felt the tension in my muscles, and he attempted to try to keep me still so he could continue to work. Being hand-picked by my Goddess, he didn't want to screw anything up. "My lady, I would strongly suggest that you relax, despite this minor inconvenience, and allow me to finish working you over. Do you wish for me to remove this distraction?"

"I'd love to see you try it, bruh." lynx stepped into his space, looking more at his chest than he was in his face. I giggled to myself, realizing that if I said the word, he would have picked lynx up and carried him away from me without hesitation.

My masseur closed his eyes and flexed his fingers, trying his best to keep calm. He looked over at me, realizing I was still naked. "My lady, say the word, and it will be my pleasure."

Oooh, I could get used to this. amani has gotten used to being the bodyguard of the family and all, but this Adonis was adding to my fantasy by flexing his taut, lean, muscular frame. As much as I wanted him to turn lynx into mush, I didn't have a choice but to call him off.

"Forgive me for stopping you, sexy, but i need to handle this before this idiot completely fucks up my vibe." I sat up from my spot, not caring that my breasts were exposed for lynx to see. He'd completely lost his mind if he thought I was going to help him. I raised my eyebrow as he sat there acting like he was convinced his request wasn't insane. "my sis has moved on from you, and you made it *very* clear why she should have."

"Look, i don't expect *you* to understand, but we've been married for ten years, and—"

"And you threw that all away when you told her you were in love with someone else!" I cut him off, shutting him down in the process. "Now, i don't expect *you* to understand, but when you tell a woman you're in love with someone else, the writing is on the wall and there is nothing else left to talk about."

"That's not the way it was supposed to come out!" lynx clenched his teeth like he'd waited for me to bring that point up. "i still love her, dammit!"

"But you haven't tried to fuck her in over six months!" I yelled back, causing my masseur to flinch again. I gave a wink at him with my back turned away from lynx, along with a sly grin and pulling him down for a kiss to put him at ease. The truth was, this whole exchange was making me wet as hell. "Guess what, hotshot, lusting after your wife instead of your wife's best friend is a good damn way to let her know you are in love with her."

"Didn't you hear me? i said i love my wife!" He tried to sound convincing, but I was curious of who he was trying to convince, me or him. The problem with his declaration was that he missed the key word in my rebuttal.

"i didn't say love, dummy, i said 'in love.' There's a difference," I snapped. "i'm in love with her, meanwhile, you just 'love' her. Who do you think she's going to want to respond to if she hears those words said to her?"

"me, goddammit!"

Who the hell was he kidding? Daddy had sajira so into him at this point there's no room for any other man. He had it like that; it was a gift. This man was more worried more about his dick than anything else, and he was too stupid to figure that out. The woman he'd married ten years ago was not the same woman that he swore he loved.

"If she does respond to you at all, it's because her body still does, but her mind has already replaced you." I felt the need to break him down to his knee pads. I had some man flesh to consume ASAP. "The last time you had sex…i can't say make love because, well… did she call out your name the way she used to when i first moved in with you?"

lynx's eyes betrayed him as he tried to remain calm. I watched the wheels turn in his mind, trying to figure out exactly where my conclusions would eventually lead him. "That doesn't mean anything!"

"Yeah, but it has you wondering, though." I laughed. "Do me a favor, would you? If you get a chance to talk to my sis, and that's not gonna happen, by the way, let me know if she admits that to you, okay?"

"Fucking bitch!" He hopped up from his spot, calling me all kinds of names as he walked away. "i don't know what i saw in you!"

"That's easy…you saw your dick in me!" I yelled after him, laughing so hard my masseur couldn't resist joining in my laughter. "Damn shame, too, you have such a beautiful dick!"

His walk turned into a jog, leaving me to finally enjoy the rest of my massage in peace. The only thing was, I was really amped up and horny as fuck now, and if his hands touched me again, I was going to rape him on the spot. So, rather than making it look like I was the aggressor, I looked up at him with a smile on my face and said, "Now that i've worked up some tension, do you think you can properly work out my pussy after you've worked the kinks out of my body?"

☥

Damn, I felt like a new woman!

After wearing out my masseur in more ways than one, it was time to get the rest of my day taken care of in enough time to get a good nap in before tonight's debauchery. My Goddess would have been so proud of me!

I began to see why paka rarely came stateside anymore. This island was addictive, especially the weather and the intoxicating atmosphere. A sistah was gonna have to heavily hint that we take a few more trips down here in the near future.

I made it to the outside tents, grinning like a horny teenager as I saw the island slave bois moving all of the dungeon furniture into the spaces. Watching them work kept me in my wanton state, the sweat rolling off their half-naked bodies causing heart palpitations that made me lightheaded.

I walked closer to the tents, making sure the spacing was where I wanted everything, taking mental inventory of what I wanted to subject myself to tonight. The pieces stoked different desires in-

side me, from the Crosses to the bondage tables to the steel cages
and everything in between. Then my heart stopped when I saw
not one, but two metallic, and motorized, suspension frames, and
two pieces of an apparatus that can only be called the "Wheel of
Torture"!

If you've never seen a Wheel of Torture before, let me see if I
could describe it for you as best as possible: if you'd ever seen
those old circus spinning wheels where the lovely assistant got on
this Ferris wheel-type contraption and the blindfolded knife thrower
spun the wheel and tried to throw the knives and hit balloons in
areas around the assistant?

Well, this was about the same premise except as you were spinning, every inch of your body was available for torture by more
than one Dominant at a time, or your body became a 360-degree
playground for your Dominant.

If the other tents looked half as wondrous as this one did, Daddy's
gonna really wonder if I had been holding back this whole time.

I wasn't holding back, honestly speaking. I always put together
my best productions, but I didn't have the dungeon furniture com-
panies in the UK and parts of Europe at my disposal, either.

I was still enjoying the bliss of my accomplishments, when a
voice popped up behind me, interrupting my thoughts.

"you know, you can be a real killjoy, do you know that?" tiger's
voice rang in my ears, shifting my mood in a direction I was not
thrilled about. "i was hoping to get some dick tonight before you
ruined it with your taunting."

Fuck! Didn't Sin have something for these bois of hers to do for
her or something?

I gave him a look that could have burned through lead. The last
thing I needed was to entertain some more drama on behalf of a
man that I'd emasculated not three hours ago.

"Damn, tiger, why do you always find a way to fuck up a wet dream?" I asked as I turned around and gave our customary air kisses to each other. "For that matter, why are you worried about one dick in this target-rich environment?"

I laughed as he flirted openly with one of the slave bois who caught his attention. He mouthed the words "see you tonight" before he finally turned his attention back to me. "What? Oh yeah, well, ummm, see, it ain't always about one dick, okay? But ain't nothing like some in-house dick, either, you feel me?"

I waved him off, watching him work his usual magic while the bois were working. He was too much, but he couldn't be anything more than what he always was, and he loved variety as much as I did. "See, i know you, boi. Remember, i was the one who got you with Sin, all right? If She wasn't so *laissez-faire* about you having whatever you wanted because it fit right in with what She wanted for Her enjoyment, too, you wouldn't be the slut you are right now."

"And i have been forever grateful for that, so ain't no point in reminding me all the damn time, trick." tiger sucked his teeth and glared at me. I love that boi to death. He'd been in my corner for a long time, and he'd always been the "Fetish Fashionista" that every girl needs, and I was glad he's mine. "But you don't get to deflect from the fact that you ruined my steady dick tonight. How would you feel if i ruined amani like that?"

"i'd kill you, so quit playing about the dick in my life." I mocked, wrapping my hands around his neck. He leaned away, almost falling on his ass. "Besides, word is, your dick won't be your dick anymore because your Mistress is dropping him the minute we get back to the States."

He gave me this "look" before he fell out laughing. "i swear, that Mistress Blaze is too much sometimes, always hedging Her bets. That's why i love that woman."

He laughed even harder when he saw I was truly confused. "Look, baby, Blaze has been salty ever since Mistress basically giftwrapped amani to your Goddess a couple of years ago. So, when She started having problems with lynx, Blaze offered to take him off Her hands."

"Wait, so why are you laughing at me?"

"Because amani gummed up that plan when he invited his frat brother down." tiger accentuated his point by fanning himself. "Lawd, have mercy, i'm shocked you haven't seen that fine motherfucker yet! Given the choice between prime filet mignon and bargain-basement sirloin, which would you choose? I know what the fuck I would choose."

"Damn, is he that fine?" He really had me curious now.

"Hell, yeah, he's that fine!" tiger kept fanning. It wasn't that hot on the beach, so I knew he was taking things to the extreme. But, with his taste in men, gay or straight, there had to be something to it. "Damn shame he's straight, though, or i'd have openly campaigned for Mistress that ass to be with us and let Blaze have lynx."

I wasn't sure if I wanted to be upset with my bro or not. I was sure he had his reasons, but it did explain why Blaze had been virtually invisible on the island except for the opening night festivities. I figured I'd check with him later tonight and guilt trip him into making the introductions.

I took a look around and was satisfied with the way things were progressing. Thankfully, everything else had gone well also, so I was about to help myself to a bit of a well-earned nap. Hopefully with a little luck, I'd be able to get rolling in time to do a little stunning tonight.

"Well, now that everything is under control, i can go nap for a little while so i can put the rest of these wannabe fetish girls on notice." I blew air kisses with him as I made my way to the family cabin. "And i'm sure you'll find a way to get your dick where you need him to be, since you've converted him and all."

tiger winked at me. "Chile, don't worry, he'll be putty in my hands by tonight. he doesn't have much of a choice if he wants to stay in Mistress's good graces the rest of the weekend. Now, go on and get you some beauty rest; you need it!"

"Bitch!" I playfully slapped him. "you know i'm a stunner; you're just jealous."

"No, chile, i call it like i see it." tiger took a closer look. "But if i was a straight dude, you could get it, and it's my job to make sure you stay that way."

"i love you."

"i love you, too, slut. See you later tonight."

THIRTY-TWO ⊗ NEFERTERRI

"you're kidding Me, baby? tiger is sure about that?"

We were in the family cabin, getting ready for the formal. After being away from amani and the girls all day yesterday to reconnect with my Beloved and recenter myself a bit, it was time to catch up with them to figure out what had happened.

From their collective body language, things were busy yesterday and for some parts of the day today.

"He's funny as hell, that's for sure," sajira scoffed. She was in a more aggressive mood than the last time I saw her. "What in the bloody hell did he hope to gain by talking to you? his dumb ass tried to fuck you behind my back!"

"sajira, baby, calm down," I cautioned her, feeling a negative vibe on her for the first time this entire trip. "There's no point in getting hyper over something that is so unnecessary."

sajira heard my voice and instantly calmed down, lowering her head and closing her eyes to gather herself before she spoke again. "i'm sorry, Goddess; i guess it still pisses me off when he's made himself perfectly clear where things stand between us. Now he wants to change his mind with the prospect of losing his Mistress is over his head. Whatever."

shamise shook her head. "Not according to tiger, sis. he is insistent that lynx isn't going anywhere, although he did say She was going to put him through more intense training to break him of his habits to embarrass Her."

"Sin never was one to give up on a project," I noted, grinning a bit. "But if what you're saying is true, shamise, that means you've been holding out on us, amani."

We turned in his direction, watching him sheepishly grin like a little kid who'd been caught trying to keep a secret. He looked all over the place, trying to find the words to figure out how to get out of the mess he'd gotten into.

shamise beat me to the questions I wanted to ask. "Yeah, bro, and the way tiger was fussing about, he's quite the cutie pie. What gives, amani?"

sajira's attitude changed when she heard her sister's remark. "Wait a minute, there's another submissive male on the island that we haven't met yet? Come on, bro, we're supposed to be closer than that!"

amani felt trapped in a corner, and it looked like he was going to shut down. I wanted to admonish him also, but I didn't want him in his feelings tonight, not when things were looking up. "amani, don't mind your sisters. you know how they get; anyone who is close to family is considered family to us."

"i understand that, Goddess, but i wasn't sure if he would be ready to meet you," he replied, shifting his body toward me. "he's been with Mistress Blaze all week, and things are really heating up between them. i promise i will make the proper introductions when we get to the formal later."

"That's My boi." I leaned down and kissed his forehead, watching his body relax now that the heat was off.

"No fair, Goddess, we didn't get to give him a hard time about it." shamise laughed in mock outrage. "i'm kidding, amani. We can wait until tonight to meet your friend. If he's half as gorgeous as tiger is claiming, he should help put a smile back on Mistress's face."

"I really hope so. I know She wasn't particularly happy when Sin dropped you in My lap, baby boi," I said, causing shamise to do a double-take. I laughed. "Sin must have spilled the beans to tiger, shamise?"

"Obviously so, Goddess, and i'm trying to figure out why You didn't?" She tried to be serious with her question. She continued to crack up, failing in her attempts to keep from laughing more. "Okay, okay, i get it, we would have done the same thing to tiger that he managed to do to me. But You know how he is, always enjoying the role of being four-one-one and everything."

"I'm sorry, baby girl, I promise it won't happen again." I kept laughing through my response. "It's not like I don't trust you three, I honestly do, but this particular piece of information was *supposed* to be limited to the women in that room at the time."

"Well, i hate to be the one to tell You, Goddess, but Sin might have breached that agreement." sajira pointed out the obvious, giggling at her contribution to the conversation. "At least You know we wouldn't have betrayed You like that, especially when *men* gossip more than women ever could."

Ramesses remained quiet as we talked. His eyes were closed and his fingers were clasped over his lips as the conversations flowed around him. He was absorbing information the way he normally did, but he also got quiet when he's mentally preparing for his usual role as Master of Ceremonies. There was an expression on his face that gave me a slight pause, though. "Beloved, there's something on Your mind, isn't there?"

We turned in his direction as he slowly opened his eyes and regarded our curious stares. "There are some things we will all need to repeat if anyone asks about Lyrical and Korina."

The mood changed quickly as the seriousness of his words sank in. amani's body language shifted to one of protection as he instinctively slipped his arm under my thigh. sajira and shamise gave each other a look before their attention focused back to Ramesses.

"If anyone asks, Lyrical and Korina found themselves in a heated affair, so heated that they were compelled to leave the island and head off to an undisclosed location," he stated. His face looked like it were made of stone, and it had us all on edge. "There is no other information to be had on where they went or anything on when they might get back to the States. You know how kinksters love their privacy."

He cracked a smile to sell the story, and thankfully it worked. The tension in the room dissipated, and he went back to his meditation. "Now, what were you saying about Blaze and Sin, sajira? Oh, you said something about men gossiping more than women?"

sajira grinned at his ability to switch his moods at the drop of a hat. "Daddy, You know good and well what we were saying."

"Doesn't mean I didn't want to hear the rest of it. I'm quite interested in learning how we gossip more than you do," he mentioned, his smile widening by the moment. "At either rate, we need to start getting dressed. I think you have some show-stopping to do tonight, right?"

I smiled, realizing the time had almost gotten away from us. "your Daddy is right, ladies and gentlemen. We have some stunning to do tonight, so let's get to it."

THIRTY-THREE ❀ RAMESSES

"Man, when You want to do Black-tie Fetish, You don't play around, do You, Sir?"

One look at the House in all its fashion splendor and it was easy to see why all eyes were on us.

amani and I followed the ladies into the grand room, where everyone gathered for the Black-tie formal social that was meant to conclude the weeklong experience for the guests. We knew everyone would be dressed to impress, but the girls insisted on stunning the group.

Based on the stares of the men in the room, they got exactly what they were looking for.

Neferterri was dressed in a crimson halter leather corset gown, a form-fitting piece which covered every curve from shoulder to mid-calf. She completed the look with a matching clutch, and rubies adorned her neck, ears, wrist, and left ankle. The crimson platform, ankle-boot heels were the envy of the women looking down at them, as though they were the only thing that mattered before they decided if they liked the outfit or not. I couldn't stop drooling before we left the cabin to even get there in one piece.

shamise didn't help matters, wearing a crimson halter leather dress, showing off her thick thighs and causing a stir of oohs and whistles as she struck mock poses to show off her body. She, too, was laced in rubies, wearing her collar with pride with matching cuff-like bracelets. Not one to resist cuffs, her heels matched the theme, showing off double-buckle ankle straps, a stacked, platform heel and a crisscross over the top of her foot, deciding to show her toes.

The showstopper that had me grinning was sajira. Our little one decided she wanted to get the best revenge on her soon-to-be ex-husband by flaunting every inch of her body and leaving *nothing* to the imagination. She wore a leather, three-buckle corset, laced so tightly that her already-accentuated curves were even more defined, accented with a leather skirt that stopped above the knee. Her ample assets on display captivated the Dominants in the room, all paying close attention to when she turned around. The grins swept the room as she showed off the back of the skirt, or lack thereof, revealing to the room that the skirt was a spanking skirt, and she'd also decided to go commando tonight. There was no point in worrying about the footwear, but the clear "stripper heels" would be the proper turn of phrase to describe them.

Michael Kors, I need to buy some stock in your company ASAP!

Not to be outdone, amani and I had the ladies swooning with matching leather kilts and military-styled leather boots, freshly shined by the island bootblacks. I wore a sleeveless leather shirt top, while amani showed off his more toned physique by wearing a fitted zipped leather vest. Now, that's not to say I was a slouch and I didn't keep myself in shape, goodness, that wasn't it, but I was a bit less muscular than our male submissive. From the gasps of the women in the crowd, I made a note to get back in the gym at the first opportunity.

"Oh, my, I wonder if they're wearing those kilts in the traditional style or not?" I heard a woman in the crowd ask aloud.

I nodded toward amani as we walked in her direction. "Why don't you reach under and find out for yourself?"

The woman blushed profusely as she slipped her hands under both of our kilts. The slick smile and unconscious licking of her lips alerted the crowd of the answer to her question. "Damn, and so gifted, too…your women must be especially proud of you two," she said as the other women in her immediate area giggled. "Would I need to…well, how do you say it…get permission to sample?"

I chuckled a bit, realizing she and her friends were part of the contingent that was invited from Nassau to witness some extra-curricular activity, and it would be interesting to see what they were capable of handling. After she reluctantly removed her hands from under our kilts, I teased her by leaning closely to her ear and whispering, "This is the Island of Evil Pleasures, love. You never know what pleasures may await you tonight…if you ask the right questions."

She wouldn't stop trembling as I walked away to join the girls at our table. I surveyed the room and marveled at some of the elegant formalwear being displayed, regardless of gender and regardless of station. To think that in an hour or so, all of these outfits would be shed in favor of lesser-clad ensembles in order to perform the scenes that would prove constricting otherwise.

Osiris and Amenhotep were the first to greet us once we sat down.

"Kid, You've done it again," Amenhotep said. "How in the world did You get all of these people from Nassau to come out?"

"I would have to give credit to Osiris and others with regard to that, Sir." I shook hands with Osiris as I deflected the credit. "The rest of the setup I can lay at the feet of Our submissives. The only thing I can take credit for is delegating the responsibilities."

"Ramesses, this week doesn't go off without You putting the right people in place to make sure things go smoothly." Osiris was always one to keep things as blunt as possible, without much room to wiggle out of it. "You should be proud, you all should be proud.

This was an absolutely marvelous week, despite some hiccups along the way."

Amenhotep stroked his beard over that statement. He gave a quick scan around the room and took notice of a couple of glaring omissions within the crowd, even with the Nassau additions. "I wonder if I should ask about the whereabouts of Sir Lyrical and Domina Korina, or am I better off not asking that question?"

"Two words, Sir: plausible deniability," Neferterri interjected as she eavesdropped on the conversation. She gave me a knowing wink before she returned to her conversation with a few guests that lingered around the table.

"You heard My Beloved, Sir. The less You know, the better," I explained. I noticed others were trying to figure out what was going on, and I was not about to arouse suspicion, so I went into theatrics. "I would imagine the happy couple is enjoying themselves quite well, to be honest. The sparks between them were so obvious that they had to cut the trip short. It is a shame. It would have been nice to see the chemistry between them in person."

I was laying it on thick for the outsiders listening in on the conversation in case someone wanted to figure out what exactly had happened to them. Unless they possessed the resources that we did, they wouldn't find out too much information, and by then it wouldn't matter. The Colombian Cartels would have taken care of one issue and Seti's associates in North Africa would have taken care of the other issue.

No muss, no fuss.

"Well, I wish them all the happiness they deserve." Amenhotep followed my cues, playing along with the routine. Thankfully, no one on the island figured out what actually had happened between my Beloved and Lyrical since the encounter had occurred while everyone was enjoying the festivities of the night. The security staff and the medical staff had a prearranged gag order, so they would be sworn by legalities to remain silent or suffer the consequences. "I've heard they decided to finish the rest of their trip in Fiji. Very sensual location, believe Me."

A few people trailed away, presumably satisfied with the gossip they could advance to the next willing ears. We did what we needed to do to take people off the scent, and for the most part, there would be no curiosities to help unhinge the rumors.

Once we were among ourselves, Osiris asked, "So, now that we've managed to take care of eavesdroppers, what did You have in mind for this last event?"

I started to answer, and the strangest thing happened.

I drew a blank.

I honestly had no earthly idea of what to do for tonight's centerpiece to the event. I looked at Amenhotep for a moment before turning back to Osiris, my mind racing to figure out what to do to make something up as I went. After the past twenty-four hours, I was genuinely out of any clever tricks up my sleeve or anything that would prove a catalyst for things to come.

"There's no need to be modest, Beloved." Neferterri slid her arms around my neck. "Don't worry, Gentlemen, tonight will be amazing."

Neferterri kissed my lips, further confusing me. I was glad I had a decent poker face, otherwise, I would have really thrown everyone off. I looked at shamise and sajira, who tried to hide the excited expressions on their faces, and then over at amani, who looked as out of the loop as I did.

"Knowing You, My darling Lady Neferterri, it should be an interesting treat, indeed." Amenhotep dismissed my bewildered look as He winked at her. "I, for one, am looking forward to this."

THIRTY-FOUR ⊗ NEFERTERRI

"Ladies and gentlemen, you are all in for a treat tonight."

When Ramesses wanted to ad lib, he took things to the extreme. The crowd was completely mesmerized by the spectacle he put on, hinging on his every word as amani was escorted to the center of the dungeon.

The girls and I took the social time that the guests took advantage of to do a crash course for the men in our lives and let them know what was about to take place.

Ramesses didn't blink once. He saw this coming and it was a simple matter of timing. To him, this was perfect timing. He simply told Osiris, who usually officiated ceremonies, and prepared for the event.

amani took the news from the girls in stride, but I had a feeling the gravity of the situation was lost on him for a moment. They tried their best to help explain to him what was about to happen and what it meant for him within the family, but it wasn't until he saw the crowd surrounding us that things finally clicked. The look on his face was absolutely priceless as they placed him on the kneeling bench facing the Cross.

The chairs had been positioned in a large circle, enclosing us and giving the ceremony an intimate feel. The lighting had been dimmed to simulate candlelight levels, with the spotlight concentrating on the middle of the circle.

"Forgive the impromptu nature of this occasion, but it has been long overdue, and My Beloved and I could not be prouder of our newest submissive, amani." Ramesses continued his spiel, making it sound like it was something he'd rehearsed for months. "Tonight, we have invited you to witness this most intimate of events, and once it is over, you will be encouraged to christen our newest addition to the House of Kemet-Ka by flogger, single-tail whip, or barehanded spanking."

Osiris made his way from the back of the dungeon, walking with keket at his side, until they made it to the center area with us. In keket's hands was amani's leather and chrome collar, complete with the padlock and key, symbolic of the permanency of his bond to the family. The crowd buzzed as those in the audience who had never witnessed a public collaring ceremony before did their best to keep their conversation to a whisper. Under normal circumstances, he would have been dressed in the ceremonial robes, as would we have been, but instead, settled on a modest leather vest and kilt with his boots, looking quite the debonair gentleman. I would have swooned over him with the other women if I weren't married to my own piece of drool-worthy eye candy.

"If I may have your attention, please, ladies and gentlemen," Osiris announced. He stepped onto the platform, motioning for Ramesses and me to join him. He waited for the crowd to quiet down before he continued. "We are gathered this evening to witness the formal collaring of amani, submissive of the House of Kemet-Ka. On behalf of Master Ramesses and Lady Neferterri, it is My honor to officiate this ceremony."

amani stayed in his kneeling position, stealing glances at shamise and sajira on either side of him. I would have corrected him on the spot, but considering all eyes were on us, I decided against it.

After all, this was a special occasion, there was no point in ruining it, and I would consider the trail of whips and floggers that would commence after his declaration a fitting punishment for his transgressions.

amani clasped his hands in front of him as though he were praying. I smiled down on him, proud of the journey he'd taken to get to this point, and curious of what the future held for him as our property. Ramesses and I took our positions, standing in front of him, nodding to Osiris to proceed with the next phase of the ceremony.

"amani will now announce his declaration, after which his permanent collar will be locked around his neck," Osiris pronounced to the crowd. I surveyed the faces, taking delight in watching the non-lifestyle people in attendance, awestruck by the spectacle.

amani took a deep breath, opening his eyes to find us standing before him. His eyes focused solely on the two of us, he said, "With devotion, i offer my body and will to You, my Master and my Goddess, to care for and do with as You will. Your desires are mine, Your will is my command."

He took another breath before continuing his declaration. "i vow to learn all that You wish to teach me to the best of my ability. i know through Your loving direction, discipline, and appropriate punishment that i will reach my highest potential as Your submissive. Master, Goddess, i accept Your collar as a symbol of my submission to You, devotion to my sister submissives, and the pledge i have made tonight. i shall wear it with pride, always."

A soft applause rose from the crowd, in appreciation of this part of the ceremony. keket presented the collar to us, allowing me to place the collar around his neck.

"I am so proud of you, My beautiful boi," I whispered in his ear as I locked the collar around his neck. He shook for a moment as I kissed the spot on his neck I knew turned him on. "I love you, amani."

"I love you, too, kid," Ramesses kneeled down to whisper. amani discreetly raised his fist to give his Master pound, their own unique way of connecting. "Welcome to the family."

"Let all who have witnessed this ceremony take note, that Master Ramesses and Lady Neferterri have accepted amani as their own," Osiris proclaimed. "he is now claimed, as his declaration of submission has been spoken and freely given. I now present to you, amani, submissive prince of the House of Kemet-Ka."

♀

"Please forgive me, these introductions are long overdue."

I was kidding when I told amani we needed to meet this friend of his. I wanted him to enjoy the euphoria of what he'd gone through and being the envy of the submissives on the island that were waiting for that moment. It wasn't as though we wouldn't get a chance to see him before we saw all of the guests off the island, and I suspected Blaze would be dying to show him off tonight also. Still, I wasn't about to stop him from following through on his promise, either.

One look at Jelani and I had to reevaluate my original thoughts.

The girls did everything they could to keep from drooling too much to keep Ramesses from chastising them for being unladylike.

I had to maintain my own decorum; despite the fact that my amani was sexy, Jelani had a body built for sin. The things I imagined doing to him in the quick fantasy flashes would have made any normal woman blush.

Thank goodness I wasn't a normal woman.

He might have been a couple of inches shorter than amani, but his body was well defined, and the Speedo shorts he wore showed off every muscle in his body. His dark-chocolate hue covered in massage oil gave his skin a sheen that caused every woman in the dungeon to take notice, whether they were compelled to do so or not.

The grin on Blaze's face let me know she was more than happy with the way things had progressed with him, and I grinned because I couldn't wait to have a quick conversation with her while amani and the girls got to know Jelani better.

"Master, Goddess, shamise, sajira, i would like for you to meet my frat, Jelani. Mistress Blaze, it is nice to see You again also, Ma'am." amani pointed us out to Jelani to give him a frame of reference. "Jelani, as you can now tell, this is my D/s family."

Jelani took my hand and kissed the back of my palm, sending chills down my spine and making me wet in an instant. Damn, I needed to get away from this man before I gave myself away. "It is nice to meet You, m'Lady. My frat has spoken a lot about You, and he definitely did not exaggerate. If i may say so, You are absolutely stunning."

"Flattery will get you everywhere with Me, Jelani." I grinned and blushed, unable to escape the way his eyes regarded me. He meant every word he said, and his body followed up the words in his mind. I struggled to keep from flirting with him, especially when his eyes gave himself away. "I will let you and amani and the girls get better acquainted, Jelani. It was nice meeting you. I'm sure we will see you in the future."

Before Jelani could say another word, shamise and sajira had already grabbed him and amani by the hands and pulled them away from us, leaving the three of us for a brief moment to chat.

Ramesses grinned for a moment before he gave me a kiss across my lips. "You're lucky I'm not the jealous type," he said. "As much as I would love to stay and chat, there are guests to disburse and scatter out to the play spaces before we have our own fun. Blaze, he has great potential, I think You will have a blast training him."

He walked away after kissing Blaze on the cheek, and the moment he was gone, we went into girlfriend mode.

"Whew, woman, how in the world have You been able to resist the charms on that boi?" I felt like I was having hot flashes he had me so heated.

"I haven't." Blaze's grin would have made a Cheshire cat jealous. "he's been so easy to mold, he's picked up on all of My simple protocols, and every time he strips down to his underwear, it's taken everything within Me to keep from raping him on the spot!"

I closed my eyes to hold myself steady as I looked back in the direction of where the girls and the bois were still talking. I looked at amani, and toward Jelani, and back to amani, and I placed a hand over my chest to regulate my breathing. "Now I see why You were pissed off with Me a couple of years ago when amani showed up for Me."

Blaze blushed. "Yeah, I was a little hot when I thought Sin had My back when we were looking at him back then. When he came and kneeled at Your feet, I had this look on My face, and Sin instantly knew She'd fucked Me over. It had nothing to do with You, though. You couldn't have known Sin and I had already talked about Your boi before She sent him in Your direction."

"Well, You can't say things didn't work themselves out, Blaze." I winked at her, preparing to state the obvious. "You know this means that You owe Me now, right?"

Blaze was incredulous. "How in the world do You figure that, Neferterri?"

"My boi introduced You to a potential submissive to serve You." The grin on my face was evident of the checkmate she didn't see coming. "After all, he could have introduced him to Me and the rest of the family before introducing him to You."

"I love You, but You can be such a bitch sometimes." Blaze laughed, but she couldn't argue with my logic, either. "Okay, I owe You, girl, You do have a point. But that also means that Sin still owes Me, too. She didn't set this sexy-ass boi up with Me."

"Exactly, Sis," I confirmed. "Not that I would hold it over Your head or anything. I also have a feeling amani and My girls will take the point in getting him acclimated to life as a lifestyle submissive, if I know them."

I looked at the way my girls fawned over them, and I saw something that made me smile. I didn't want to jinx it, so I didn't speak it into existence. Some things develop in their own way, without interference.

I snapped out of my thoughts to switch gears and get into the proper headspace, and I knew Blaze was in that same mode. "Okay, Sis, we need to go ahead and get some play time in before we both spontaneously combust from the sexual heat we're giving off. I'll see You in the morning."

THIRTY-FIVE & RAMESSES

"Are you ready for what you're about to go through?"

It really didn't matter whether she was or not; it only felt like a fun question to ask.

The first phase of her gauntlet consisted of a masochist's dream: being suspended while being whipped by some of the most renowned Masters in the scene, six of them to be exact.

I was there to make sure she didn't float too far away. Normally, I would have joined in the "Circle of Pain" with my fellow Dominants, but a conversation sajira and I had before the scene was set up changed things:

"i can't get these thoughts out of my head, Daddy. i need something to erase the tapes in my head."

"How far are you willing to go, baby girl? It's going to take a lot, and it will get intense if you're not careful."

"As far as You can push me, and then farther than that. i don't wanna feel anything by the end of the night."

"you don't wanna feel anything, sajira?"

"Well…i wanna feel You, Daddy. Every inch of You."

"you will, baby girl. By the end of the night, the last thing you will feel will be My dick deep inside you."

"You're so nasty, Daddy…i need nasty tonight."

I don't think she would understand what my Beloved and I would have in store for her, but she would find out soon enough. Some of it she would see and some of it she wouldn't see.

I led her out to the apparatus that would become the symbolic scene of her escape from the torture in her mind: the motorized suspension frame.

Her face lit up the moment she saw it, and the grin spread when she saw the men and women who would make up the circle. At least two of the men she would have picked for her "circle" stood in front of her, and the sight of Mistress Sinsual as one of the two women she wanted made her night.

"Okay, precious, now that you're done drooling, it's time to get you rigged up," I told her.

She lowered her head, smile intact. "Yes, my Master. Your wish is my will."

The slaves I'd chosen to help with the scene brought the ankle and wrist cuffs, placing them on her body and leading her under the base of the suspension frame. The cuffs were then linked to the quick-release locks, ensuring she was in place. I walked over to the switch and flipped it to turn on the winches to raise her arms over her head. The slaves kept her balanced once I turned on the wenches to lift her legs. By the time I was done and had her in place, she was suspended in a prone position.

"Ladies and Gentlemen, you may begin," I announced as I stepped to assume my position. I took a seat below her head, making sure she could focus on me as the whips began their collective assault.

Osiris and Seti took their positions on either side of her near her upper back, while Sin and Blaze positioned themselves near her thighs and ass. Menes and another Dominant, Sir Jazz, were at her feet. Once everyone was in place, they commenced their whip action.

The idea of the "Circle of Pain" was the idea of multiple Dominants leaving whip marks on the submissive at the center of the circle, rotating every few minutes to a new area on the submissive, to cut down on any monotony during the scene. The scene was over when the Dominants were back in their original positions.

As the stings of the whips began to make their presence known upon her skin, I smiled at the beautifully painful faces she made as each of the whips made contact seconds between each other.

"Are you still with Me, sajira?"

"Fuck…yes, Daddy…owww…i'm here with You."

"Does it hurt, baby?"

"Yes…mmmmmm fuck, yes…it hurts, Daddy…i don't…don't make them stop, please."

I moved my index finger in a circular motion over my head, indicating to the circle to rotate and continue their onslaught. Being suspended in the air with nowhere to go, sajira could do nothing else but scream as the whipping became more intense and increased in its frequency.

I caressed her face and kissed her lips at different times during the scene, keeping her mind here with me instead of letting her take off into space. I took great care to watch her flight, determining when she could and could not hit higher altitudes. The next rotation brought her closer to the pain/pleasure threshold, reducing her ability to speak to nothing more than moans and whimpers and nonverbal yes's and no's.

"you're going to enjoy the next phase in your gauntlet, baby girl," I teased, knowing she really couldn't hear me. "Well, you won't be able to see what's happening to you, but your body will love what will happen."

Her moans had their effect on me, but she always got to me quickly. I tried to resist acting on my urges, but I wanted my submissive badly.

"Daddy…i…i wanna come…my clit…is throbbing… for You."
She was so far gone now, the only thing she wanted was to be
fucked and put to sleep. "It feels…so good, Daddy… the whips…
feel like…kisses…on my…skin."

It took a lot to resist the look on her face. She mouthed the
words, "Fuck me, Daddy," while lunging toward me to kiss me,
even while the whips continued to strike and sting against her
skin. She made the most sensual faces when she was in ecstasy,
but I had to make sure she continued through her gauntlet. My
Beloved would be awaiting her arrival soon, and I needed to end
the scene so Sinsual and Blaze could rest a bit before they par-
ticipated in the next phase.

I closed my hand into a fist and raised it over my head, which
clued the Dominants to wrap the scene up. I nodded toward the
ladies as they withdrew from the scene to head to where Neferterri
was stationed. I signaled the slave bois to get into position to take
sajira down to carry her to where she would go next.

She resisted being taken down, her body still acting as though
it were still being whipped and wanting more. The bois were having
some trouble maneuvering the quick releases because of her resistance.

"Don't take me down yet, Daddy," she begged.

"It's time to come down, baby. Let the bois take you down."

"But they're still whipping me, Daddy. i don't want them to stop
yet. i'm almost there."

"sajira, I won't say this again; stop struggling so they can take
you down," I growled in her ear to make sure she understood this
wasn't one of her dreams where she could resist and no harm would
come to her. "I will stop your gauntlet if you disobey Me."

That shook her out of her haze. "Yes, Daddy, i will obey," she said. Seconds later, she held as still as she could as the bois used the quick releases to unhinge her from the suspension cables. A few moments later, one of the bois had her in his arms as he carried her to her next destination.

Osiris sat down next to me as one of the slave girls placed a water bottle in his hand before placing a glass of rum and Coke in mine. He had worked up a sweat, along with the other Dominants involved in the scene, and the smile on his face was indicative of an enjoyable time. Seti, Menes and Sir Jazz soon joined us, their smiles mirroring Osiris's.

"I didn't know sajira was such a pain slut," Osiris remarked as he took a swig of his water. "Usually she would have called for her safeword by the time we'd rotated the second time. To get to My original spot before You ended the scene, I'm impressed."

"You're not the only one, Osiris," Seti chimed in with his thoughts. "I haven't been put through a workout like that since the grand opening night when I put slave amirah through the paddles in My bag. I am also very impressed by her stamina."

They were right; under normal circumstances sajira would have called out her safeword within minutes of being stroked with the first few whip lashes. I think that was what concerned me most. She might have had some bad memories from the past year that she wanted gone from her mind, but it felt like more than that. It felt like she wanted to erase the last ten years of her life from her psyche. She said she wanted to be pushed beyond her comfort zone, but what I had her subjected to was only the beginning, and she took the first phase like a seasoned masochist, not a relatively new submissive that once cringed at the crack of a bullwhip.

I only hoped the next phase would help in that endeavor.

Whatever her husband did to her to provoke this purge, God help him if she even recognized him after tonight.

"sajira's not a pain slut, Gentlemen, and these aren't the usual circumstances, either," I answered as I downed the glass in one gulp. "she has some demons to release tonight, and I have a feeling it will take a lot to eradicate them once and for all."

THIRTY-SIX ⚯ sajira

"Take me, Goddess. Your wish is my will."

My nerve endings were beyond sensitive. I felt like if anything or anyone touched me, I would explode. I didn't care who had me anymore, I didn't want this feeling to go away.

lynx tried to get my attention all night, showing up all over the dungeon whenever I was around someone scening or if I was chatting with a friend or two. His presence threatened to mess with my head, and I didn't want to be in the wrong headspace in the event I wanted to perform a scene or three. I wasn't in love with him anymore, but my body still craved his touch, regardless of how repulsed I was by his actions.

I needed away from that vibe ASAP.

Going through the suspension whipping scene was exactly what the doctor ordered. From the moment I heard the winches lift me into position, something in my mind clicked and I was able to zone everything, and everyone, out.

Everyone…except my Daddy, that is.

Watching his eyes, I knew I could fly as high as I wanted and he would be able to reel me in. His eyes were always so intense and arresting. It felt like I developed tunnel vision as my body went through more than my mind would have ever allowed.

The grin on his face as I made sexual faces at him made me wetter by the second. Each lash of the whips that hit my body felt like kisses caressing my skin, sinking me deeper into bliss.

I needed to feel him inside me. I wanted him to make me his, to remove any lasting traces of my husband's essence from me and replace them with his own. I begged him through the tears of the pain I felt to take me away and ravage my body before sending me to my next destination.

His eyes smoldered, showing me the fire within him, a fire I would have given anything to be consumed by. He slowly shook his head in response to my pleas, mouthing only one word, "Later."

Damn, what that man does to me…well, you know the rest.

There was a method to their madness, and I'd come to trust that madness implicitly. After the events that had occurred after my collaring ceremony last year, I knew what the potential consequences of not trusting them would be, and there was no way I would go back to feeling that way again.

"Put her down right here on the bed, slave," I heard my Goddess command him. He lowered me ever so gently onto the plush comforter, stepping away quickly to move on to the next directive.

I heard her giggle for a few moments before I heard the other voices in the room.

"She looks like she was put through a really intense scene, Neferterri. Do You think she's ready for this?" I heard a voice I didn't recognize ask of my Goddess.

"she was, but I know My sajira, and she can hear everything that's going on around her; isn't that right, baby girl?"

"Yes, my Goddess, i'm here, i hear You, and i'm ready," I responded as though the last hour never had happened. "i'm always Yours to command."

"Yep, she's a trooper, all right." I heard Sin's voice. "she took everything we threw at her and smiled with each lash that hit her skin."

"That's My girl," my Goddess whispered in my ear. She caressed my face for a moment, making me feel warm and tingly. "you won't be blindfolded for this phase, precious. Do you understand?"

"Yes, my Goddess." My body trembled at her touch. "i want to be able to see and feel everything."

"Good girl, that's what I thought you might say." She tapped my ass and said the command, "Down dog."

I immediately slid my legs up and out, perching my ass in the air while arching my back in the "down dog" yoga position. I began swaying my hips, acting like a bitch in heat, awaiting my first sexual partner of the night.

I didn't contain the grin on my face as the women admired my ass and the way I presented it. Sin and Blaze were the most vocal, obviously because they knew what to say without pissing off my Goddess.

"I swear, that ass gets prettier every time I see it, Neferterri," Sin commented.

Blaze chimed in, "she has a body built for sin and debauchery, Sis. You should be proud of her."

"I am proud of her, especially once she endures what we put her through tonight," my Goddess said. After a few quiet moments, she finally smacked my ass and announced, "Ladies, You may take her now."

I felt Sin's familiar hands gripping my hips first, sliding inside me with her strap-on. Hearing her moan as she eased every inch of her dick inside me ignited my inner slut. "She" realized there would be more to come and delighted in the unknown count she would have in her mouth and pussy before this scene was over.

The new-found masochist in me delighted to feel nails tracing the welts on my body, welcoming the shivers of pain that mixed with the pleasure of being pounded by Sin. Her delight heightened at the presence of another pair of hands and the distinct feeling of cold, sharp steel slicing across my welts, causing screams to escape my lips. I yelled out for Sin to fuck me harder, feeling my mind preparing to take flight again.

"Shit, this bitch is gonna make Me come!" Sin announced as the other two hands continued to take and slice across my skin.

"Come, Sis, so I can have a crack at her!" Blaze replied. "I wanna see that beautiful ass in motion when I take her!"

Sin slid out of me without warning, her orgasm paralyzing her. In the recesses of my mind, I recalled the women adopted the FeelDoe® strap-ons because they caused G-spot orgasms. I was jealous because I remembered how powerful my G-spot orgasms could be, but I wasn't in the right position to achieve that yet.

It didn't stop me from coming, though.

Between the knives I felt, the nails tracing over my whip marks, and my ass getting slapped as my walls were invaded, only a cold and unfeeling being would be unable to orgasm at least once.

I was quickly losing count with each convulsion my Kegel muscles suffered through. No matter what the cost my body would pay for in the morning, it was worth the purge my mind would enjoy at the end of this gauntlet.

"Fuck me, Ma'am, get this pussy!" I yelled out, not knowing who the next woman would be. I heard other women moaning in the room, but I didn't bother looking up. I was selfishly focused on my own wantonness and pleasure, grateful to my Goddess and my Daddy for allowing me to.

I heard Blaze growl as she entered me, laughing as she heard how slick I was. "Damn, you're still wet, slut? Fuck, I'm really gonna wear this pussy out now!"

She slammed into me with enough force to make me wonder briefly it a man had actually taken hold of my body. The fury of her strokes rocked me back and forth, causing me to grab the sheets and brace for the impact of her pelvis against my ass.

I felt the attention focus on the two of us as the sounds got louder and my screams got more pronounced. In fact, one person's attention cut through the noise in the room and instantly had my attention.

"Damn, Blaze, I know she gets You hot, but be careful with My property!" Neferterri's voice balanced me a little, but Blaze had my body humming, with yet another tsunami wave crashing through me, threatening to render me unconscious.

"Fuck...she's...got...fuck, I'm coming!" Blaze wailed as she shook violently while inside me. She tried to keep going like she had something to prove against what Sin did to me, but her strokes no longer had the force they possessed only minutes ago.

"Move, Blaze, it's My turn!"

"No, I got her next!"

"Damn that, she belongs to Me now!"

I didn't care if it sounded staged or if it were real, but to have Female Dominants fighting over who got to fuck me next was the boost I needed to take off into the stratosphere!

One after another, each woman tore into me as though I were the last piece of ass they would ever get in life. I think it might have been at least three other women who had their way with me. Each one couldn't believe I was still wet and didn't need any lube, but this was a rare night for something like that to occur. Usually, I would have needed to stop and use some lube after Blaze was done fucking me, so, at least for tonight, my body and mind synced with the same objective in sight:t get rid of every bit of negativity in my mind, body, heart and soul, for tomorrow would begin with a clean slate.

While I didn't hear her voice during the scene, I felt my Goddess's presence near me the entire time. I was convinced she was the one slicing over my body with the knives because she would never trust anyone outside of Daddy to keep from breaking my skin. I had been switched into different positions to give my knees some rest, but I was never on my back, by her instructions. That was reserved for her.

In my mind, it would be the perfect sendoff.

After the last woman eased out of me, I was flipped onto my back. Her comforting, soothing hands gripped my weary legs and pinned them back as far as they would go. One more dollop of lubricant-laced fingers caressed my swollen lips. I softly cried out from the pain and soreness before my walls were invaded yet again.

This time was different.

My Goddess had come to reclaim me.

The reason why this last position was reserved for her was so she could end the scene and send me back to the family cabin to rest. Before she could do that, she needed to retire the slut and reclaim the slave who belonged to them, and I was ready to be reclaimed.

At least, I thought I was.

"Hi, precious."

"Hi, Goddess."

"It's time for you to come back to us, sajira," She cooed in my ear as she slowly stroked me.

"i know, my Goddess. Is it safe to come out?" I asked as I wrapped my legs around her waist, deepening our connection. My pussy didn't feel so sore while she was inside me. "Where's Daddy, is He okay, too?"

"Daddy's fine, baby girl, you will see Him soon enough," She reassured me while kissing my face and lips. Her slow and rhythmic stroking inside my sex had a soothing effect, providing more peace of mind as each moment passed. "We will all be there by the time you wake up. Now, let's enjoy our time together before I have the slave boi take you to the cabin. I love you."

"i love You, too."

She continued to stroke me and caress me until the exhaustion from the two scenes slipped me into dreamland. The last thing I remembered before passing out were the strong hands and arms of the slave boi who brought me to my Goddess lifting me from the bed and taking me to my final destination to rest, until I was awakened when the rest of the family got back.

I sank deeper into the arms of my courier, who took great care in not disturbing the contents of the precious cargo he was entrusted with delivering. Letting my body succumb to a much-needed power nap, I chose to enjoy the bonfire raging in my dreams.

Smiling at the memories turning to ashes before my eyes...

THIRTY-SEVEN ⚯ shamise

"i've been waiting for this all week, Daddy."

I couldn't take my eyes away from the fire as it flickered from his fingers. I was mesmerized by the beautiful sight, helpless to stop his fingers from touching my body. I didn't want him to not touch my body with his fire-laden, gloved hands, but I wasn't about to admit that I was looking forward to this. It was only a matter of time before my body would move in sync with the rhythm of the dance, despite my being bound to the Cross.

He had to move swiftly, as the alcohol mixture that glistened on my skin rolled toward sensitive areas on my body that he knew he didn't want to have singed.

That was what the vat of wax warming in the jars over the fire was for.

I loved fire play scenes because of the intimacy between partners and the fear of getting burned was an aphrodisiac for me. I got wet whenever I was watching or participating in a scene; it didn;t matter to me because I was a fire slut like that. Being an Aries, we're already drawn to fire, so it was second nature to me to enjoy this type of scene.

"you've been a good girl for Me and your Goddess, My darling little one." He kissed me softly across my lips. "I've been looking forward to this all week, too, precious."

This was what all the work we did this week boiled down to, and I was so glad it was finally over. The release tonight would be explosive, and after I'd overheard what my sis was subjecting herself to, I felt the need to play "can you top this" by seeing her suspension and whip scene and her all-girl gangbang and raise her with my fire and wax scene.

If I were lucky, I might have coerced Daddy into fucking my brains out.

The heat of the flames licking my skin aroused my senses, and his kisses against my skin aroused my libido. It didn't matter where his lips were, my body responded. It felt like silk grazed against me as his hands moved over my arms, up to my shoulders, and caressing my neck before he turned his palms up and let the flames lick at my nipples, never touching my skin the entire trip.

"Mmmmm, Daddy that feels so good." My eyes narrowed, giving me an intoxicated look. He matched my stare, realizing the fire had its effect on him, too. I strained against my binds as he continued to drip the alcohol mixture onto my body and letting the fire blaze the trail along my skin, my eyes flashing along with the trail, trying to figure out its final destination.

Taking his free hand and drying my skin to keep it from igniting in areas without his knowledge, Daddy's body language gave himself away. He wanted me, I felt him, and the feeling was more than mutual, even before we began this scene.

My wrists and ankles might have been bound, but my hips weren't. I swayed them back and forth, enticing him to end this scene early. The belly-dancing classes were definitely worth the investment as I watched his eyes move with my sway, seriously considering my silent plea. The way the heat of the fire affected me, all he had to do was tell me the scene was over and we were heading to the cabin with all due haste so I could properly put him to sleep.

He tried to ignore my movements, even blowing fire onto my skin from the torch in his hand to get me to stop. I arched my back and moved in rhythm with the direction the flames traveled, causing him to smirk with the realization that I was flirting with him during the scene.

"you think you're slick, don't you?"

I batted my eyelashes, trying to play innocent. "i don't know what You're talking about, Daddy."

He slapped my hips, the source of his attention. "So, these shouldn't be moving if you don't know what I'm talking about, precious."

"Do You wish for me to stop moving them, my Master? Are they distracting You?"

"you better not stop them from moving, baby girl, or I might have to punish you."

The grin on my face was evident now. I was this close to having him where I wanted him. "i'd have to be a bad girl for You to punish me, Daddy. Have i been a bad girl?"

His eyes found mine as the flames in his hand found my nipples again. He held the torch there, daring me to moan, daring me to move or sway. He slowly moved from my nipples, lower to my panty line, the flames tickling the sensitive skin around my bikini lines. I was so tempted to give in to his dare, but I didn't want to move; his eyes took me prisoner and weren't about to let me go. I subconsciously licked my lips, one of my defense mechanisms when I wanted to moan or scream and I wasn't given permission to do so.

The heat danced near my clit; I felt my pussy getting wet from the prospects of my sex being caressed by the flames. I started trembling, fighting the urge to slide my hips forward to consummate the union of fire against my nether regions. All I needed was for the flames to hit my clit just once and I would have been in pure heaven from then on. I would have welcomed whatever, and I do mean *whatever*, he would have wanted me to do, as long as I could feel it…right…*there*.

As I contemplated moving despite the consequences, he pulled the flames away, stepping away from me and extinguishing the glove.

The sneer on his face told me he intended to take the heat away from me. "you haven't been a bad girl yet, but if I have My way… and I will have My way…you will be before the night is over."

If I didn't think it would get me killed, I would have screamed in frustration! I forgot how much of a sadist he could be when he knew I wanted something so desperately that I would gladly breach protocol to get it. I willed myself to keep my back against the Cross, even though every fiber of my being wanted to do the opposite.

He saw my quandary and smiled.

Damn Sadists.

"I see you want to be a bad girl after all, shamise," he said. I looked down and noticed the vat of wax in his hand, along with a foam paint brush. "Good, I like My girls when they want to be bad, it makes it easier to do this—"

Before I knew it, he'd dipped the paint brush in the hot wax and stroked the brush across my right breast, covering my already sensitive mound and nipple.

I moaned loudly this time, unable to contain myself due to the immediate pain coursing through my nipple, followed by the familiar burn and crossover into the pleasure centers in my brain, welcoming the tingling sensation along with the searing heat that made wax so addictive. I wanted more, my eyes expressing themselves to him, feverishly begging him to take me deeper into the abyss.

"Mmmmm, I think she likes it." He grinned as I continued to shiver against the sensation the wax had on me. "Do you want more?"

"Yes, Master, please!"

"Ask properly, sexy," He commanded as he let drops of wax fall on my shoulders.

"Master, please cover me in wax, i beg You."

"That's better, baby girl," he replied as he applied the wax on every square inch of bare skin available to him so meticulously I was convinced by the time he was done, I would have a wax bodice to take off for display.

With each stroke on my skin, I purred with satisfaction. I closed my eyes to focus on the way my body reacted to the stinging sensations once the wax was applied. The anticipation of where he might place the paint brush next added to the heightened sensitivity once the brush made contact. I gasped at the way the wax coated, the fleeting, burning sensation before the warmth on my skin presented itself.

Before long, I was covered from my neck to my knees in wax, with every possible area of my skin adorned.

I felt so hot...oh, God I was so hot...I felt the beads of sweat forming on my forehead and down my back.

Daddy took one of his knives out of a bowl of ice to cut and scrape the wax from my skin. The cold steel pressed against my warmed skin was a welcomed shock as I felt the dried wax pulling from my body, along with the sharpness of the blade slicing along the newly exposed skin.

My body tingled, my demeanor shifting from ecstasy to pure

lust. My desires turned to primal, appetent, hurry-the-fuck-up-and-get-me-off-this-fucking-Cross sex. The type of sex I didn't want to wake up from until at least sometime after midday.

Based on the way he took the wax off me, Daddy had the same sense of urgency. He never said a single word during the wax purge, not even caring about the shavings hitting the blanket. For all I knew, he already had someone at the ready to clean up the mess the minute we disengaged from the play area.

The minute my ankles and wrists were freed from the Cross, he kissed me so hard my clit jumped at the meaning behind it.

His eyes gave him away, and for once, I didn't care. I wanted him to say the words that would have me wet the rest of the night.

"I'm gonna wear you out when we get back to the cabin…I want my slut *now*."

THIRTY-SEVEN ⊗ NEFERTERRI

"I'm gonna beat the shit out of you!"

You know, under normal circumstances I would have said those words were music to my ears. Coming from Sin's mouth, I would have sat down and asked one of the island slaves to bring me a bowl of popcorn and a glass of Moscato while amani massaged my feet so I could enjoy the show.

The tone in Sin's voice was what startled me.

She'd never sounded that evil.

After taking a look in her direction and noticing the source of her condescension, it made all the sense in the world.

lynx was already locked in to the suspension frame and howling as Sin gave him the whipping of a lifetime. He wiggled and flinched and flopped around like a fish out of water as she tore into his flesh with two chained floggers, each one at least fifteen falls thick!

For those that might not understand, let me say this: if I was a little worried about him, you should be, too. Hell, even tiger flinched with each swat on lynx's body.

With everything that he had done to incur Sin's wrath, I was shocked this didn't happen sooner than it did. Part of me took some pleasure in watching his torture. After all, he treated my sajira dirty with his actions this week.

The other part of me wanted to feel sorry for him.

Notice I said I *wanted* to feel sorry for him? I hoped she beat the black off him.

I was heavily engaged with amani on the Wheel of Torture, watching his exposed and naked body rotate for me to take aim with any number of implements at my disposal. Hearing lynx's screams of pain only served to enhance my high from torturing my boi, albeit for different reasons.

The other sight catching my attention was Blaze doing her thing with Jelani. I finally got a chance to see him in all of his glory, and to tell the truth, I saw the reason why she'd kept him under wraps all week until she had an idea of whether he would be into her or not.

That boi was stacked!

Not that my baby wasn't, of course, but my boi took care of Blaze and then some with that fine specimen of a man. The muscle definition alone would be intoxicating to the touch, after a few marks were put on it for good measure.

I returned my focus to the task at hand, watching amani slowly spinning before me, every inch of him available to be groped, stuck, pinched, whatever my heart desired. That took my mind off Jelani for a few moments, but Blaze decided she wanted to start trash-talking in the space.

I ignored her for a few moments, but then she got louder, stoking my competitive nature. She wasn't about to outshine me, and I was determined to make sure she didn't.

"Sound off, amani!" I yelled as I began striking him as he spun.

"One, Goddess! Two, Goddess!" He counted off as he felt the buffalo hide hit different areas. "Three, Goddess! Four, Goddess!"

"One, Mistress! Two, Mistress!" I heard Jelani yelling out as Blaze struck him.

We kept up our own version of "Dueling Banjos" for a few minutes, trying to figure out which boi would be able to sound off the loudest. Meanwhile, lynx had them both beat because of the sheer nature of the floggers Sin used and the type of force she exerted to get him to scream louder than our bois put together.

The bois managed to get into the act, wanting to make their Dominants proud and declared the unofficial winner of the duel. amani heard Jelani, Jelani heard amani, both heard lynx and tried to amp things up to keep up with him.

The whole scene became so much fun I didn't care who won whatever we were supposed to "win." All I knew was three bois were feeding the sadistic nature of three Female Dominants while being masochistic sluts getting their own rocks off. It was a win-win situation for everyone involved.

That was until Blaze upped the ante in a way we never thought possible.

She unbuckled Jelani from the work bench she bound him to, tapped him on his shoulder and whispered something in his ear. I couldn't make out the command, but I soon found out as he lay on the blanket near where they were, face-up, and prepared as Blaze lifted her skirt and positioned her pussy over his face and mouth.

"Now, lick Me, slut!" She bellowed as she rested her full weight on his face. The rapturous look on her face was so palpable it caused Sin and me to stop what we were doing so we could watch her. I rotated the wheel so amani could watch his friend as he was being queened.

"Mmmm, yeah, that's it, boi, lick it all up!" She lost herself in Jelani's fervor. She rolled her hips, riding his face harder, relentless in her pursuit of her sexual eruption.

Seconds later, her normally mezzo-soprano-pitched voice tuned up quickly to soprano, letting everyone within shouting distance know she'd arrived at her destination.

Sin was perturbed. "Fuck, Blaze! Really?"

Blaze was still grinding, oblivious to the other people in the room. Her breasts spilled out of her bra, and she was still in the grips of the climaxes Jelani elicited from her body. Pinching her nipples in an effort to prolong her trip, she shouted to any deity who would listen, damn near speaking in tongues as her words became unintelligible.

Sin was enraged at her question being ignored, although I couldn't imagine why she was. Blaze hadn't been this lewd in years, and I was happy as hell for her. I guess my grin was a bit too toothy because Sin glared in my direction, acting like I was supposed to be on her side.

"Quit hating, Sis," I answered her icy stare. "You gotta admit this is hot as fuck, Sin. I mean, look at Her."

We looked back in Blaze's direction and we were shocked to realize the scene had changed dramatically.

Blaze deftly slid off his tongue and was balls-deep on top of Jelani, riding him like she was a jockey at the Belmont Stakes.

"Okay, hooker, now You're just showing off." Sin waved her hand dismissively as she flipped the switch to lower lynx down from the suspension frame. Once she and tiger unbuckled him, she attached their leashes and led them out without saying another word.

Blaze slowed down long enough to realize Sin left the area. She looked up at me for an explanation, but all I could offer was a shrug and a grin. She shrugged and went back to wearing Jelani out.

I felt the desire to leave them to the afterglow of the scene they'd performed, and I wanted to take care of the growing urge growing within me.

As I unhooked amani from the wheel, I kissed his cheek. "Did you enjoy the show?"

"Very much, my Goddess, thank You for stopping the wheel to where i could watch," amani replied. "Watching them has me horny, if i'm allowed to say."

I grabbed his leash and attached it to his collar, glancing at Blaze and Jelani one last time. Blaze looked up, blew a kiss at me and mouthed, "See You in the morning, Sis," before getting back to riding her prized stallion.

If we didn't get to the cabin so he could fuck me, I would explode!

I tugged on amani's collar and rushed out, heading in the direction of the cabin. "you're not the only one who's horny, baby boi. I need you to take care of Me ASAP."

THIRTY-EIGHT ⚯ sajira

We were undressed before they had a chance to command us.

It's difficult to explain, but there was a comfort and freedom with being among family as opposed to being in public. Sure, we did our thing regardless, but it felt like we always held back a bit, like the things we did were more comfortable when it was only Daddy and Goddess watching. There's a need to please and make them smile whenever we performed for them that heightened when no one else was watching.

Tonight, and more importantly, this moment, was unabashed pleasure personified.

Goddess sat in Daddy's lap as they indulged in watching the three of us enjoy each other. The smiles on their faces made me so wet I knew amani would slip right in the moment he was given the chance.

My sis and I had been dying for the chance to have our submissive brother sexually, but we knew we had to wait until they gave permission to do so. All week long we'd been flirting with him, fondling every inch of his body while he returned the favor, and building ourselves up into a ridiculous lather with the hopes that before we headed back home, we would be able to have him.

Daddy nodded in approval, his eyes focused on the way amani grinned as we engaged him, taking turns kissing him before shamise laid him down so she could take care of her oral fetish. I continued kissing him, moving to his nipples to bite and suck on his chest. amani moaned and shook with the two pairs of lips and hands hitting the spots he'd so graciously revealed to us during our more explicit conversations over the past year.

shamise got lost in her oral fetish, her up and down strokes causing amani to cry out from her skills and how she made him feel.

"Is she sucking you good, baby boi?" Neferterri teased, watching his face contort as shamise sat up for a moment to tie her hair back. I grinned at her when she did that. It meant she was just getting started.

"Yes, she's sucking me so good, my Goddess!" amani replied, trying to get the answer out before feeling shamise's mouth devoured him again. "Oh my God, her tongue is so good!"

"I think he needs something to keep his mouth occupied, precious," Ramesses commented. "Sit on his face so he can put that tongue to good use."

He didn't have to tell me twice!

I sat over his face, making sure I was still able to watch my sis hard at work getting his shaft slick and wet. Feeling his tongue focusing on my lips and my clit and watching her stroking him with her mouth, I found it difficult to stay upright. I wanted to suck, too, and I leaned down for a moment to make eye contact with her to let her know what was on my mind.

"Switch," I heard Daddy command. "shamise, sit on his face. sajira, make him come."

Fuck, I was *this* close to getting mine when he uttered the order.

I reluctantly pulled my sex away from his mouth as shamise mounted him, and I knew she was already close because when she performed orally, she could come from the sensation alone.

I moved up and down on his dick, determined to make amani

come all over my hands and mouth before Daddy commanded us to switch again. I tightened my lips around his length, sucking him deeper with each up and down motion, feeling his hips tightening, giving me the signs he was almost ready to explode.

"Make him come, sis, he's eating me so good!" shamise trembled from the pending waves of orgasmic bliss ready to overwhelm her. "Daddy, he's gonna make me... can i come, please?????"

"Should we let her come, Beloved?" Daddy kissed Goddess as he made the inquiry.

"Daddy, please?!?!?! amani's got me there; please, i've been a good girl, i promise!"

"Yes, I think it's okay for her to come, Beloved," Goddess responded. It wasn't hard to figure out they were in a sensually sadistic mood, reminding us that they were still in control when it came to our pleasure. Even in this threesome, they directed every scene, every position, for their pleasure.

I felt amani bucking under me, ready to explode. "Daddy, amani's almost there...do i?"

"Milk him dry, precious," Daddy replied, a smirk on his face as I looked back to seek his permission. "he's been dying to have you both, so let him have his wish."

I rapidly flicked my tongue over his head while my fingers jacked him off. His hips lifted off the floor, and the warmth of his eruption spilled over onto my fingers. I could tell it had been a minute since he was allowed to come because the second load shot in the air and landed on his stomach.

"Fuck, no fair...i was...supposed to...come!" shamise tried to breathe through the shockwaves that hit her. She braced herself against amani's tongue, realizing he wasn't about to stop until he was told to. "Oh fuck oh damn oh fuck oh shit oh my God!"

"Switch." This time, I heard Goddess speak, but I felt the sex dripping from her voice. I stole a glance and saw she was slowly riding reverse cowgirl on Daddy, trying to sound like she wasn't enjoying herself. "shamise, doggie-style. sajira, spread so your sis can make you come. amani, you better fuck shamise well; your Sir is watching."

We switch as commanded, and amani was inside shamise before she was able to get me into position. I lay down, positioning myself under her face, the aroma of my sex mingling in the air. I had a bird's-eye view of her ass bouncing as amani pounded into her pussy, making her scream out before she buried her face in my wetness. She tried to concentrate on licking me deep, but amani's directive to fuck her senseless had her body concentrating more on bracing for each stroke. Unable to focus on her oral skills, she moved to slide her fingers inside me, fingering me deep and stroking against my G-spot. First two fingers, then she slid a third one, even while amani held her body prisoner, determined to even the odds and make sure I wasn't the only one who didn't come yet.

The way she finger-fucked me, she had my spot and had me coming in no time.

"Daddy… Goddess…please…she's got me there!"

"Let it go, sajira! you deserve it!" Goddess's voice trembled. I looked up, and Goddess was on all fours getting fucked on the floor near where we were. She looked so damn good getting fucked by Daddy that I lost it.

I screamed out loudly, my body contorting and moving to get away from my sis, who had a lock on my walls and continued to piston her fingers in and out of me, causing me to squirt all over her hand and wrist.

"Damn, sis, give it to me. Fuck, he's fucking me so deep!" she said. "He's…i'm coming…fuck, his dick is so good."

"Switch." Daddy tried to sound like he was still in control, but the way I saw it, he wouldn't be for long. "sajira...shamise...switch."

amani grabbed for me, his urgency to feel me stoking my desires for him to be inside me for as long as his body would let him. The moment we merged, I shook and adjusted to his girth.

No wonder shamise was screaming to the heavens. This boi was blessed! It's one thing to have something that big in your mouth, it's quite another to have him so deep inside you that you can feel him in your stomach.

"Damn, baby, get it!" I cheered him on, feeling him increase the pace and force inside me. I heard my ass slapping against his pelvis, and I lost the ability to get my sis off. "Damn, sis, he's fucking the shit out of me!"

She moved close to me, kissing me deeply as she rocked with me to absorb the force of his strokes. "Yeah, sis, just take it baby, he's a monster...let him beat that pussy up!"

I heard Goddess screaming out that she was coming, and it wasn't until then I remembered they were even engaged in their own personal time together. Hearing her enjoying herself fueled me; being stuck between shamise and amani getting my back blown out was pure bliss.

amani kept up the pace, holding my hips in place as he tore into me. It took everything within me to hold on to shamise as he got into some sort of zone and forgot we were there with him. My ego took over, encouraging him to give me everything he had if he wanted to get some again.

I felt the pressure building and I wanted to get my nut so I could pass out.

"It's coming, isn't it, baby?"

"He's got me coming again, sis...fuck!"

"Don't fight it, sis, just let him have it."

amani growled, unable to really form words at that point. He pulled out of me and fell back on the floor, completely exhausted.

We weren't done with him, though.

We took turns sucking him, at times kissing each other through the blow job we gave him, ready for him to come. He couldn't take much more, growling deeper, his grunts more guttural now; it was only a matter of moments before we'd be rewarded with the fruits of our labor.

He shook like we'd taken electricity and sent the current through him, his climax taking him down little by little, the explosion less intense than the first one he had, but copious nonetheless.

I grabbed the blanket nearby, content with sleeping on the floor on one side of amani while shamise snuggled on the other side. We looked up, noticing Daddy and Goddess had already snuggled together on the couch, smiling at the spectacle we'd made of ourselves.

"Get some rest, you three. We have guests to see off the island in the morning," Goddess informed us. "More than likely we'll stick around for a few more days to rest and relax before heading back ourselves, but tomorrow is going to be exhaustive, so sleep well. Good night."

EPILOGUE ⊗ RAMESSES

I had the strangest case of déjà vu.

Yeah, I know, we've done this before, but it never got old.

The slaves served brunch.

The Mimosas were flowing.

Groggy and exhausted island attendees were dragging themselves into the grand dining area to grab food and listen to the outgoing speech before packing up and taking the yachts back to Nassau to head back to their respective home locales.

Gratefully, another endeavor had completed, but not without some bumps and bruises along the way.

Osiris and Seti walked past me as I sat at the main table. A knowing nod from Osiris and a wink from Seti gave me unspoken information that loose ends had been tied up permanently. We would never speak of it again.

Amenhotep enjoyed his role as the support host, instead of being front and center as the eye of the storm that normally happened when things wound down after a large-scale event. He held His glass in my direction, a salute for a job well done. I held my glass in His direction, acknowledging the man who'd made me the Master I was.

Dominic was happy that things were finally over with, and he made sure the security director he'd left in place was more than prepared for anything that would come down the pipeline. After this week, we were definitely at the point of expecting the unexpected. As long as he remained vigilant, things would work out well down here.

I wasn't stupid, though.

He needed to get back to his girls and the firm. It's nice to travel for business, but there's no place like home.

My Beloved kissed my cheek. "It's time to get this over with, Beloved. We don't want them to miss their flights."

I stood at my spot, tapping the side of my glass with a spoon until the crowd quieted. Once they did, I cleared my throat before I spoke. "Good morning, everyone, and we sincerely hope you were able to enjoy the island to the fullest. Thank you all for helping to make the grand opening of the *Isle ne Bin-bener* a success. We hope you are able to come back soon, and as a token of our thanks, My Beloved and I extend a discounted return engagement to all of you."

The crowd buzzed over hearing this news, and I smiled at Neferterri as I continued my speech. "This discounted package is contingent upon returning to the island within one year, otherwise, you will be subjected to the normal rates that will apply. For those of you who have memberships to NEBU, Deshret, or Thebes, the discounted packages will not expire, so long as your membership is in good standing. On behalf of My Beloved, along with our House and the island staff and personnel, we wish you a safe journey home, and we'll hope to see you again soon."

☥

"This was a wonderful debut, kid. Congratulations."

Amenhotep, Neferterri and I were on the balcony of the main

building, watching the yachts sailing toward Nassau and enjoying a few mixed drinks to keep the buzz going from the Mimosas earlier.

"So, what do You have up Your sleeve next, youngster?" He gave me a look for a minute like I'd already had something planned out. "I have a feeling it's going to be hard to top this endeavor; I know that much."

I shrugged. "I put so much attention and energy into getting this place up and running, I don't have a thing figured out. All I want to do is go home, see my daughters, decompress from this hellacious week, and I can think about the next big thing after about a month of not doing any real thinking."

He laughed at me, taking a sip of His drink. "Well, it has been a busy couple of years for You, and You still have that security firm to run, too. Maybe You and Neferterri need to take some time off and just let the compounds operate without any major events for a few months?"

Neferterri shook her head, stepping in front of me to lean against me as she faced Amenhotep. "You boys can take a break if you want to, but the ladies and I have already gotten to thinking about what we plan to do."

The grin spread across Amenhotep's face as the prospect already intrigued Him. "What did You have in mind, My dear Neferterri?"

She turned around and kissed my lips, her grin as wide as Amenhotep's. I already had a funny feeling I wasn't going to like what she had to say. She had "that" look in her eyes. "We can discuss the details later, but let's just say, You gentlemen will not be needed for this particular event."

ABOUT THE AUTHOR

Known for his mind-twisting plots and unique prose, Shakir Rashaan rolled onto the literary scene as a contributing writer to *Z-Rated: Chocolate Flava 3* in 2012. His raw, vivid, and uncut writing style captured the attention of the Queen of Erotica herself, Zane. A year later, Rashaan made his debut with *The Awakening*, opening to rave reviews and a "recommended read" accolade in *USA Today*'s Happy Ever After literary blog. The follow-up in the Nubian Underworld series, *Legacy*, has garnered even more success, with its third installment, *Tempest*, poised to burn up the pages, making the series one of the most unique in the erotica genre.

Upcoming projects from Rashaan include the upcoming *Kink, P.I.* series in 2015 and a few new projects being developed under the pen name, P.K. Rashaan. With his prolific writing prowess and openness on his social media platforms, Rashaan has plans to be a mainstay within the erotica genre and beyond.

Shakir is a Phoenix, earning his Bachelor of Science degree in Criminal Justice/Communications from the University of Phoenix. He currently resides in suburban Atlanta with his wife and two children. You can see more of Rashaan at http://www.Shakir Rashaan.com.

Twitter: http://twitter.com/ShakirRashaan
Facebook: http://www.facebook.com/Shakir.Rashaan
Instagram: http://instagram.com/ShakirRashaan
Email: shakir@shakirrashaan.com
Blog: http://www.medium.com/@ShakirRashaan

IF YOU ENJOYED "TEMPEST,"
BE SURE TO CHECK OUT

Obsession

BOOK ONE OF THE *Kink, P.I.* SERIES
BY SHAKIR RASHAAN
COMING SOON FROM STREBOR BOOKS

ONE

Hate me or love me, I get results…

I'm damn good at what I do. Sure, I bent the rules a little bit, but what cop hasn't? But I was never…I repeat, never…dirty. You can ask any of my old partners, and they'll tell you that for a fact.

But when your childhood partner in crime comes calling and says the words *I got something I want you to run for me*, and then backs it up with capital to keep me happy and away from the P.D., you jump at it quick. That's what I did a year ago, and I haven't looked back since.

He and I go way back; in fact, we were damn near partners on the force together. That is, until he decided to start doing his photography thing, and we went our separate paths. I never held a grudge against him about it, though. The way I saw it, things have a funny way of working themselves out, and he always said he would find a way to get me out of the P.D. before he figured that he had to bury me.

Oh, by the way.

The name's Law...Dominic Law. But you can call me Dom. My now business partner Ramesses called me that when we were in high school and the nickname kinda stuck. But now, instead of Detective Law, you can call me by a different moniker now...

Private Investigator...so you can't tell me shit now.

Actually, it's more than that; I run the P.I. business, yes, but I'm also the head of Ramesses' security detail at the *Palace* and Neferterri's security detail at her club *Liquid Paradise*, so they keep me quite busy with everything that goes on.

But that's not all; thanks to Ramesses I got a lot of cases that the various P.D.s can't always deem high priority, especially when sometimes the cases aren't always "normal" by mainstream standards. After a while, I got the rep for being the "Kink Detective," and sometimes I could be brought in on a consult for the unusual sex crimes around the ATL area.

Couple that with the fact that because of all these kink-related crimes, I found myself immersed deep inside the BDSM community here in Atlanta, which was fine, because it wasn't like I wasn't already into the shit to begin with. I can thank Ramesses and Amenhotep for that. I honestly didn't think that I would want to be *that* deep, but when you see how women like Ramesses' girls and the slaves at the Palace treat a brother, it is very hard to resist learning how to get that same treatment.

Just to be clear, my boy has damn near converted me; my problem, as he saw it, is that I'm the new meat on the scene. Add that with the fact that I'm a heterosexual black man and my best friend (that is mentoring me, by the way) happens to be one of the power players in the Atlanta POC BDSM community, and the women on the scene drool over me because I was a cop at one point in time.

The problem, you ask?

Technically there is no problem, except an ex-wife that happens to be into the same thing that I, when we were married, could really never be a part of because of my occupation. I mean, come on, a cop in the Deep South trying to be discreet doing "kinky shit"?

It's not gonna happen; in fact, it's one of the "irreconcilable differences" we had when she filed for divorce. Now, not only am I a newbie in the community, but I have to occasionally run into her at munches or at the *Palace* when a larger community function is going on, and then hear her damn mouth about it after the fact. I'd dwell on this some more, but you couldn't probably care less. If you're like most Americans, you're simply going to lump me into that collection of oddballs that you think of as "the strange people." I find it offensive to be lumped into the same group as Jehovah's Witnesses, and I'm sure they feel the same way about me, but go ahead; I'm used to it.

I'm one of the popular people at the local munch. Oh, yeah, that's right; you don't know the "strange person" jargon. A munch is short for a meet and lunch and that is the proper, and original, term for a gathering of people in the bondage, dominance and sadomasochism lifestyle. Take a minute to add leather to your mental label for me. Go ahead, I'll wait. You're wrong, though. Not everyone into BDSM, the lifestyle we call it, is a leather-clad freak. A lot of us, including Ramesses and Amenhotep, I'll grant you, but not all of us. Not me.

It's not like that won't stop Ramesses, though.

Look at me…sounding like Ramesses again.

Damn it.

Well, he's got me convinced now, but I had no intention of sounding like a damn tape recorder, either.

Munches vary in tone. It's all to do with the people involved.

The South Fulton munch is mostly well-educated and well-employed, so the only difference between one of our gatherings and a meeting of your local Kiwanis Club is...well, damned if I know.

The tone is set by the group leaders; in this particular munch it is Ramesses, Neferterri and Mistress Sinsual, generally the folks who have been around the longest. Mostly people dress casually, blue jeans, dresses, skirts and blouses, clean sneakers, and even the occasional suit.

I tell you this so you can understand why I wasn't surprised when peaches sat down across from me. Of course, peaches' not her real name. Let me rephrase that; peaches is her real name in the sense that it's the only one she'll answer to because it's the name her Master gave her. Don't worry about understanding everything, just keep up with Ramesses and me and let the otherness sort of wash over you... like a golden shower.

Sorry, I couldn't resist.

When I thought about it, I was surprised to see peaches here, much less anywhere outside of *Inner Sanctum*, one of the local dungeons. The South Fulton munch was a place for people to socialize among other lifestylers and Lord Aris and his harem weren't really capable of getting outside the lifestyle. He thought it was a waste of time, except to collect more girls for his personal enjoyment. Ramesses and his mentor, Amenhotep, never could stand the guy. Hell, come to think of it, I hadn't run into anyone that really held any affinity for the man, except for the subs that were with him. But in the interest of keeping harmony in the community, most people tolerated him.

Not exactly what I would do if I know the man ain't worth two dead flies, but I digress.

Upon examining the situation further, I couldn't recall in my limited experience ever seeing one of Aris' slaves at a gathering where he wasn't. Lord Aris was a controlling asshole, but women mistook his misogyny, control-freak attitude and lack of social skills for a commanding air of dominance, and they flocked to him like moths to a flame. He had to beat them off with a stick, which he loved. Hell, what man wouldn't?

I took another sip of the tea and waited. peaches wanted to talk to me, but the protocol that she's under prohibits her from speaking to a Dominant unless spoken to first. I should have respected that protocol as a courtesy to her Master, but I didn't. In case you haven't been paying attention, I don't much like Aris, and he'd been clear and vocal about his disdain for me because of my association with Ramesses, nothing more.

So fuck him, and fuck her.

I let her sit there and make eye contact with the table while I waited for her to decide which was more important: Aris' protocol or her need to talk to me. It was torture for her. Call it a sadistic side of me, but I enjoyed watching her squirm.

"May i speak, Sir?" she finally asked.

"Yes, you have permission to speak, slave," I replied, following the proper etiquette that I had been learning from Ramesses.

"i can't find Master. i haven't seen Him in over a week and He's not returning my phone calls."

I shrugged. Like I give a fuck, it's not my problem.

"Aris is not exactly known for letting his slaves down easily," I pointed out. "Perhaps He's simply just incognito for a day or two?"

"No one has seen him for a week," she amplified, a slight bit irritated at my indifference. "He was supposed to have a session with slave maia on Thursday and he didn't leave the key for her, Sir. I tried calling his work number and got the answering machine.

I know he's not your favorite person, and I understand if you do not want to, but can you find him for me, Sir? I know that you and Lord Ramesses are close, and he is an honorable Dominant, so I know that you are of honor as well."

Damn. She pulled the card of my mentor out on me, which made the prospect of saying no even harder. Truth be told, I'm a softie when it comes to women who are in earnest need of help. Some habits never die; after all, I was a cop before. But now, I was a businessman, and a businessman gets paid for services rendered.

"slave peaches, the fee is one hundred dollars per hour, two-hour minimum, plus expenses which will amount to a least another hundred dollars. I don't promise any results."

I almost put my prices up enough to put her off. The key word is almost.

"Lifestyle discount?" she asked tentatively.

"Mind your place, slave," I roughly answered, trying to sound like I knew what I was saying. Truth is, I really wasn't sure if I was or not, but I didn't care if I was being contracted; she was not about to lose her protocol just because I decided to help.

"Please forgive me, Sir," she sheepishly answered. She colored a little, embarrassed, and pulled some money out of her purse. She counted out three hundred dollars in neatly folded twenties and fifties and put them on the table. I counted them and put them away and then put my notebook and pen on the table in front of her.

"I'll need your Master's home address and a list of all the submissives he worked with, as well as submissives that are currently under his charge," I instructed her. Normally, I'd have asked about enemies, but with Aris, we might be talking all week. Besides, this was typical Aris; I'd probably find out that he'd gone to Vegas for a week or something like that, while he waited for the subs he'd chosen to get rid of to get the message.

"I'll need your home info," I told her. "I'll send the contract to you there."

"Could you go ahead and start looking today?" she asked. "Please, Sir?"

I considered making her beg. I'd enjoy that. She'd enjoy that. But this was a public munch. Discretion is the term that applies and Ramesses and Mistress Sinsual get very unhappy with people who make the vanillas squirm, and it's not a pretty sight. The only nice thing about being "in the know" is that you aren't actually an outcast. It's hard to find the kind of women I like in vanilla circles.

I texted Ramesses to keep from drawing too much attention to peaches; it was difficult enough as it was, considering that she was wearing a skirt just short enough to cover her ass and a halter top and sandals. Not conservative, but she was a youngster and she knew she could show off her body and no one would complain… at least except those of the straight female persuasion, that is.

He texted me back about a minute later, telling me that I had the afternoon to handle business, but I needed to do a quick check at the Palace before the night was out. That gave me a few hours to do some preliminary work.

I put my smartphone back in its holster and told peaches, "Sure. I'm not doing anything this afternoon. I can at least get some quick follow-up done. If I figure out anything, I'll let you know."